I0757859

PRINCES ARE WILD

REGENCY ROYALS BOOK 3

JESS MICHAELS

Copyright © 2021 by Jess Michaels

All rights reserved.

No part of this book may be reproduced in any form or by any electronic or mechanical means, including information storage and retrieval systems, without written permission from the author, except for the use of brief quotations in a book review.

For Michael: Thanks for staying in this house and continuing to rock my world. (Sorry babe, I told you I was gonna).

AUTHOR'S NOTE

There are a lot of conversations about the concept of Content Warnings in books and for other media. Having suffered from panic attacks that were triggered by trauma, I would NEVER wish that on my worst enemy. I want you to enjoy what you're reading, never be pulled away because you were surprised by triggering material. So, I will do my best to include Content Warnings in an author note in each book from now on. Also, look to my website for them, so that you don't accidentally buy a book that might give you pause.

Content Warning: emotional abuse (described and on page)

CHAPTER 1

Summer 1817

The Island of Athawick

Prince Remington of Athawick stood on the terrace outside of his chamber, staring out at the sea as the sun dipped down to its edge, turning the water orange and pink. It was good to be home after two tempestuous months in England. Despite what some in his family would argue, Remi loved Athawick. He loved her sandy shores, he loved her stormy seas, he loved the people who occupied this place, made it exactly what it was in all the best ways.

Coming home should have brought him a little peace, but it didn't. A sigh escaped his lips as he turned away from the beauty of the scene before him and he smoothed his jacket. Exiting his large chamber, he moved down the hall a few doors to his sister Ilaria's room. He knocked once before walking in without waiting for leave.

She stood in the middle of the chamber, but she was not alone. Her fiancé, Captain Jonah Crawford, was with her, his arms around her as they kissed passionately. When Remi pressed the door shut loudly behind him they broke apart, breathless, and pivoted to face him.

He grinned. "Tsk, tsk. It is one thing that everyone knows you two can't wait to marry, but quite another to keep flaunting it," he teased.

Ilaria shot him a glare. "I don't think it's considered flaunting anything when you came barging into my chamber."

"I knocked," Remi said, and then turned his attention to Jonah. "And you…here we are, home at last. What do you think of the place —is it just as you remember?"

A flutter of a smile crossed Jonah's normally serious face. "It's been two years since I was privileged to be in Athawick," he said. "And because I was on the Prince Regent's honor guard, I might not have been so free to explore as I shall be this time. I look forward to it."

"I'm sure you do." Remi's words elicited a huff of playful frustration from Ilaria and a laughing shake of Jonah's head.

Jonah caught her hand and lifted it to his lips. "I should get settled in before the evening's events. I will see you later, though."

To Remi's surprise, Ilaria tittered and blushed. It was a funny thing, love. He was getting to see it far more closely than he'd ever imagined since Ilaria's engagement and the marriage of their adopted sister, Sasha. Love had never been something he had faith in. Pleasure was wonderful—he sought that as often as he could. But love?

"Your Highness," Jonah said with a small bow toward him.

Remi pulled a face. "At some point you're going to have to stop being so formal, you know."

Jonah laughed as he headed for the door. "You'll be Remi to me the moment I am officially wed to your sister. Good evening."

As he exited the room, Remi called out, "Good evening, *Jonah*." Once he was gone and the door shut behind him, Remi turned his attention on his sister. "He thinks me a fool, doesn't he?"

She laughed softly. "It's the role you play so well. But no, he doesn't."

There was some comfort in that answer, alongside a dose of truth. He did play the role of fool. He created an image of himself that no one could touch. Rakish, layabout prince...no one expected anything of that sort of person. "I'll try harder then," he murmured.

Ilaria paced away with a snort of laughter, moving to her wardrobe to examine the gowns arranged there. As she flicked through them absently, he asked, "When is Grantham doing the thing?"

She glanced over her shoulder and blinked in what appeared to be true confusion. "The...*thing?*" she asked.

"Isn't he making Jonah a duke or a squire or something for his great bravery in saving your life in London?" He said the words with his usual playful air, but felt anything but nonchalant about them. Ilaria and Sasha had both been attacked in London and had been saved by the men who loved them. For his bravery, Jonah was to be given a title. It was also a way to elevate him so that his marriage to the princess would be more...how had Grantham put it...*palatable* to a populace that was already uneasy.

"He's making him a count and you know that," Ilaria said. "I think it will be later in the week. Before the wedding."

Remi found himself smiling. Ilaria probably didn't know it, but when she said the word *wedding*, her entire being lit up. His sister had always been beautiful, but now she was stunning.

"Look at you, about to live your happily ever after," he mused softly.

Her eyes widened a little. "I didn't think you believed in happily ever after."

He shrugged one shoulder. "Only yours and Sasha's. I will believe in those because it's impossible not to believe when you're both so joyful. And I am glad for you." Her expression softened as if she was becoming emotional at his statement, and he cleared his throat quickly. "And there is the wonderful bonus that you thwarted our brother's plans so perfectly. *That's* always fun for me to witness."

Ilaria shook her head and laughed, diffusing the deeper emotions from a few seconds before. "You say that, but you might not feel it soon enough. After all, if I didn't marry a titled person of the British Empire in order to provide a buffer for their interference here in Athawick, then the next logical choice for that type of union...is *you*."

She said the words playfully, but Remi's reaction was anything but. A full-body shiver worked through him at the thought of being tied down, forced to marry, potentially despising his chosen bride... having it devolve into the relationship he'd watched between his mother and late father.

"Luckily we're not in England anymore," he said.

She tilted his head. "You think that makes you safe? There are dozens and dozens of English men and women arriving on our shores this very moment. Yes, to celebrate my marriage, but certainly some have also been brought here in an effort to tempt you."

"God's teeth," Remi grunted. "Why doesn't Grantham marry an English girl himself if he wants a fucking alliance so badly?"

Ilaria's eyes went a little wider. "Well, you needn't bite my head off about it, Remi."

He was about to deny he'd done so, but he couldn't. His tone had gotten far harsher and his sister had been on the receiving end. But there were things he could tease about and things he couldn't. Still, none of it was Ilaria's fault. Nor her responsibility to fix.

"I hope you're not going to be in such a foul mood for the ball," she continued.

"No, no." Remi waved off the concern and the negative emotions with one sweep of his hand. "I won't be. I must captivate all those guests, mustn't I? Tell me they aren't all crowding into the palace."

"You don't even listen to the briefings from the courtiers and Dash, do you?" Ilaria said with a laugh. "Most are being housed in the inns and the homes of our gentry. But about a dozen or so will be here in the palace, yes. The prettiest women on offer, I'm sure."

Remi rolled his eyes. "Do you think *King* Grantham would murder me if I simply ruined them rather than wed one of them?"

"He might not," Ilaria said after a fraction of a moment's consideration. "But Mama, though..." She trailed off with a significant look.

They both dissolved into laughter for a moment. When it passed, Ilaria waved him toward the door. "Now go away, will you? I must get ready. Oh, and pull the bell on your way out."

"Yes, Your Highness," he said with a ridiculous bow as he departed her room, tugging the bell pull before he did. But as he stepped into the hallway, he expelled a long breath.

Over the years, he had become very good at pretending to be far more nonchalant than he felt. A perfect way to maintain distance, to keep away unwanted attention. Only right now his emotions were so tumultuous that he feared he might not be able to hide them. Which meant he'd have to work all the harder at it. Prince Remington of Athawick was a playboy prince. He would inhabit that role completely, by God, and never let anyone see anything else.

Miss Priscilla Linfield spun around the room, her hands grasped in those of her best friend, Lady Ophelia. When they stopped, dizzy and laughing and breathless, she clutched a hand to her breast. "I cannot tell you how wonderful it is to be invited to Athawick as a guest of your family. You were so kind to make me part of it, Ophelia. And the Duke and Duchess of Gilmore were wonderful to agree to your schemes."

Ophelia squeezed her hand gently. "You know my brother and Abigail feel just as attached to you as I do, Pris. I couldn't have thought to do this without you at any rate."

Priscilla paced away, her hands fluttering with the excitement of it all. She turned back with a grin that felt like it would split her cheeks. "Just think, *I* shall be some small part of what everyone knows is the event of the decade!"

Ophelia shook her head slightly and her smile fell just a fraction. "So they say."

Priscilla tilted her head and looked her friend up and down. Two more opposite people there could not be. While Priscilla was quiet and often shy, Ophelia spoke her mind and seemed to have no care about it. Priscilla buried her nose in books and facts and history, Ophelia drew the eye of every man in every ballroom. Even their looks could not be more opposite. While Priscilla was fair-haired and curvaceous, Ophelia had dark, smooth locks and a slender frame.

And yet, despite all their differences, she and Ophelia had been friends for years, since they were girls. They had seen each other through thick and thin. Being around Ophelia always made Priscilla a little...braver. And she hoped she was sometimes a calming influence on her friend.

"You cannot truly be as nonchalant about this as you pretend to be," Priscilla said with a laugh. "Not even you. We are staying in a *palace*."

Ophelia looked around the fine chamber they would share and nodded as if reluctantly agreeing with Priscilla. "Fine, I will admit it is not every day that one gets to say that. My brother encountered King Grantham several times during the Athawick royal family's stay in London. And here we all are as a result."

"I am thrilled to be with you," Priscilla said. "And to be away from London and my family."

Ophelia's expression shifted and she lunged forward, catching Priscilla's hands once more. "Oh, Pris, is it terrible?"

Priscilla's arms began to tingle at the question and she had to draw a few long breaths to calm herself before she spoke. "Yes," she admitted softly. "As always."

Ophelia drew her to the settee before the fire and they sat

together. Her friend leaned closer, exploring her expression. "When you did not speak of it during the voyage here, I had hoped things had improved."

Priscilla sighed. "I was...I was trying to hide it from you, I admit."

"Why?" Ophelia asked, her eyes growing wide.

"Because I hate being your sad, pathetic friend with her sad, pathetic life," Priscilla dipped her head. "Always going on about my hardships does not make me a very attractive person, I know."

"First off, you can always be honest with me," Ophelia insisted. "And second, you are anything but sad or pathetic. You are the most lovely, brilliant and kind person I know. So tell me about it, then."

"When Papa declared his desire to remarry two Seasons ago, I was supportive of the idea. After all, Mama died five years ago. And I thought that if he were distracted, some of the pressure would come off of me." Priscilla worried her hands before her. "But then he didn't choose someone at all appropriate for his age, but someone closer to ours. Two years older than I am and one of the nastiest women I've ever met. Since their marriage in the spring, things have gone from bad to worse."

Ophelia pursed her lips. "I worried about that. Caroline was always a terrible person—I could not imagine that marriage would improve her."

"It has not. I tried to reach out to her as a friend, as a..." Priscilla pulled a face. "...*daughter*, but I've been rebuffed at every turn. She encourages my father's further disappointment in me, sometimes through outright lies. And I am aware that she is trying as hard as she can to produce a male heir for him at last, then push me out entirely." She bent her head. "I can only think of...of two ways to be free."

"Which are?" Ophelia asked slowly, her tone laced with concern.

Priscilla couldn't look at her. "Marriage, of course. Though I've failed at that consistently for the past seven dreadful Seasons."

"And what is the other mode of escape?"

Priscilla opened and shut her mouth. She had intended to be completely honest with Ophelia when this topic was broached during the trip, as she'd known it eventually would be. She'd wanted her best friend's advice and support. But looking at Ophelia now, she hesitated. What if she told her and Ophelia was disgusted? What if she turned away? Priscilla had so little to cling to, she didn't want to risk losing her friend.

"Why don't we focus on the marriage option for now?" she said, voice trembling.

Ophelia moved closer. "What is the second option, Pris? Become a lady's maid, perhaps? A governess?"

Priscilla shifted. She'd considered those options, of course, but she had no experience in service or with children. Sometimes she felt entirely useless. And if she made the attempt to enter into service, she was certain her family would thwart the efforts. Caroline would whisper and it would be as bad as a poor reference.

But if she was to become a man's…lover…his mistress…she doubted anyone would be asking for a reference then. Did she know what she was doing any better in that arena than the other? No. But she'd found a book that was quite…enlightening. She could learn. She would have to.

"Something like a servant," she murmured. "But I'd rather fully explore the marriage option before I put too much effort into the other. I have a thought."

Ophelia looked like she wished to discuss the other topic further, but she nodded slowly. "I cannot wait to hear it."

"Perhaps my problem is that I have been out so long at home. All the gentlemen know me, they see me as unwanted. But here in Athawick…"

"You are the mysterious English rose," Ophelia finished with a slight smile. "A very good idea. At the welcome ball tonight, we could make a list of potential gentlemen for pursuit. Starting with those in court."

"King Grantham?" Priscilla repeated in shock. "You cannot be serious."

"I actually meant Prince Remington," Ophelia said. "And some of the titled men in the court. Certainly I would never suggest the king."

Priscilla bent her head. "Oh. You…do not think I could be attractive enough to him?"

Ophelia snorted out a sound of derision. "On the contrary, I cannot believe *you* would consider *him*. Because he and my brother became friendly while the family was in London, I was *forced* to observe him far more closely than I would have ever desired. He is stern and cool and distant. He's…he's…ill tempered."

Priscilla's eyes went wide at the passion with which Ophelia discussed the man. "He's also handsome."

Ophelia snorted as her gaze darted away. "I suppose he *is* handsome. One can hardly deny that fact."

Priscilla gripped her hands before her. She could not deny that during the recent royal visit to London, she had made a deep study of the Athawickian royals. They were the center of every piece of gossip for months, after all. It had been an enjoyable pastime to read all about them and try to catch a glimpse of any of them across the ballrooms and parlors of Society. Both the king and Prince Remington were devastatingly handsome gentlemen. The prince's eyes, especially, were intensely beautiful.

"It is silly to talk about it," she said with a shake of her head. "I am *not* attractive enough for a king."

"You are too!" Ophelia insisted and caught her hands. "Great God, Pris, don't let your stepmother's cruelty or the idiocy of the men of our Society make you think you do not deserve whatever you desire."

Priscilla pondered that a moment. "The king is certainly different from the gentlemen in our acquaintance. He's supposed to be very intelligent, everyone says so, so he might value a woman like me who prefers reading and study to parties and balls."

"Ugh," Ophelia muttered, not altogether too softly. "Why not think of the prince?"

"Prince Remington?" Priscilla repeated. "Gracious no! He is far too wild for me. He would not notice me more than he would notice a fly, I would imagine. No, if I were to dare to reach so high, to make this last attempt at the best match possible, it would *have* to be the king. On paper, it makes sense, I think." She sighed because she could not believe she was even considering such a thing. Ophelia did make her believe in herself so much more. It was why she adored her. "And he is not in London, which means I would also escape my family."

Ophelia bent her head. "And me."

"But you could visit me," Priscilla suggested. "Imagine being best of friends with a *queen*, Ophelia!"

"I am already best of friends with a queen," Ophelia said softly, and squeezed her hand. "Fine, so you would ignore all the warning signs that this man is a terrible bore and only focus on his better qualities. Then what will you do to win over the illustrious King of Athawick?"

Heat rushed to Priscilla's cheeks. "Well...perhaps *you* could help me. You've met him, as you said."

"God help me, yes," Ophelia said.

The wheels in Priscilla's mind began to turn. She was desperate, after all. If she were desperate enough to think of becoming a man's mistress, couldn't she turn that same effort and energy into catching a husband? The ultimate husband, at that.

"Are you well enough acquainted to be able to introduce me to him?" she asked slowly, trying to picture how that might go. "A more personal introduction, not just a brief curtsey in a receiving line? Or perhaps your brother and Abigail might do it if you asked?"

Ophelia pulled a face. "Ugh, I suppose that could be arranged. But I would only do it for *you*, Pris."

Priscilla let out a breath she hadn't realized she'd been holding. This was a plan, at any rate. One that could keep her from the very scary position she might be in next if she failed. "Thank you. I will not waste your extremely noble sacrifice." She got up and moved to the wardrobe. "Now help. I need to figure out what to wear."

"Oh, I have the prettiest gown—you would look divine in it," Ophelia said, jumping to her feet and joining her.

Priscilla pivoted toward her. "We have not worn the same size in years, Ophelia." She motioned to her fuller breasts. "Would it not be more than a bit...tight?"

Ophelia laughed as she pulled out a red gown with golden stitching throughout. A gown certainly fit for a queen and far prettier than any of the dresses Priscilla had brought.

"If you are trying to catch the attention of a man," Ophelia said as she held it up to Priscilla, "that might not hurt your chances."

Priscilla giggled at her friend's quip and hurried to ring the bell for their maids to help them prepare for the night's festivities. But as she did so, she couldn't help but feel nervous. Suddenly there was so much on the line now, the very path of her future. And she could only hope she would make the right impression, the right choices, and set herself free.

CHAPTER 2

Remi stood in what felt like a never-ending receiving line as dignitary after dignitary made their greetings. Because this was an event celebrating Ilaria's impending nuptials and Sasha's recent ones, his sisters were placed ahead of him in the line and he could watch his entire family as they interacted with their guests. All of them looked happy.

Well, *Grantham* didn't look happy. But the king was always serious during these events. All the time, actually, since he'd taken the throne. Once upon a time Remi had had fun with his brother, but things had changed, tension had risen.

The others seemed happy, though, including Queen Giabella. She hadn't stopped beaming since they arrived home in Athawick.

Remi, on the other hand...was bored. God, he was so fucking bored of all of this.

He shook another sweaty hand, smiled pleasantly and then groaned beneath his breath. Surely this damned receiving line had to be close to finished. At least in the ball he could have a drink or two, dance a bit, sneak off if he needed space.

He glanced down toward his brother to see if the crowd was thinning and found that a small group of people had approached the king. Three women and one man, and for once Grantham actually looked warm, welcoming as he spoke to the man. Remi wrinkled his brow. The gentleman did look somewhat familiar and he wracked his brain to come up with some details as their party moved down to greet the queen.

His mother leaned forward, as kind as always, and as she did so, Remi caught a better look at the women in the party. One lady clung to the arm of the man—his wife, obviously. She was very pretty, with dark hair and a warm smile. Beside them was another dark-haired woman, stunning and with a somewhat knowing expression. Normally that was who he would be drawn to, but instead his gaze flitted to the final lady in their party. She was blonde and petite, with a full, curvaceous figure. The color of her eyes was unreadable from the distance, but she kept flitting that stare back toward his brother.

And yet Remi couldn't take his gaze off of her. She was very pretty. And not just that. There was something else about her, something he couldn't quite place. But he kept his attention focused on her as the foursome made their way through the rest of the family and finally settled at him.

"The Duke and Duchess of Gilmore," one of the courtiers helpfully supplied from behind him. "And Lady Ophelia and Miss Priscilla Linfield."

"Prince Remington," Gilmore said, extending a hand as the ladies curtseyed in time. "I don't know if you recall, but we met at my club while you and the family were in London."

"Yes, the club," Remi said, shaking the gentleman's hand firmly. "I could not place it and you have saved me. A pleasure to see you again, and your lovely companions."

"The pleasure is ours, I assure you," the duchess said with a warm smile.

He barely heard her, because at that moment the blonde turned toward him and their eyes met. Hers were green, a lovely dark green that put him to mind of deep, humid woods.

"A warm welcome to you all," he said softly as she dropped her gaze to the floor, her cheeks brightening. "And where are you staying?"

"We are lucky enough to be situated in the palace," the duchess supplied. "Your brother and mother were very kind."

Remi's brows lifted. He knew only a handful of guests were to be placed in the palace and he couldn't say he was disappointed this group were some of them. After all, Gilmore seemed a good enough sort, and the interesting Miss Linfield would not be unpleasant to look upon across a breakfast table.

Not that Remi made it to the breakfast table all that often.

"We have taken up too much of your time," the duchess said.

"I look forward to you taking up even more of it, Your Grace," Remi said, placing just enough flirtatious teasing into his tone that the duchess tittered softly.

Their group swept away into the ballroom. There were a few more guests to meet and then the family followed at last, entering the ballroom to the blaring of trumpets. His brother said a few words, Remi didn't pay attention to them, and the festivities truly began as the music rose.

Ilaria and Jonah, as well as Sasha and her husband, the Earl of Bramwell, led the dancing with a waltz. Meanwhile, the queen headed into the crowd to greet her friends and favorites in a more leisurely fashion.

Which left Remi standing by his brother's side. Grantham was glaring across the ballroom, his gaze focused. When Remi followed the stare, he found the Duke and Duchess of Gilmore and their charges, Miss Linfield and the duke's sister. Remi couldn't remember her name at present.

"I thought you liked the duke," Remi said, elbowing Grantham in the ribs gently.

His brother turned the heat of his glare on him now and nudged him back, not quite so gently. "I do."

"Then why are you glaring daggers into their party?" Remi asked.

"Hush," Grantham grunted. "They are coming across the floor to us. Do try not to make a scene, if you are capable."

His brother's order made Remi want to do the exact opposite of the edict. God, wouldn't it be fun to make a scene right here, right now, in the middle of his brother's crowded ballroom? Dance on a table or kiss the fetching Miss Linfield directly on the mouth. It would drive Grantham to the brink.

But it would also harm Ilaria and Sasha...and irritate their mother. So he pushed those wild urges down and instead forced a bored smile for the Gilmore party as they reached them.

"Good evening again, Your Majesty, Your Highness," the duke said.

Grantham's glare faded and was replaced by genuine warmth, which left Remi even more confused. What was so troubling to Grantham, then? "I'm so pleased you and your wife could join us, Your Grace," he said. *"Truly."*

"And we are thankful for the invitation," the duchess said with a brief smile for her husband. "Both because such friends are always well met, but also because it is a help to us."

"And once I'm happy to provide, Your Grace," Grantham said with an even warmer smile toward the duchess. "I'm happy you approached—these things are such a crush and there is never any time in the receiving line to say anything but the emptiest of platitudes. I hope your journey to Athawick was uneventful."

"Wonderful," the duke said. "And what a glorious introduction to Athawick as we sailed in this morning. Your shores are as beautiful as all rumors would have implied." The duke's sister cleared her throat gently, and for a moment the man's attention shifted to her. "I also wished to take the opportunity to more fully introduce you to our charges for the trip. You have met my sister, Lady Ophelia, before, of course."

To Remi's surprise, Grantham's brow furrowed slightly and he held his gaze on Lady Ophelia's face for a second too long. "Indeed," he said, his tone strained.

"But I don't think you might have had the pleasure of making Miss Priscilla Linfield's acquaintance."

"A pleasure, once again," Grantham said. "And of course, this is Remi...Prince Remington."

Remi stared at his brother. He never made the mistake of formality when they were meeting those outside of their family. He would definitely have to address that later and try to pry out of his brother exactly why he was so distracted.

"It is truly a pleasure, Your Majesty," Miss Linfield said, edging forward. "I read all about Athawick during your family visit to London and I could not believe such a fairyland truly existed. But here it is and I cannot wait to explore it further."

She leaned a little closer to his brother, and Remi watched her. Her body language was far too obvious. She wanted to make a good impression as she stared up at Grantham, all but batting those long blond lashes and lifting her green stare to be offered to best advantage.

Of course, Remi knew something she didn't: his brother was made of stone when it came to ladies. He was Remi's polar opposite in that regard. Oh, he'd had his dalliances, of course. He was no monk. But Grantham barely let his family past his defenses. He certainly had never allowed a woman to see anything but the kingly mask he wore.

Even now he glanced down at Miss Linfield and there was... nothing in his expression. "I believe the queen has scheduled a special tour of the capital city and surrounding countryside at some point before the nuptials. So you will likely get your wish. Now, Gilmore, I do hope we can talk more as the days pass. I know you are invested in some shipping ventures and I think we could both benefit from an alliance of sorts."

Lady Ophelia arched a brow. "So much business to be had at a supposed family celebration."

The entire party's gaze pivoted to her and Remi's eyes went wide. Not many people challenged his brother, and he could see Grantham didn't appreciate it. "That is why I said we would discuss it at a later date, Lady Ophelia. Perhaps I wasn't clear enough."

"I think you're perfectly clear," Lady Ophelia said with far more sweetness in her tone than was reflected in her eyes.

Grantham cleared his throat. "I should excuse myself, I have many people to speak to tonight. Enjoy yourselves."

He nodded vaguely to the group and then turned away. When he did so, the duke turned to his sister and glared. "Will you excuse the duchess and me, Prince Remington, Priscilla? We would like to have a chat with my dear sister."

Lady Ophelia sighed and the threesome slipped away, leaving Remi with Miss Linfield, who now looked entirely deflated. It seemed she had put a great deal of pressure onto her meeting with his brother, and Grantham's lack of interest, coupled with the odd exchange between him and her friend, made her sag a little.

"So what do you think of our little circus, Miss Linfield?" Remi asked, keeping his tone light.

She almost physically shook away whatever emotions she was allowing herself and looked out over the ballroom. "I was being honest when I called this place a fairyland, Your Highness. It is truly beautiful. Even the ballroom is finer than any I've ever been in. Look at the gauze and the beautiful candelabras and the livery and this design on the flooring is stunning."

Remi wrinkled his brow and looked at all the things she had pointed out. He was so accustomed to his home, he sometimes forgot how bright and beautiful it might be to a stranger. He smiled as he saw it through her eyes.

"We like it," he said.

She lifted those same eyes to him, and he was surprised when his breath hitched. Good Lord, but that stare was something. She hadn't fully turned it on him since they met but now he couldn't turn away. Her eyes were such a stunning green. When he didn't look away from her, her cheeks brightened with the hint of a blush.

He cleared his throat. "Would you like to dance with me, Miss Linfield?"

Her lips parted as if she were startled by the request. Truth be told, he was a little startled himself. He normally had to be dragged into dancing with the eligible ladies and limited himself to those he could seduce without consequence.

"Er, are you asking me to dance, or only if I'd *like* to do so?" she asked.

The question truly confused him. "Why would I ask if you'd like to and then not mean to follow through?"

She blushed again, but this time it wasn't a pretty flush of nervous attraction. It was something far sadder, more embarrassed. "It has been known to happen. As a jest or a tease."

He arched a brow. "I think you'll come to find out, Miss Linfield, that I am a rogue, *not* a cad. Let me rephrase. Will you do me the great honor of dancing the next with me?"

Her mouth opened and shut, but finally she nodded. "Y-Yes. I would like that, thank you."

The timing of her response was perfect, for the first dance had just ended and the floor was emptying of one set of revelers and filling with the next. He extended a hand and she glanced up at him once more before she took it. He guided her to the center of the floor and they waited together there.

"Everyone is watching," she said softly.

He glanced around. Indeed, she was correct. While his sisters had danced the first with their husbands, he was the first royal family member to choose a partner outside their realm. He should have realized what a stir that would cause.

"Are you a good dancer?" he asked.

"Fair," she admitted, her breath a little shorter.

He extended a hand again as the music rose and drew her closer. "Then you'll just have to trust me to lead you."

They spun out into the steps together. For the first few turns, she was a little stiff, but she relaxed as they turned. Once she did, he realized how she had undersold her talent on the floor. She was actually a very good dancer, with natural grace and a smooth fluidity to her movements. She could adjust easily when he maneuvered her and never lost her rhythm even when they had to dodge less talented dancers around them.

"Are you related to the Duke and Duchess of Gilmore then, that they would bring you with them to such an event?" he asked.

She shook her head. "No. I would think you'd know that from looking at me and Ophelia—we are nothing alike."

"Plenty of people are nothing alike to their blood siblings," he said, glancing toward Grantham briefly. "But yes, you two do look night and day."

The light in her gaze flickered a little, and for the first time, she stumbled in her steps. He firmed his arms around her, keeping her from tripping. Now why had that bothered her so much?

"Well, that may be true. But Ophelia is my oldest and dearest friend. And like a sister, no matter how...how much lovelier she is than me."

He wrinkled his brow. Ah, so she believed he'd compared them and found her lacking. Or else she was fishing for a compliment. But no, that didn't seem correct. She wouldn't look at him and her cheeks were filled with high color.

"I never said she was lovelier," he said simply. "I never thought it, either."

Her lips parted, but she still refused to lift her gaze to him. She just continued to turn in his arms and her fingers, which had been resting lightly on his shoulder, tensed slightly.

"You—you must be happy for your sister," she stammered.

He smiled and allowed the subject change. "I am. For both of them. Ilaria is my blood and I am happy for her joy. Sasha was adopted, but she is just as much my sister, as has been proven by the fact that she will be coronated a true princess once the royal wedding has taken place. I could not be more pleased for both of them, nor love them more."

She stared into his eyes and shook her head slightly. "Those are lovely things to say, to feel. They are not quite your reputation."

He choked on a laugh at her unexpected cheek. "Oh really, Miss Linfield?"

She caught her breath and staggered again in the steps. "I'm so sorry, I should never have been so forward with you, Your Highness."

He arched a brow. "If you are so aware of my character, you should know that I like forward. I like unforeseen depths like the ones you just showed." He leaned a little closer and caught a faint whiff of her scent: vanilla. Simple but warm and surprisingly intoxicating. "Now tell me, Miss Linfield, what exactly have you heard my reputation to be?"

"Oh...I...I couldn't..." she stammered.

"Nonsense. I demand you tell me," he teased. "By royal edict."

The music was beginning to slow and she swallowed hard. "Wild," she said, so softly that the one word almost didn't carry. "You are wild. Untethered. That you care for nothing but fun."

While he might agree with the first two adjectives, her last descriptor stung a little. She might not be the only one to believe it, but he hated to hear it.

"I do care about my family, Lady Priscilla," he said.

She nodded. "I can see that. I'm sorry I assumed incorrectly."

He chuckled. "Oh no, the rest is absolutely correct. I *am* entirely wild, completely untethered. I hear that is the attraction." He was holding her too closely now. He knew it. He couldn't seem to stop it. "Sometimes a little wild is what is needed, wouldn't you agree?"

The song ended with one crashing crescendo and she jolted as if startled. Slowly, she extricated herself from his arms and managed a shaky curtsey.

"Thank you for the dance, Your Highness," she said, keeping those green eyes away from his. "Good evening."

She backed away and then departed the dancefloor unsteadily. He still felt all the eyes on him and straightened up as he left the dancefloor in the opposite direction.

She hadn't answered his question, of course. When he asked it, he hadn't been expecting a response to be honest. He'd just been teasing her, playing the game he always played. But now he wondered how she would answer if pressed. He wondered what a woman like her would do with wildness if she caught it.

CHAPTER 3

Days passed quickly in Athawick, as packed as they were with activities. Since the welcome ball three days before, Priscilla had partaken in a bowling tournament on the magnificent south lawn of the palace, watched a presentation of traditional Athawickian boating trials on the lake and had a luxurious tea hosted by the queen, Princess Ilaria and the new Countess of Bramwell, themselves.

But there had been little chance to interact with the gentlemen of the party. She had only seen Prince Remington at supper since their dance at the ball. He'd been seated on the opposite end of every table from her and only sent her a few smiles or quick glances.

"You do look very pretty. Even the most boring king in the world would have to notice you," Ophelia said.

Priscilla jolted. She had not been attending to what her friend was chatting on about as they stood together in the parlor, awaiting the gathering of the rest of the guests. But now she was pulled to reality. Ophelia was talking about the king. The king Priscilla was supposed to be...would one call it wooing? She didn't know of many women in her acquaintance who wooed a man, but she supposed that was her goal. Or at least make him notice her.

Only he wasn't the royal gentleman who kept entering her mind. She had barely thought of *him* at all during the last few days. She really had to get her mind sorted or she would miss this opportunity.

"I hope so," she said, glancing down at herself and the pale green silk gown stitched with yellow flowers at the hem and intricate latticing on its short sleeves. "My grandmother used to say that she liked this color on me, so perhaps others will think the same."

Ophelia adjusted one of Pricsilla's curls so that it hung just so to frame her face. "Green has always been your color. It brings out your eyes."

She might have said more, but there was suddenly the rumble of a deep voice from in the hallway. "I understand the issue, Blairford, I am not so much a fool as you seem to think me to be."

"King Grantham," Ophelia whispered closer to Priscilla's ear.

Priscilla wrinkled her brow. *Was* that him? She did not yet recognize his voice so instantly as her friend seemed to do. "He sounds angry," she whispered back.

Ophelia rolled her eyes. "He always sounds angry, doesn't he? Come!"

She caught Priscilla's arm and dragged her toward the door. Priscilla pulled back. "What are you doing?" she whispered.

"Hurtling you into the path of a king," Ophelia grunted before she hauled Priscilla into the hallway and did just that. She gave Priscilla a not-particularly-gentle shove toward where King Grantham stood with his head courtier. His face was slightly flushed and he was talking closely with the man.

Priscilla came to a staggering stop. He really did look upset—she didn't want to interrupt him. She was about to slink back to Ophelia when she heard her friend call out, "Oh, there you are, Your Majesty."

Her voice drew his attention and he glanced down the hallway.

He looked past Priscilla at first toward Ophelia. His gaze flitted as if he were looking her up and down and then his lips pinched before he focused his attention on Priscilla, standing like a fool not ten feet from him.

"Your—Your Majesty," she stammered, swallowing hard as he stared at her.

"Take care of it...*please*," he said to his frowning courtier and then moved toward her. "Good morning, Lady Ophelia, Miss..." He hesitated as if he were struggling to recall her name.

"Linfield," she supplied.

"Of course, forgive me," he said, and inclined his head slightly. "I see you are both ready for...what has my mother planned for our guests today?"

Priscilla stared, her mind not allowing her to form coherent thoughts, let alone sentences. Not because the man was so handsome—he was, of course—but because he was so...he was *intimidating* in his presence.

"A tour of Athawick," Ophelia said when she could not, and stepped up. "I know Priscilla is very much looking forward to it, aren't you?"

Priscilla nodded. "Yes."

They both waited for her to elaborate, and when she didn't, Ophelia laced her arm through Priscilla's and squeezed gently, as support or inducement, Priscilla wasn't certain. "She researched so much of your island over the last few months that she will truly enjoy every moment. I'm sure you would be a fine guide for her."

He blinked down at them, his gaze on Ophelia rather than herself. And Ophelia stared right back, clearly not intimidated at all. It was almost as if Priscilla wasn't in their presence, hovering awkwardly between them.

"The entire royal family is happy to share their information about our country," he said at last. "And I'm sure my mother is also employing other guides."

"But none is a king. Certainly you must know every in and out, don't you, Your Majesty?" Ophelia pressed. "You do love your country to distraction, I have heard."

His brow furrowed. "And the distractions are why I am afraid I am not joining the group," he said, his tone a little sharper. "I'm certain you and Miss...Miss Linfield will have a fine time. Excuse me."

He pivoted and walked away without even so much as a backward glance. Priscilla stared after him, blinking as the chill his presence settled upon her dissipated.

"That ridiculous, pompous..." Ophelia shook her head.

Priscilla caught her arm and squeezed. "He will hear you!"

"I don't care," Ophelia said with a glare in the direction the king had disappeared into. "Could you possibly *want* such a man, Pris?"

"A king?" Priscilla hissed.

Ophelia pursed her lips. "A king who is so cold he cannot even come down from his throne for five minutes put together? So grouchy and self-important he feels a need to...to loom up like he does?" Her tone became faraway as she stared off after him. "I would want better for you. In fact, I forbid such a match."

"Forbid it?" Priscilla repeated, uncertain if she should laugh or be offended. "*You* suggested it!"

"I did no such thing. I suggested you pursue someone at court and then didn't argue strenuously enough against the idea of the king. Which I do now, as your dearest friend and confidante," Ophelia said with a certain nod of her head. "We will find another way. Another man or another path entirely. There are so many things we can find for you to—"

"If I cannot find a man to marry by the time I leave Athawick at the end of the month, I'm...I'm considering becoming a man's mistress."

That stopped Ophelia mid-sentence. Her friend stared at her, eyes wide with shock. "Priscilla," she said at last.

Priscilla shivered at her tone. "So do you...hate me? Judge me?"

Ophelia stepped forward and wrapped an arm around her. "Of

course not. You know I have no place to talk when it comes to such matters."

Priscilla bent her head. Four years before Ophelia had become involved with a man. It had ended poorly, but not before her friend had let things go too far. No one else knew it. Even her sister-in-law was in the dark.

"You have the best place to talk, considering you know the consequences," Priscilla said softly. "I do not consider this lightly, I hope you know."

"You never would," Ophelia said, her voice a mere whisper. "I just didn't know things had become so...desperate. What do you think about going to a man's bed like that? Would you be...be ready for what that meant?"

To Priscilla's surprise, her mind pulled her to an image of Prince Remington, his hands tight around her on the dancefloor, his gaze locked with hers as she was lost in his handsome face. She blinked to clear it and stepped away. "I...I don't know."

Ophelia clearly had a great deal to say on the subject, but before she could speak, the rest of the party began to enter the hall and move to the foyer in preparation for their tour. Ophelia squeezed her hand as she waved to the Duke and Duchess of Gilmore to join them.

"We will speak of this more later," she promised.

Priscilla nodded and tried to force a smile, a much more difficult thing when Prince Remington entered the foyer, the queen on his arm. He scanned the crowd and his gaze settled on her for a brief moment. He gave her a smile and then a cheeky wink before he pivoted away.

She closed her eyes and drew a long breath. Her future felt so cloudy that it was terrifying, so she tried to focus on this one day, this one moment...and hoped she'd find a solution to the rest before it was too late.

~

Remi had somehow managed to position himself at the end of the large crowd of royal guests, which gave him the best vantage point of them as a whole as they strolled down the long lane leading from the palace. His mother had intended for them to walk down to the village just below the castle. It was a beautiful place where lucrative businesses of trade and fishing created prosperity for a kingdom.

It also had a fine tavern where Remi had long snuck away to drink in disguise and occasionally whore his way to oblivion so he could forget who and what he was.

Today, though, he didn't long to do those things quite as much. Today found himself staring off into the crowd, attention firmly focused on Miss Priscilla Linfield. She walked with Lady Ophelia and her family, but while their group was happily chatting, Miss Linfield seemed distracted. Her shoulders were rolled slightly down, her gaze focused on the path ahead of her instead of her company. When the group stopped so that the queen could say something about the beautiful iron gate that led to and from the palace, Miss Linfield fell away from her friends and stood to the side, fussing with a loose string on the edge of the long sleeve of her pale blue spencer.

He found himself moving toward her as the rest of the party began down the path again.

"Good afternoon, Miss Linfield," he said as he reached her elbow.

She jumped as she glanced up at him, as if she had not noted his approach. "Your Highness," she said with a brief curtsey. "I-I did not see you there."

"No, for you are leagues away," he said, and leaned a little closer. "Thinking of some man?" He meant it to tease her, but he was surprised when her gaze darted away and her cheeks brightened with color. "Oh, I have hit upon a truth. Fascinating."

"You are being ridiculous," she huffed, voice trembling as they fell in step together at the back of the group as they continued down the path toward the village.

"Am I?" He chuckled. "Let me see if I can guess. You are troubled, that much is clear from the way you're holding yourself. So this is not a happy thought. In fact, I would wager you are disappointed."

He frowned as his own words pierced and he realized exactly what she was disappointed about: his brother. He'd guessed she might have an interest in Grantham when he first saw her with him, but had pushed that thought aside after their dance. The one he couldn't stop thinking about for some blasted reason. But now... now he knew his first instinct had been true.

"I-I'm not disappointed," she said. Lied.

"Of course you are, just as every lady must be," he drawled as he put a little more space between them. "After all, His Majesty has not deigned to grace us with his presence, has he?"

He heard the chill in those words and hated himself a little for it. Normally he didn't let such emotion rule him. No, for all his...what had Miss Linfield called it...wildness? For all that wildness, he was just as reserved as his brother when it came to letting emotion, especially painful emotion, rule him. He just suppressed it with far more entertaining methods than Grantham did.

Miss Linfield cleared her throat. "I...I suppose if your brother had joined us, it would have given me...given all of us...a chance to get to know him. To see him interact with your city, with your countrymen and women. Seems a good way to understand a person if one wished to do so."

She was hedging, and not very effectively. "I'm sure you're right, since country is all he gives a damn about," Remi said.

Her gaze jerked toward him. "You think so?"

"I know so, *Priscilla*." He emphasized her given name and watched as the color to her cheeks grew even higher. She stumbled a bit and he caught her elbow to steady her. She pivoted into his chest as she tried to catch her balance and her hand came to rest there, just above his heart. She stared up at him and he down at her, as close as they had been the night they danced together. Only he could not pretend that to pull her a bit closer was proper or for any other reason but that he liked the way her full curves molded to him.

Her breath became short but she didn't pull away. She just stayed there a fraction of a moment too long before he dropped his hand and she stepped back.

She was going to walk away, probably find an excuse to wend her way back into the group, and he didn't want that. For some unfathomable reason, he found himself wanting to spend more time with her. With her, this woman who was trying to convince herself that she liked his brother. This woman who was so innocent that it practically dripped from her and certainly kept her from being his type.

Despite all that, he said, "I could show you."

Her lips parted and her voice was rough as she whispered, "Show me what?"

There were at least two dozen inappropriate answers to that question, but he waded his way through them all to the one he'd meant. "The island. *His* island," he said. "I could show you."

She glanced up the path toward the group, which was now a few carriage lengths away up the road and growing farther with every moment that passed. "We're...we're on a tour, Your Highness."

He chuckled. "Yes, and my mother will make sure you hear all about the history of the church tower and the docks and God knows what else. I'm talking about the *real* Athawick."

She worried her lip for a moment, making them delectably pink and kissable in the process. Then she nodded slowly, with great uncertainty. "I suppose knowing more than the official facts about the island would be...interesting."

He didn't wait for her to talk herself out of that decision. Without another word he caught her hand in his and tugged her away from the path and the group.

"Wait," she said. "They might not notice that I've vanished—I'm invisible to most of them—but won't you be missed?"

He frowned at her description of herself, but then shrugged. "If I am gone, my mother will assume I hustled off to escape the crowd, which is true. Or went to do something wicked."

"Remington," she gasped, and he jerked his face back to her. She was red as a plum and she shook her head. "Your Highness, I'm so sorry, that was entirely inappropriate and I shouldn't—"

"Remi, and I want you to," he interrupted as he continued to urge her from the path, rather like some villainous cad in a gothic novel or fairytale. But then he'd always been more wicked villain than upstanding hero.

Her brow wrinkled, but she fell into step beside him despite what he knew had to be her misgivings. "You do?"

"Yes. Do you know how absolutely irritating it is to spend a lifetime being Your Highnessed and Princed and bowed to?"

She shook her head. "I suppose not. I'm hardly anyone at all back in London. As important as a flea."

He glanced down at her. "I doubt that, Priscilla."

She shifted at his use of her first name again, a fetching pink filling her cheeks. "If you were to wager, you would be wrong. But truly, you cannot expect me to call you Remington…or worse, Remi. You may dislike being a prince, but that doesn't change that you *are*. I have no right to call you by a family nickname. Or be anything less than formal with you."

He stopped walking and pivoted to face her. "Right now you and I are sneaking away from the main group together. Is *that* proper?"

She glanced back over her shoulder, and for a moment he thought he had overplayed his hand, that she would insist they go back to the others. But instead she sighed. "I suppose not."

"Then there is little harm in calling me Remi and I calling you Priscilla when we are alone together, is there?" he asked. "In private where no one would hear or judge you."

"Very well," she said after a long pause. "Then lead the way."

They walked together for a while, on a winding path that took them not directly to the village, but in a circuitous route around it and down to the sea. It was a secret path that led down a steep bluff to the beach. He moved down the shifting sands first and then turned back to extend a hand to help her. She looked at his fingers for a moment, then gripped them for balance as she came down the sandy hill.

"Will we be able to get back up?" she asked.

He smiled. "We'll go back up a different way. So what do you think?"

She drew in a deep breath and he watched her as she took in the view. It was glorious—he'd never met any person who didn't think so. This afternoon the sky was cloudless, the sun brilliant above them. This particular section of beach was comprised of soft sand, not like some of the wilder, rockier shores on the southern tip of the island a day's journey away by carriage. Here the waves lapped gently, not crashing and whipping up spray.

"It is almost unbearably beautiful," she said softly as she stepped closer, almost to where the waves would dampen her slippers and the edge of her gown. "Did you ever swim in it?"

He laughed. "Many times. It's such a short jaunt from the palace that my brother and I used to sneak out many a night and take a dip in the waves."

She pivoted to face him. "King Grantham did this?"

"He wasn't King Grantham then," he said with a shake of his head. "He was just Grantham to me and not quite as stuffy as he is now. My father hadn't quite beaten that into him."

She drew back a little. "Beaten?" she repeated, eyes wide.

He flinched. He shouldn't have said something like that. He was drawn to this young woman, but she was still a stranger. "*Encouraged*, if that word suits you better," he corrected.

She held his stare for a long moment, and he thought she might press him, might go digging in the mine of the past and its various pains. But instead she bent and let the water come up over her hand.

"Oh, it's cold," she said with a laugh. "Though I suppose it is the same sea as touches England's shores. I don't know why I thought it would be warmer. You two were brave to swim in it."

"It was part of the challenge," he said. "Who could stay in the cold for longest. He always won, the arse." He laughed and realized it was the first time in years that he'd done so when referring to his brother.

She smiled. "Why? I would think you would be driven to defeat him."

"You think so?" he asked, arching a brow. "And why is that?"

"You just seem the sort who likes to win," she said.

"Hmmm, you might be right at that," he admitted on a laugh. "But in this case, I think the answer would be discipline. He had enough to stay in the cold water just to see me dart out first."

"Well..." she said slowly. "Discipline is a fine quality in a king and a person."

He frowned. Why was it that any time she spoke highly of his brother that it irritated him so much? He didn't care if she pursued Grantham...and surely she would be rebuffed. His brother seemed in no hurry to wed, but to see his siblings shackled first. And Grantham was almost impossible to turn from a path once he had taken it. Thanks to that same discipline that Priscilla apparently valued so bloody highly.

"I wouldn't know, I am not king," Remi said, perhaps a little sharper than he had intended. "Come, we'll walk a bit farther up the beach."

He walked away from her then, expecting she would follow. Which, of course, she did. But he felt ill at ease. Usually he was effortless when it came to ladies, but this particular one set him on his heels a fraction.

And he had to do everything in his power to fight that. To keep from letting her see any side of him that he didn't want to reveal. This was a game, after all. One he wasn't going to lose.

CHAPTER 4

Priscilla wasn't certain of what to think of Remi's "tour" now that it had been going on for three-quarters of an hour. On one hand, he was utterly charming as he showed her the clusters of cottages outside of the main city where most of the residents of this part of Athawick lived. He had stories for so many of his people and that had been surprising by itself. He was supposed to be a ne'er do well, wasn't he? But there was clearly more to him than that. There was plainly a man that cared for his people, as much as his brother was rumored to do.

But then there was the other side to him.

His tone occasionally grew sharp when he mentioned King Grantham. It was evident that there was strain between them and her questions about his brother did nothing to ease it. In fact, sometimes his annoyance seemed higher when she pressed about the king's favorite pastimes or books or music.

And then there was the way Remi looked at her.

He was doing it right now as they strolled through a beautiful wooded grove on a path that seemed to be leading back to the castle in the distance. He was focused in his regard, his eyes always lingering on her face. It was almost as if he could see...deeper. Past whatever walls she erected, past however she held herself apart from him and most other people.

She shivered as she tried to ignore the attention. His regard, after all, could mean nothing in the end. It might even be little more than a game he was playing.

"You have told me stories about your family," she said quietly. "And the people of your island. But I have heard very little about *you*, Remi."

He arched a brow. "I thought your purpose in running away with me was just to hear all about my brother from an unbiased source."

She gave a soft laugh. "You think you are unbiased?" she asked. He didn't answer and she huffed out a breath. "Well, *I* would not say so."

"What *would* you say?" he pressed.

She tilted her head and examined his expression more closely. This might be a place where a more intelligent person would mask the truth, but she had never been one to lie. He had asked a question, she would answer.

"I cannot truly tell if you even *like* your brother, though your stories about your mother and sisters are warm. Your father I haven't heard a peep about aside from an offhand comment nearly an hour ago."

His jaw set as she spoke and a storm entered his gaze. She should have apologized and backed away. And yet she was further drawn in by that uncharacteristic show of emotion.

"I...*like* my brother," he said after what felt like a very long pause. "He is decent and there are few enough people one can say that about in this world, including myself. If he likes me is another story. Not unlike everyone in my family and more than half our kingdom, he thinks me a hopeless fool. And perhaps I am."

There was pain in that last statement. She felt it rippling under the surface and it changed everything she'd thought she'd known about this man. Now when she looked into his eyes, she saw the emotions. They were far back, hidden behind boredom and playfulness and flirtation, but they were there nonetheless.

His expression shifted as she looked at him. Discomfort flitted over those incredibly beautiful features and then he smirked and all of it was covered. Erased. Buried. "And what about you, Priscilla Linfield? What do *you* think of me?"

He wanted her to laugh. To call him a cad, to break the tension that now lingered in the air. Instead she said, "I think you are more than you wish the world to know, Prince Remington."

His smile faded and his jawline hardened again. He stepped up to her, closing the distance that separated them in one long step. Now he was too close. She felt his heat, she scented the woodsy smell of him. It was like when he'd caught her when she fell or held her when they danced, only this time there was no denying he used his nearness to unbalance her.

Her breath felt helplessly short in her lungs, like she couldn't draw a full gasp of air. He tilted his head, his gaze intently locked on hers. He appeared...*surprised*, but she had no chance to consider why that might be, because he lifted a hand and touched her, gliding his bare fingers along her jawline, his thumb tracing her lower lip ever so gently.

"Remi," she gulped out, unsure what else to say. How else to respond when he put his other arm around her waist and drew her closer.

His mouth lowered toward hers, and it was clear what would happen next. She could have pulled away. He held her loosely enough to allow escape, and she didn't think he was the kind of man who would force a kiss.

But she didn't. Instead she found herself lifting ever so slightly on her toes, trying to reach him faster, trying to feel this unexpected connection on a deeper level.

His lips brushed hers, gently at first. Just a featherlight exploration, but it was explosive, setting off reverberations of sensation through her body. He touched only her waist, her cheek, her lips, but she felt the echo of him in all her limbs, in her blood, between her legs.

Her lips parted and he probed deeper, his tongue pressing inside her mouth. He tasted like tea, like mint, like something irresistible, and she wanted more. She gripped the lapels of his jacket, clinging for purchase, using them for leverage to lift even closer.

He was…tasting her. There was no other way to describe what he was doing with that wildly talented tongue. And though she had never been kissed like this, she reacted with some natural drive she'd never felt awakened in her before. She wanted to be closer, to drive deeper. To feel more of this dizzying desire that he awakened in her with his mouth.

This prince. This brother of a man she had made some clumsy effort to pursue.

That dragged her out of the fog his kiss created, and she gasped, breaking the contact of their lips. He released her immediately, his blue gaze tracking her as she staggered backward a few steps.

"W-we shouldn't do that," she choked out.

She somehow expected him to react, but all he did was arch a brow. He looked…bored. Like it had all been meaningless from the kiss to the rejection of it. That was utterly confusing considering how passionately he had claimed her mouth.

"I suppose not," he drawled. "After all, you want my brother, don't you?"

Her lips parted at both the words he said and the edge with which she said them. "W-want?" she repeated.

He tilted his head. "Don't lie to a liar, Priscilla. Your goal is to land a king, is it not?"

She caught her breath. Everything in her knew that she should deny his claim, but he already knew. He knew her thoughts, it seemed. Her desires. And that was as terrifying and intoxicating as his kiss.

"I…on paper King Grantham seems a good match for me," she admitted slowly. "After all, we're both studious sorts."

He snorted but made no verbal comment beyond that. She glared at him before she continued, "I have heard that he likes some of the same things as I do: music and books and the like. Only…"

She dropped her gaze. This was a ridiculous conversation. No, it was a ludicrous situation entirely. She shouldn't have run off from the group with Remi, she definitely shouldn't have kissed him, she most certainly shouldn't be speaking words of confession to him.

"Only what?" he asked, his tone sharp enough that she glanced back up at him.

He had folded his arms across his broad chest and his lips were pinched, almost in irritation. But if this exchange bothered him so, if he thought her foolish, why did he not just march her back to the group and forget about her? Why did he push?

She licked her lips and his pupils dilated slightly. "Only he does not seem to notice me," she admitted, and hated how heat flooded her cheeks. "It is a humiliation to concede, and I'm sure you will laugh at me, but I was somehow imprudent enough to believe that I could somehow make a *king* notice me when no one in my own country did for so many years."

Her voice caught and she cleared her throat. She was not about to have an emotional collapse in front of Remi of all people.

"I might laugh," he said softly. "But only because that is what one does when considering fools."

That stung, and she turned away slightly. "I would not disagree that I am a fool."

"Not you." He sounded like that was the most absurd notion. "Them. And my brother, if he has not cast his gaze upon you with any interest."

She allowed herself to look at him. He seemed serious, not like he was teasing her. This man who could have any woman he wanted…had had a great many, if his reputation was correct…said she was desirable.

He smiled slightly, and she shivered. "You—you are a flirt, sir," she gasped out.

"And *you* need to be," he retorted with a shake of his head. "You are hopeless, absolutely terrible at it."

She wrinkled her brow. "Well, that is direct."

"Direct is the best way to be in these situations, isn't it? And do you deny that you have little skill in...in seduction?"

She had *no* skill in seduction, but he had gone from petting her to...well, he was insulting her, wasn't he? And all in the span of a minute. "You *did* kiss me," she retorted.

His eyes went wide at her peppery tone. "I did do that. But I promise you had very little to do with it. I did it only from my own wicked volition."

He winked as he said it, and she couldn't help but laugh at his teasing. He did turn her on her head over and over. Normally such a thing wouldn't be attractive to her. She liked when people and situations were predictable. But this chaotic, handsome man made her toes curl a little in her slippers. More than that, he made her comfortable to talk to him about a subject she dodged with everyone else, even Ophelia, in some ways.

Priscilla sighed. "But how does one...flirt? You are not wrong that I've never been good at it. It all feels so false to me, so forced. How did you learn to be so proficient at it?"

He shook his head. "I just...I just am, I don't know. I didn't have lessons, Priscilla. It isn't elocution or dancing."

"*Isn't* it like dancing?" she asked. "And doesn't it make sense that perhaps a master of the art...someone like you, perhaps, could teach a novice like myself?"

In every other scenario, Priscilla had felt that Remi was entirely sure of himself. But right now he stared at her like she had grown a second head or like he'd just realized he was in a dream, not reality. He looked confused and uncertain and...intrigued.

"Me?" he asked. "Teach you to flirt?"

She nodded. "Yes. You seem the best person for it."

"Why not Lady Ophelia?" he asked. "You two are close."

"Close as sisters, but first off, Ophelia doesn't flirt. She doesn't need to draw people to her—they just naturally come to her." She tried not to be jealous of that fact as she continued, "And secondly, I don't think she approves much of your brother."

His mouth dropped open. "Is *that* what she said?"

Priscilla considered him a moment. "Would you have her beheaded for impertinence?"

"Of course not. Locked in a tower, perhaps. But never beheaded," he teased.

"She thinks him rather…boorish. And sometimes rude. And far too grumpy for me. So she will not be an ally in this. Which leaves me with you."

"You think *I* would be an ally in this?"

She nodded. "I'm sure you wish your brother to be happy."

He narrowed his gaze on her and then walked away, rubbing his chin as he did so. "I'm not certain of my position on his happiness. Your friend might be right that my brother is bound to avoid such a frivolous thing. But I *would* like to see him married." He glanced back at her. "If only to keep him from springing the same trap on me."

"You think he would force you to marry?"

"He tried it with Ilaria in London," he said with a shrug. "I am the next in line for such machinations. But if he were to make his godforsaken alliance first…well, then I would hardly even be a spare anymore." His expression fell a fraction. "I would be almost nothing at all."

"You are quite the mercenary," she said.

"No, I'm clever," he corrected. "And you are certain you wish to win him?"

Certain…well, she felt considerably less certain when she could still taste Remi on her lips. When her stomach still fluttered in a way she didn't fully understand when she looked at him.

But this prince had been very clear that he had no intention to marry. And kiss or not, she could certainly not be his type if he ever did. He'd want someone like Ophelia certainly, as cocksure as he was, as playful and confident.

"I-I suppose," she said.

He pondered her for a moment. "Then I'll help you," he said at last. "I'll teach you everything you need to know to land a man. More specifically *that* man."

She worried her lip. This seemed like the worst idea, even though it had been her own not three minutes before. After all, she'd kissed this man, and he wasn't exactly an uninterested party. But the threat of her future still hung over her like a guillotine waiting to fall.

If this could help...?

"Thank you," she said softly. "Truly. You don't know what this means."

His brow wrinkled, as if he had caught a glimpse of her utter terror. The one she tried to hide. But he said nothing about it, merely motioned back toward the path. "Come, if we go this way, we will be able to rejoin my mother's party as they make their way back to the castle. Not a one will be the wiser."

She wasn't certain of that, but she felt too off-kilter to launch an argument. So she merely followed him through the woods, back toward reality. Back toward whatever future she could make for herself, with his help or without it.

CHAPTER 5

People had always thought that Remi was reckless. At least that was the charge his father had often thrown at him, and his brother sometimes said the same.

What they didn't realize was that often Remi knew exactly the trouble he was getting into. He didn't stumble into it—he walked in willingly, accepting the consequences because the rewards made sense.

But now, a day after his pledge to Priscilla to teach her how to flirt, he was less certain of himself than he'd ever been. This was a mistake, there was no denying that. He'd been thinking of her more often than he should since their searing kiss in the woods the previous afternoon. Normally when that happened, he backed away as swiftly and quietly as possible so as not to form a bond he'd only have to break.

But Priscilla didn't want a bond. Not with him anyway. So pushing her off on his brother was the perfect solution. It solved his problem of being forced to marry for position and it gave her what she wanted. Everyone would win.

In theory. In practice, he felt a little sour inside every time he thought of Priscilla kissing Grantham like she had kissed him.

He shook the thoughts away and set his teacup on the sideboard in the Blue Parlor. Tonight was the second ball of the royal wedding celebration, and Remi had arranged to meet with Priscilla in…he glanced at the clock on the mantel…twenty minutes so they could talk a bit about flirting. When he was with her, he surely wouldn't be so taken in anymore. That would solve the problem.

He moved toward the door, ready to make his way to the ball-room where he had intended to help her practice, but before he could make his way out of the chamber, the door opened and his mother stepped in, followed by her longtime personal secretary, Dashiell Talbot.

"Mama," Remi said, coming forward to kiss her cheek. "Dash."

"Good afternoon, Remi," the queen said with a quick glance toward Dash. "I am sorry we didn't see you this morning at break-fast. There were a few guests asking after you."

Remi pursed his lips. "Were there now? And did you tell them I'm a wastrel who always sleeps until noon or beyond? Did any of them faint dead away at the idea of marrying such a lout?"

His mother was trying to suppress a laugh. Remi smiled, for he loved doing that. He loved pulling down her royal mask a fraction, even if it was just to stick his tongue out at her. And she loved it, too. The rest of the royal children always whined mercilessly that Remi was her favorite.

"Not a one, I'm afraid, so your campaign to make yourself less attractive is failing miserably," Queen Giabella said.

"A campaign, she calls it," Remi said with a quick wink toward Dash. He had always liked the man. He was serious, but he took care of Remi's mother. He protected her at all times, against all comers.

Dash shook his head. "Your failure to appear *was* noted, though, Your Highness. All joking aside, these next few days are critical to—"

"Grantham's great plan to unite one of us for political gain?" Remi asked, and wished he sounded less bitter about it.

"No," Dash said gently. "It is critical to Princess Ilaria's future."

The queen took Remi's hand. "You know that tomorrow is a big day for her. Grantham will be officially granting a title to Jonah before their wedding next week. And with the unrest in the kingdom continuing, it is important that we present a united front for her *and* for your brother's sake."

Remi bent his head. "Yes. I will try to do better, Mama."

She smiled up at him. "Thank you, love. Will you join Dash and me for tea? We were going to discuss some scheduling, but that can wait, can't it?"

"Of course, Your Majesty," Dash said softly.

"I wish I could," Remi said. "But I have another appointment to attend to and it starts just now."

Giabella's brow wrinkled. "Another appointment? What other appointment?"

Remi chuckled. Good God, if he told her what he was doing with Priscilla Linfield, she would have an apoplexy. But in the end, it could result in help for the entire family. When she spoke of unrest, it made his stomach turn. Grantham, for all his stuffy faults, was a good man and was already a good king. That some were determined to undermine that was vexing.

But if Grantham married…would it not appease the populace in some way? Ilaria's royal wedding was already enrapturing the people—Grantham's could only make it better. And Priscilla would be a good choice for that kind of calming effect.

"Your Highness?" Dash asked.

Remi blinked. He'd been woolgathering. "Don't worry yourself, I promise I'm not getting into too much trouble. And I might even help the family." He lifted his mother's hand to his lips and kissed it briefly. "Now I must rush off. But you will save me a dance tonight, won't you, Mama?"

She smiled and it lit her face up so beautifully. God, he loved to see her happy. The years with his father, especially the later ones, had been so miserable, and he liked to see her come back to life. "Of course. I will put it on my dance card immediately."

He squeezed her hand, saluted Dash and rushed from the room. He moved down the hall, past a few parlors, where he heard guests talking, and prayed they would not waylay him. But at last he came to the ballroom. The door was cracked and he slowly pressed it open.

The staff had already finished their cleaning and decorating for the night's festivities so the only person there was Priscilla. She was early, but of course she would be. Remi almost laughed at his foolishness to think he'd beat her there.

She stood at the glass terrace doors, staring out with a pensive expression on her lovely face. Her blonde hair was pulled back in a simple style, with curls framing her cheeks. Her dress was also simple, a pale blue silk with a feather pattern that fell along the skirt. It highlighted all her curves rather perfectly, and he couldn't help but think of how she'd fit so beautifully against him the day before.

"Oh, Your Highness," she said as she turned toward him with a jolt. It was one he shared, because when she looked at him, it was sort of like being hit by lightning.

He ignored the feeling and stepped forward, forcing a playful smile to his face. "Miss Linfield," he said. "I should have known that on time would be late for you."

A fetching pink blush filled her cheeks. "I know it is a bad habit, for isn't it just as rude to come too early as it is to be tardy?"

He wrinkled his brow. "Perhaps for a small supper party, but certainly you coming to the ballroom a few minutes early is no crime." She blushed deeper and his eyes widened. "How early were you?"

"Er, an hour?" she said slowly, as if drawing out the answer would make it better.

"An hour?" he repeated. "Great God, Priscilla, why?"

"I was nervous," she admitted on a laugh. "And I couldn't focus and Ophelia started asking me all kinds of questions. I thought it would be better to walk off my nervous energy here in the ballroom. And I admit, it has been nice. Not one person has come in here until you did, so I got to gather my thoughts without being intruded upon."

"Do you need me to leave?" he asked, half meaning it even if he said it playfully.

"No!" she burst out. "You're the one I've been thinking of." Her eyes went wide. "I mean…I only meant I've been thinking about our agreement."

He cleared his throat. The idea that she'd been thinking about him hit him directly in the chest. "Yes, I've been thinking about it too. Trying to gather my thoughts on how to flirt. It was more complicated than I thought it would be."

She seemed as relieved as he felt to get to the crux of the matter. "That doesn't surprise me. You are such a natural when it comes to how you interact with people, and with women especially. You must not even think about the actual mechanics of how you do what you do."

He thought about that. "Yes. That is likely true."

"I made a study of you last night," she admitted, and blushed. "Not too obvious, I don't think. But I watched you at supper, and later when the gentlemen rejoined the ladies after their port."

"A very silly tradition we only did because the English gentlemen seemed to think it ridiculous that they wouldn't get some time away from the ladies," Remi said. "In Athawick we normally all break together after supper."

She smiled slightly. "Yes, you have a very different view of men and women entirely, I think, than the English do. You hold your women at a higher level, see them as closer to equal."

"I would say that my mother and sisters are far more than my equal," he said. "I hold them in much higher esteem than I do myself."

"That is lovely, but you have so many good qualities, Remi," Priscilla said, stepping toward him. "You make people comfortable. I watched it last night. You are so genuine, so welcoming. You've never met a stranger, or at least it seems that way. And when you are with someone, you are truly with them. You're not looking off to your next stop—you are present, and that is rare."

Remi swallowed. In some ways he did all the things she described to hide in plain sight. That she was observing them felt... uncomfortable. Like a mask had been stripped from his body and left him naked.

"Perhaps we should begin with the lesson," he said, hearing how rough his voice was.

She hesitated, but then nodded. "Of course. I did not mean to take up too much of your time."

He could have corrected her. After all, he had been looking forward to this time with her all day. But at the moment, that felt too vulnerable, so instead he beckoned her closer.

"There is a trick to flirting," he said as she stepped up closer. Not close enough, but somehow still too close. It was a very confusing thing. "And you hit on it a moment ago when you said that you want to make the person you are with feel you are truly present." He hesitated. "Even if you aren't."

He watched her expression fall slightly as those words sank in. He had implied, of course, that his connection was an act, or potentially so. And he could see her running through their interaction the day before and wondering if he had been truly there with her or already planning his next interaction with some other person.

He hadn't been, of course. But she didn't need to know that.

"I see," she said softly. "And how do you do that?"

"Contact," he said. "It's all about contact. Giving it and removing it. Implying it and enacting it."

She looked confused, and so he reached out and let his hand brush her forearm briefly, just the lightest brush of his fingers. "You do look lovely in that gown, Miss Linfield," he said as he pulled his hand away.

Her pupils dilated and her tongue darted out to lick her lips. His traitorous body, the one that should not have wanted her, reacted of its own accord, sending a flash of hot desire through his veins.

"The words are simple, benign," he choked out. "And the touch is brief. It could be construed as meaningless. But it is a connection."

"I...see," she whispered. "You held my gaze as you did it, too. It did feel like it—like it shrank the world a little."

She wasn't wrong. In this moment, the world did seem small, boiled down to him and this woman, in this quiet room where no one else existed. That he couldn't let that be was something too easy to forget.

"If the touch seems too difficult," he said, backing away from her mostly for his own sake, "or too informal when my brother is so stiff and staid, then there are other ways to connect without it."

Her gaze darted to the floor and she nodded. "And what are those?"

He slipped a finger beneath her chin and lifted it, making her look at him.

"Eye contact," he said softly. "The first way to draw someone to you is to look into their eyes. You can do it from across the room, you can do it when you're talking about the most benign subject. But you'll notice most people don't look others in the eye, so when you do it, it is the first step of being present."

She seemed to consider that a moment. "I suppose that's true. I don't meet the eyes of many people except those I'm comfortable with. And...and you."

He smiled despite how dizzy this entire conversation was making him. "You don't feel comfortable with me?" he teased.

She shook her head. "Never. I'm entirely off kilter when I'm with you."

He swallowed hard. The feeling was most definitely mutual, but what was the point of saying that? It had nothing to do with their current lesson and would only muddy the waters and push them both further from their mutual goal.

"Here, let me stand back a touch," he offered. "I'll go to the punch table here and we'll pretend I'm getting a drink. Approach me and let's just try what you've learned thus far."

She nodded, though he could practically see her head spinning. He stepped away and positioned himself at the table. There was nothing on it at present, but he made a show of pouring himself pretend punch from a pretend bowl into a pretend cup. When he pivoted back, he found her smiling at him, somewhat indulgently.

And he wanted to kiss her so badly that he could almost taste her. A feeling he ignored.

"So I am Grantham in this scenario," he said. "Allow me to get into character." He furrowed his brow and scowled and grunted, playing an over-the-top version of his brother.

She giggled, but then smoothed her hands over her gown at is she were trying to put herself in character just as he was. She turned away and then slowly pivoted back. From a few feet away, she met his eyes and let a small smile tilt her lips.

He was lost. Those green eyes were so wide in that moment, so bright. His lips parted as he stared into them and saw...

But no. He saw nothing. This was a game and one she intended to win with a different man. He had to remember the outcome he was hoping for, the result he needed to come to fruition.

"Very good," he said, his voice too rough. "Now approach me."

She did so, slowly but not too hesitantly. "Your Majesty," she said softly.

"Miss Linfield," he grunted, trying desperately to stay in the character of his brother so that this wouldn't be so very real. "Are you enjoying yourself tonight?"

She smiled, just a flutter of expression, and nodded. "Very much so. The ball is perfect."

He nodded. "Yes, perfect."

She cleared her throat and edged closer. "So you are suggesting, Remi, that I might find a way to...to..." She reached out and rested a hand on his forearm briefly. She kept the eye contact as she did so, and the world began to spin just a bit faster and more out of control as he stared down at her. Her fingers were only pressed lightly to his arm, but even through the layers of clothing, he felt the burn of them as if she branded him with her touch. God's teeth, it was confusing. What woman had ever enthralled him so completely and without even knowing she was doing it?

He cleared his throat and backed up a step, breaking the contact before he caught her around the waist and kissed her thoroughly, ruining the entire plan before they'd even fully started.

"Yes," he grunted, and this time it wasn't to play the role of his brother, it was because he couldn't form a cogent sentence when she was looking at him like that. "Only I would be very brief if I were you. Grantham is obsessed with propriety."

"As he should be," Priscilla said, and turned away slightly. Her breath was coming short now, as if she had been as moved by this game as he was. "As we all should be, I suppose." She worried her hands before her. "Are there…are there any special topics of conversation that I might wish to bring up to him? Something that would make him feel a connection?"

Remi wrinkled his brow. God, what did his brother like these days? Once upon a time he would have said fishing or riding or boxing, because he and Grantham had done all those things together. But in the final year of their father's life, in the year since his death, their bond had frayed more and more. Now he wasn't certain he truly knew Grantham at all.

"He's fond of a raspberry tart," he offered weakly.

She rolled her eyes at him. "*That* is your grand suggestion? That I bring up raspberry tarts like a fool?"

He chuckled at the idea. "It would make you stand out."

"I suppose that is true," Priscilla said with a broad smile. "Well, I don't know if this will work, but I will try. Thank you for the help."

He nodded. "Of course. And I will try to help you further tonight. I'll corral him toward you as soon as I can. And grease the wheels by extolling your many virtues."

She pulled a worried face. "Oh, don't build me up too high or I shall surely disappoint him."

"You could never," he promised.

A blush darkened her cheeks and she bent her head. "You have more faith in me than I have in myself. But I will try so that your time and your assistance won't be wasted. And now..." She backed away. "I will trouble you no longer. I must go start to ready myself for tonight."

"I look forward to seeing you," he said. "Oh, and Priscilla?"

She stopped and turned back at the door. "Yes?"

"Wear something green," he suggested. "It will bring out your eyes."

"You think he would like that?" she asked.

"I would."

Her lips parted and the blush brightened. Then she nodded and slipped away.

When she was gone, he let out his breath in a whoosh. He had done what needed to be done and perhaps she would be successful in her pursuit. If she wasn't, he would level the blame at Grantham, not her.

But if she was...

Well, he was going to have to start figuring out how to be less intrigued by Priscilla. Because their goals, though similar, could not allow him to track her as he was doing. Could not allow him to want her as he was doing.

He just had to remember that fact before he destroyed three lives by wanting something he could not have.

CHAPTER 6

Priscilla smoothed her gown for what felt like the tenth time since she and the Duke of Gilmore's party had entered the ballroom. The royal family had not yet joined them, but she found herself staring toward the door every few moments as if she could conjure them. Conjure one of them, at any rate.

And she feared it wasn't the king that she wished to draw to her, despite her plans. She just wanted to see Remi. As if his chaos could calm her somehow.

"You are pale," Ophelia said, sliding an arm around her waist. "Are you well?"

"I am," Priscilla said. "Just a little nervous."

Ophelia wrinkled her brow. "Nervous about what?"

"Well, we all must make a good impression, mustn't we?" Priscilla said after a pause. Ophelia would not approve of her plans, she knew. She disliked King Grantham so completely. The last thing she wanted to hear was yet another diatribe about the man's lesser qualities, which was what always happened when his name came up.

"I suppose," Ophelia sighed. "Oh look, here comes the family now so we can begin at last."

King Grantham entered the ballroom first to a fanfare of trumpets. The room as a whole curtsied and bowed to him. His lips pinched as if he didn't enjoy the attention and he swiftly scanned the room. His gaze fell on their party, and Priscilla held her breath as she tried to do as Remi had taught her: catch his eye. Only the king didn't seem pleased and he barely looked at her before his gaze moved on.

She let out her breath in disappointment. So much for the first effort. The queen entered behind him, and then Princess Ilaria and her fiancé, Captain Crawford. They looked deliriously happy as they smiled at each other. Behind them was Remi, and Priscilla's heart thudded traitorously. He was so handsome in his full formal attire, even if his hair was rakishly mussed. Did he do that on purpose, or had he just been absentmindedly running his fingers through those thick locks?

Unlike his brother, when Remi found her across the room, his attention lingered. He gave her a brief smile and a nod, shoring her up before he stepped aside and allowed the Earl and Countess of Bramwell to make up the rear of the party. Another happy couple that looked at each other with pure adoration.

For a moment Priscilla's heart revolted against her mind. She wanted that. She wanted the connection she saw with those couples in love. She wanted head-over-heels devotion and passion, not the vague regard of a man who married her to connect himself to her grandfather and his title.

She pushed those desires down. The only end to that path was one of ruin and despair. She'd had plenty of chances to find love and it just...it just hadn't been there for her. Now she had to protect herself at all costs, and *this* was the way to do it.

The royal party broke apart, spreading to separate corners of the room to greet guests. The earl and his new countess stepped onto the dancefloor to take the first turn of the night. For a moment Remi and the king stood together, talking with their heads close together. Remi looked uncharacteristically serious and Grantham shook his head. But at last they began to come across the room toward her.

"Abigail, would you dance with your husband?" the Duke of Gilmore asked, sliding an arm around his wife's waist.

Priscilla let her gaze move back to her companions. Yet another example of deep and abiding love was being played out before her. There was a spark between Abigail and Gilmore. A flame when they thought no one was looking.

"I would like nothing more," the duchess said softly as she stared up at him with pure love.

"Excuse us, ladies," Gilmore said to her and to his sister, and then they moved off into the crowd.

"They truly adore each other," Priscilla said softly.

Ophelia nodded. "They went through a great deal what with the… with everything. But they came out so happy with each other. I could not have asked for a better wife for my brother or sister for myself."

There was something sad about Ophelia's tone as she said that, but Priscilla didn't get a chance to say anything, because in that moment Ophelia noticed that Remi and King Grantham were rapidly approaching.

"I certainly do not have the energy for *that* man right now," Ophelia huffed. "I'm going to get some punch—would you like to come with me to escape him?"

"Him, King Grantham?" Priscilla asked.

"Yes," Ophelia said with impatience.

"No, I'll greet him and the prince. You run away if you need to."

Ophelia swiftly ducked away without another word, leaving Priscilla to stare after her. Perhaps it was best that her friend wasn't standing with her when the men reached her. Ophelia tended to draw all attention to herself without even meaning to do so. Aside from her dislike of the king, she was a jolly sort, friendly and quick witted. Plus, she would certainly note any attempts at flirtation that Priscilla made and comment on them later. At the moment, Priscilla wasn't ready to dig deeper into the fraught topic of her future with Ophelia.

"Good evening, Miss Linfield," Remi said as he and the king reached her. She shook her thoughts away and smiled first at him and then at the king.

"Your Highness, Your Majesty," she said as she executed a quick curtsey.

She glanced at Remi, but he gently flicked his chin toward the king, as if reminding her of her path. She forced her gaze back to him, trying to meet his. An almost impossible task when he was looking off into the crowd in the direction that Ophelia had gone.

"You recall Miss Linfield, do you not, Grantham?" Remi said.

That did the trick. The king did look at her now, though not in the eye. His gaze flickered over her, impassive, disinterested. "Er, of course. Lady Ophelia's friend," he said, and then shook his head. "You came in the party of the Duke and Duchess of Gilmore."

"I did. They are old friends. Ophelia is my dearest friend."

The king pursed his lips. "How...interesting."

She shifted slightly. He sounded exactly the opposite of interested. In fact, he looked rather annoyed. "You—you know, I took a tour of part of your island the other day," she said, trying again to catch his eye. "It is a beautiful place, you must be very proud of it."

His brow wrinkled. "I am."

He was standing close enough that she could probably touch him, just as Remi had explained during their lessons on flirting. Only she could think of nothing clever to say when the man was looming up over her, his attention only half on her. Touching Remi had been easy, but this was something else entirely.

"I would...love to talk to you more about it," she said. "I find myself fascinated by the history and the people of Athawick."

Remi smiled slightly, a faint encouragement that told her she had chosen the correct topic. It buoyed her, and she again tried to find the king's attention. She smiled up at him.

"Er, yes," he grunted. "There is a great deal to love here in

Athawick. I'm certain one of the courtiers could direct you to a book on the subject in the library."

He looked away, back into the crowd, distracted from her yet again. The truth hit her in the chest: this man would *never* look at her, not directly. Not with interest. Good on paper had not translated to anything beyond that. Now, whether that was because she was fundamentally unattractive to men or just this man didn't really matter in the moment. In the moment, it just felt like humiliating failure.

She backed up, dropped her gaze at last. "Of course, I'll ask someone about that. I have taken up enough of your time, I fear, Your Majesty. I shall leave you to the rest of the guests. Good evening."

She pivoted, refusing to look at Remi. She worried she'd see his disappointment in her performance, or worse, his pity. And she didn't want to see any of that. Right now she didn't want to see anything or anyone until she'd gathered herself after that humiliation.

She rushed away, trying to maintain a composed expression as she weaved through the crowd and finally managed to escape the ballroom. She just needed a moment to herself, that was all. And then she'd have to pretend again. Pretend she was fine, pretend she was unbothered, pretend she wasn't making a thousand of the most desperate plans for a future that felt terrifying blank at present.

Because she certainly wasn't going to be saved by a king.

Remi watched as Priscilla left the ballroom and his heart swelled with the humiliation that was clear all over her face. She had tried to do what he asked and now she was in pain.

He turned his attention back to Grantham. His brother seemed to hardly notice that the young lady had departed. He was still staring off on the ballroom floor, where the couples were dancing.

"Oy," Remi growled. "What the hell is wrong with you?"

Grantham jerked his gaze back to him. "I beg your pardon? You would do well to recall that you are speaking to your king in public."

"I'm speaking to my brother, and I can do it privately if you'd prefer," Remi snapped.

Grantham let out a grunt, then caught Remi's arm. They stalked across the ballroom together and entered one of the alcoves along the back wall. It wasn't entirely private, but that was probably good. What Remi wanted to do right now was punch some sense into his brother and he didn't think that would go over well.

"What are you going on about?" Grantham asked.

"You just humiliated Priscilla," Remi said, stepping up closer to his brother. Grantham had a few inches on him, but they'd always been evenly matched when they fought. "You selfish, pompous arse."

Grantham flinched. "How? I spoke to her, did I not? I was cordial."

"You were so distracted, you didn't even notice the young woman has an interest in you," Remi said. God, he almost choked saying those words.

Grantham jerked back as if he *had* been punched. "What?"

"You bloody idiot. You didn't see her gazing up at you with those...those incredible green eyes? You didn't see her trying to catch your interest with talk about the island you supposedly love?"

"I do love it," Grantham retorted sharply. "You have no idea how much. But the concept that Miss Linfield would have any interest me is ridiculous. That I would have interest in her, even more so."

Remi fisted his hands hard at his sides. "Why is that?" he asked through clenched teeth.

"Because she is best friends with the most inappropriate woman I have ever seen in my life." He moved to a part of the alcove that allowed them to see the ballroom floor. "Look at Lady Ophelia."

Remi did so, finding the stunning, raven-haired beauty easily in the crowd. She was dancing a country reel with the others, a wide smile on her face, her steps light and lively. Almost every eligible man in the room was tracking her, and half the married ones.

"I am looking." Remi shrugged. "What of her?"

"Were I to express an interest in Miss Linfield, were I to have *any* interest in her, it would only set me firmly in the path of that... that..." Grantham's voice got softer. "Impertinent, headstrong...hoyden."

Remi's eyes went wide. There was something about the way his brother shifted, the way Grantham's gaze focused so entirely on Ophelia, that made the truth clear. He was attracted to the woman. Powerfully so. And that hadn't happened in years, at least so far as Remi knew.

And it closed the door firmly on all of Priscilla's hopes, no matter if Grantham would ever pursue that desire for Ophelia or not. It was odd because relief washed over Remi as he realized that. Too powerful, too overwhelming.

Of course, that was just because he'd kissed Priscilla. That would have made things awkward had she ultimately married his brother. That was likely the only reason he felt relief.

"You are an idiot," Remi said, but there was little heat to the comment.

Grantham shook his head. "That is entirely possible. Why so interested in what happens to Miss Linfield?"

"I'm not," he lied. "But I do think that hurting her was not well done."

Grantham drew back. "It was not my intent to hurt her. I just don't want her."

That made Remi flinch. It was how Priscilla saw herself, after all. A woman men would not want, at least for marriage. "Then you're a fool. Now go back to your party and your scowling at the sunshine, and I will go back to my games."

"And we'll pretend we never had this conversation? Pretend we never danced around...around whatever truth marks us both?" Grantham asked, and for a moment he met Remi's eyes evenly.

"We always do," Remi said, and walked from the alcove without a backward glance at his brother.

He ought to have just mingled back into the crowd. Perhaps found an amiable widow to dance with. But instead he looked toward the door where Priscilla had left a few moments before. He had to follow her. It was like a drive that burned inside of him, pulling him toward her even when he ought not go there.

But he had taught her the flirting, hadn't he? Didn't he owe her the courtesy of telling her she hadn't done anything incorrect beyond pick the absolutely wrong mark for her attentions?

It would be better to hear it from him, at any rate.

So he followed where she'd gone, exiting the ballroom, roaming down the long hallway. Almost all the doors to the various parlors and studies were closed, but there was one near the stairway that was cracked, a sliver of light coming from within.

He pushed the door open slowly and found Priscilla. She stood at the window looking out on the dark garden below. Her head was bent, resting in her hands. And she was...she was crying.

And suddenly all he ever wanted in this world, in his life, was to make that stop. So he entered the room and shut the door behind him.

CHAPTER 7

Priscilla didn't want to cry. It had never been in her nature to gnash her teeth and weep. Very few in her life cared if she was hurt, and showing her underbelly like that generally only led to vulnerability she could scarcely afford.

But as she stood at the window in the study, thinking about the disastrous encounter in the ballroom, her mind raced. It brought back every memory of every moment of rejection that she had experienced since her debut seven long years ago. There were so many.

Ophelia had been a diamond. A sparkling jewel who refused every offer that crossed before her. But Priscilla had been the wallflower, cowering against the wall, praying to be noticed and yet hoping to never be seen. She could hear the vicious tone of her father as he picked apart every flaw. And of course she had known Caroline, her father's new wife, during that time. They had only been a few years apart in age, after all. She had felt Caroline's contempt for her then and even more of it now that she was Priscilla's stepmother. They both felt she was a failure.

Were they wrong? Ophelia always said so—it was part of why she'd demanded Priscilla come on this adventure, to free her from that cruelty. But when it came to men, the best response she had from them was the one King Grantham had given: bored indifference.

It would destroy her, in the end. Whatever failing made her so unwanted would come back to England with her and make her an old maid with no prospects and little affection from her family. And if Caroline succeeded in making a male heir with her father? Priscilla could only assume it would get worse.

She heard the door behind her close and turned to see who had found her. She expected Ophelia, but jolted when it was Remi who leaned against the shut door, watching her through a hooded gaze.

Good God, but he was handsome. The most beautiful man she had ever spent more than five minutes with, altogether. All those lovely angles, every confident line…he was like something out of a fairytale or a romantic novel. So far above her in stature, and yet he sometimes looked at *her* like *she* was some sweet treat he wanted to sample. He had kissed her, for heaven's sake, and that memory would likely be the only one to sustain her for a very long while.

"I suppose you feel you wasted your time on me," she managed to whisper. "As you told me a few days ago, I am a hopeless case."

He flinched at his own words, repeated back to her. "I didn't mean it as anything but a playful tease, Priscilla. I think you anything but a hopeless case. My brother, on the other hand…"

She felt the burning heat of embarrassment creep up to her cheeks. "He could hardly look at me."

"It isn't because of you," Remi assured her as he stepped closer and the distance between them shrank. "He is…he carries a great deal on his shoulders. It's easy for me to forget from my useless perch so far away. And he is also…" He dropped his gaze. "It isn't because of you."

"It is kind of you to say," she said slowly. "But I have to believe you are wrong."

"I'm not," he insisted. "And there are other men here, Priscilla. Give me a day or two to consider the options and—"

She held up a hand. "Oh, please don't make this humiliation even more complete. It isn't as if King Grantham is my debut attempt at catching the attention of a man. I must be realistic. I have been out seven years with not even anything close to success. I am a failure at a match. When I return home I will either be relegated to old maidenhood and forgotten entirely or...or I suppose they might force a match if my father can convince my grandfather the marquess to throw, as he would put it, good money after bad."

"That is not fair," Remi said.

"And neither is the world." Priscilla turned away. She didn't want him to see her when she said the next thing, but she did have to say it. For her own understanding as much as for his. "I had another option in mind, but I now think it is as much folly as this one."

He was silent a moment, and then she heard him move even closer. When she turned to look at him, he was only a stride's length away now. He was staring at her intently, focused entirely on her. Such a strange thing to experience such regard while she was talking about how little of it she had earned in the past.

And this regard could come to nothing. For some reason this perfect man had taken her on as a pathetic project. Certainly now he would lose interest and find some other, more successful woman to push into his brother's path.

"What is the option?" he asked.

She lifted her cold hands to cover her suddenly hot cheeks. "I-I had thought to become a man's...lover."

He was quiet for so long that she began to think he hadn't heard her. But then he shifted and cleared his throat. "You're talking about finding a protector. A man to take care of your needs financially...physically."

Hearing it from his voice made her feel even more foolish about the thought. "Yes, but how could I? If no man wants me as his wife, who would wish for me in his bed? And I have no experience in such things. I assume a man would want an experienced lover based on what I've read."

His eyes boggled. "What have you read?"

"There's this book, *The Ladies Book of Pleasures*—Ophelia had a copy and we looked at it a few summers ago. She probably still has it. But it was clear as I read it that I was out of my depth with such things. So it is yet another strike against me."

"First off, you are *not* unwanted," he said. "I have watched you the last few days and I am not the only one."

Her brow wrinkled. "You needn't placate me. I know what I am."

"You don't know what you are." He threw up his hands in apparent frustration. "I have no idea why no man has been intelligent enough to take you to wife, but I'm guessing it may have more to do with whatever your family has offered to come along with you, not because of you. When it comes to taking a lover, a man can choose what he wants. It does not have to be political or financial like a marriage."

She swallowed. He might just be attempting to be nice to her. To let her down easily. But she still clung to the hope those words provided. "You would be more expert on those matters than I."

He chuckled, but the sound was rough. "Oh yes, indeed I would. So you must listen to me as the authority, Priscilla. You *are* desired. You could tap into that if it was your wish."

"But I don't know how," she repeated.

He hesitated and then licked his lips. There was something about that tongue darting out, tracing the mouth she still remembered the taste of, that made her body tense. She could hardly breathe as they stood there, so close and yet not touching, talking about something so inappropriate as how she might take a lover.

"I could teach you," he said softly.

She stared at him. She must be dreaming because he could not have said such an inappropriate thing to her in the middle of a parlor in his palace. Not with his family just down the hall. Not this man.

"You...what does that mean?" she squeaked.

He edged even closer and reached for her. He was wearing

gloves and so was she, but when he took her hand, she still felt the electric jolt of contact.

"It means exactly what I said. If you want to learn about pleasure, Priscilla. If you want to gain some experience in the world you think you wish to pursue, I would teach you."

"Why?" she choked out.

He tilted his head. "Because I failed you in one arena and I want to help. And that is the right answer, but the real one is that I have not been able to stop thinking about your taste since I kissed you a few days ago. I wake up rock hard in the night with that flavor on my tongue. And I want to know what the rest of you tastes like. I want to wake up all that sensuality that I see in you. I want to help you learn the pleasure you so richly deserve. Because I'm a cad walking around in the garb of a prince."

She blinked at those words. So direct. So erotic. She didn't fully understand what he meant, couldn't picture it, but the emotion, the pleasure that rushed through her body was easy to decipher. It was animal and instinctual. It was desire. Something she'd felt before from time to time but never like this.

"I-I don't know what to say," she whispered.

He arched a brow and caught her hand a second time. This time, though, he drew her closer. Her skirts tangled around his legs, her chest brushed his, and when she looked up at him, it felt like he was the only thing in the world.

He trailed his fingers down her cheek, then tilted her face toward his. She watched as his mouth lowered, her heart pounding with anticipation as she waited for the brush of his lips to hers. When it came, slow and gentle, she melted against him. She lifted her hands to press against his chest, steadying herself as she parted her lips and let him inside.

He took the invitation with a rough groan and then he was tasting her, their tongues tangling, at first slowly and then with increased fervor. His hand gripped into a fist against her back, like he was just barely clinging to control, though how that was true, she didn't know.

What she did know was that her own sense of control was fraying to the brink. She wanted to rub against him, she wanted to force him to pull her closer, she wanted to feel his bare skin on hers. These were powerful desires, more powerful than anything she'd ever felt before.

He was offering her all of that. He was offering to give her pleasure and to make her ready for a future that might just save her. A terrifying thought, really. Because once she took this road with him, a great many others would become closed to her.

She stepped away from him at that thought. His breath was short as he stared down at her. "You don't have to decide anything tonight," he said. "Think about it."

Her lips parted and she nodded. "I-I will," she whispered. "But I...I must go now. I can't...I can't be here with you and think."

She didn't wait for a response, but simply rushed past him and into the hallway. She looked toward the ballroom. Even from so far away, she could still hear the music. How could she walk back into that room with all those people and just pretend that everything was fine? Normal? She couldn't. She'd never been that good an actress.

So instead she went the opposite direction, back toward the stairs that led to the guest wing of the palace. Back to the big, beautiful chamber she was sharing with Ophelia. Her friend would eventually notice her missing, but they could talk later. Right now she just wanted to be alone. To think about what Remi was offering.

And to try to come up with a more reasoned response than to simply launch herself at him like a wanton and beg for everything a man like him could provide.

~

R emi re-entered the ballroom a few moments after Priscilla's dramatic exit from the parlor. He searched for her in the crowd, but she was nowhere to be found, and he scowled.

"Oh, that look is usually on our brother's face, not yours," Sasha said as she stepped up and slid a hand into the crook of Remi's elbow. "Don't tell me it's contagious."

Remi forced a smile as he looked down at her. The royal family had adopted Sasha when she was a girl and he'd never seen her as anything but his sister, equal to Ilaria in all ways that mattered. In London she had met and married the Earl of Bramwell, and the two were deliriously happy. Remi was happy for her.

But they had always been close, and he feared that she would look up at him like she was right now and see…

"What's wrong?" she asked, proving his worries warranted. "Remi…"

"Nothing," he lied. "Now, have you promised every dance to Bramwell or may I have this one?"

"You may," she said, but still sounded concerned as he guided her to the dancefloor.

He thanked his lucky stars that the current dance was a traditional Athawickian passing dance, so they would not be close too often for conversation. They began with their hands clasped and he felt her staring him down, deep into places he rarely showed, her concern lining her lovely face. He pulled her close briefly, but they were forced to part as they skipped away down the line. He twirled a different lady, skipped through a line of gentlemen. It was all very lively and light, sort of the way he lived his every day life, really.

Finally they came back together, hands sliding past each other while she twirled. By the time the music was over, everyone on the floor was laughing and breathless, including himself. He bowed to Sasha and she curtseyed in return, and he hoped she had been distracted by the fun of the dance.

Instead, when she slipped her hand into his elbow again, she squeezed gently. "Take a turn with me on the terrace, won't you?"

He pursed his lips. He couldn't refuse her. Normally he wouldn't want to. "Of course," he said.

They exited the warm ballroom and out into the cool night air. The smell of the sea floated even up this high, and he released her as he leaned upon the barrier of the terrace and breathed it in deeply.

"Why are you not yourself?" she asked.

He shut his eyes and didn't face her. "I am always myself, Sasha. Who else would I ever wish to be?"

She didn't laugh but touched his hand lightly. "Remi."

He faced her. "We are all a bit out of sorts, aren't we? After all, our return to Athawick is only recent, there are two relationships to celebrate in our family and there is still unrest amongst our populace."

Sasha shivered. She and Ilaria had both been victim to that very unrest, in separate attacks in London. The faction of their people who wished to see Grantham step down as king might be small, but it was vocal. It was violent from time to time.

"You worry about Grantham," she said softly.

He hesitated. "Yes," he said at last. "We may not be as close as we once were, but I would never see my brother come to grief."

"Of course you wouldn't," Sasha said. "And I suppose it would be polite for me to simply accept these explanations and then let you go back to your fun inside. But I know you, Remi. I can see there is something more happening here. You've been out of sorts for days now. Distracted. Is there something else happening?"

Remi thought of Priscilla. The way she had lifted into him when he kissed her. The taste of her lips in the parlor that very night. He thought of how desperate he was to have more of her. He didn't *do* desperate. He'd never had a reason to before. And yet here he was, trying not to fantasize about the moment when she might breathe the word "yes" to his proposal.

He stared at Sasha. He could tell her all that. She wouldn't judge, at least not outwardly. And perhaps she would have some advice that would set his head back on properly. But she would also tell Ilaria. And the word would spread and suddenly everyone in the family would be in his business. They would all see it as fodder for a trap to get him wed.

And then there was Priscilla. She was far too sensitive not to pick up on their knowledge. It would humiliate her further after tonight's disastrous attempt to catch Grantham's attention. Remi couldn't do that to her.

"I promise you," he said. "I am perfectly fine. And if my distraction is an issue for you or for any other family member, I will try my hardest to be more present. Or as present as I ever get."

Sasha smiled, but he could see she was not satisfied with the answer. God's teeth, did he really seem so bad off for all this?

He cleared his throat. "Now tell me, are you excited to be properly crowned a princess of Athawick?"

"All the formalities will be done as soon as the Ilaria and Jonah wed," Sasha said. "And then the official coronation will be early next year, I suppose when it can get what Mama calls 'the attention it deserves'. I don't know that much will change. After all, Ilaria and I will go back to London soon enough to live our normal lives with our husbands."

Remi jolted at that thought. He'd known that was true, of course. Both Jonah Crawford and Thomas, the Earl of Bramwell, had duties in London that couldn't be fulfilled from so far away. But when his sisters were both gone, only to visit from time to time…

Everything really would have changed. He would be alone here in Athawick, doing…what? What the hell was his place anymore? He wasn't a king like Grantham. And his brother would not ask for his counsel, certainly. There was no duty beyond the occasional appearance. His mother would probably encourage him to find a cause to be figurehead for, but then…what?

God, it was utterly depressing.

"Remi?" Sasha pressed.

He leaned down and bussed her cheek. "I will miss you very much, Sasha," he said. Then he smiled over her shoulder as he watched the Earl of Bramwell step out of the ballroom. "And here comes your love, so I shall leave you two alone to enjoy the moonlight."

Sasha didn't look entirely pleased by that suggestion, but she greeted Thomas with all the affection in the world on her face. Her worries would fade with a little focused time with her husband. And it allowed Remi to slip away into the ballroom.

But even as he fell into the role the world expected him to play: lighthearted prince, flirtatious rogue, he couldn't be settled in his heart. Because everything was changing and he had no idea what that would mean for him tomorrow, next week or next year.

CHAPTER 8

Priscilla paced her chamber, worrying her hands together with every turn. In the other room she heard Ophelia getting ready, chatting happily with her maid. Her friend had not yet seemed to notice Priscilla's anxiety, and that was a good thing. She couldn't talk to Ophelia about what had happened between her and Remi. It was all far too humiliating and shocking…and intimate.

But that left her fully responsible for her own decisions. Ones she would have to make soon, because she would surely see Remi again this afternoon. She'd avoided him last night by not returning to the ball, and this morning by staying in her chamber instead of eating breakfast. But this afternoon the royal family was hosting a game of battledore and shuttlecock, and there was no way to get out of that. Not without rousing more concern and attention.

Ophelia stepped into the room with a smile. She was wearing a gorgeous afternoon gown in a pink lawn fabric with a little flower pattern. She spun around to show it off and then laughed. "I am well armored to trounce my competition today."

Priscilla laughed and it did not have to be forced, despite her spinning mind. Ophelia was notoriously competitive in these kinds of lawn games. Or card games, or any game, actually. But she was such a happy and light person that no one ever seemed to mind losing to her. "I'm certain you will win the day."

"Of course I shall." Ophelia looked pleased with herself as she tied her straw bonnet around her chin. "Imagine King Grantham's annoyance when he must crown *me* the winner of the day and present me with my prize. His grumpy countenance will be legendary."

Priscilla shook her head. She hadn't thought of King Grantham at all since his rejection the previous night. Odd, for she normally rolled such humiliations around in her mind over and over. But no, not this time. This time she'd been far too distracted by Remi.

"Are there to be prizes?" she asked.

Ophelia gasped and her gaze lit up with absolute glee. "Oh, that's right, you weren't there. There are, indeed, prizes. Queen Giabella was talking about them with Abigail and me last night at the ball when the subject of the tournament came up. The winner of the game gets a little trinket, a medal, I think."

"And what of the other places?" Priscilla asked.

Ophelia blinked. "You mean the prizes for those who are not the champion? I wasn't paying attention. I want that medal and I shall wear with great pride."

"You are always so certain of yourself," Priscilla said with a sigh. "I wish I had that talent."

"Not everyone considers it a talent," Ophelia said, her bright expression fading a fraction, but only briefly. "And now I must ask if you are up for this afternoon. Your headache must have been terrible to remove you from both the ball and breakfast. Are you feeling better?"

Priscilla nodded but didn't meet her friend's gaze. She wasn't very good at lying and she didn't want Ophelia to push further than she already was. "Yes, thank you. I'm much better now. Ready to face...well, whatever comes."

Ophelia wrinkled her brow, and it seemed she might ask something more, but before she could, the Duchess of Gilmore entered the room. Abigail looked lovely, her cheeks a bit flushed and her eyes bright with pleasure. She smiled at them both. "Are you ready? I fear we will be more than fashionably late if we don't head downstairs now."

A reprieve found, Priscilla followed the rest of their party downstairs where the Duke of Gilmore waited for them. They stepped out into the garden as a foursome and then beyond the flowers and pathways, onto a large lawn space in the distance. Laughter already drifted up from those gathered there, ladies and gentlemen clustered up, talking and drinking tea and enjoying the sunshine. There was so much more of that here, where it seemed the sea breezes blew the clouds away more than was possible in England.

Priscilla glanced around, trying to tell herself she was simply interested in everyone who was already gathered, but when she found Remi in the crowd, her heart leapt. He was standing with a few ladies, chatting and…well, it was obvious he was flirting a little. Her heart sank slightly. Not that he had any obligation not to do so. It was his nature to be playful and light with others, especially ladies. She had begun to understand that. But she still felt much more jealous than she had any right to.

She was about to turn away when he lifted his gaze to her across the lawn. Their eyes met, and something in his posture shifted. He said a few words to his companions and left them, crossing the lawn toward her in long, sure steps.

She swallowed, heart suddenly racing and hands shaking at her sides. She'd never had a man come toward her with such purpose, such focus before. It was rather something to have all that directed at her.

He reached her and smiled at the rest of her party. The one she had all but forgotten was standing with her.

"Your Graces," he said with a slight incline of his head. "Lady Ophelia. And Miss Linfield." There was something about the way he drew out her name that made a shiver work through her. "Good afternoon."

"Your Highness," the duke said, and the party all bowed or curtsied accordingly. "A fine afternoon for the entertainment."

"Fine, indeed," Abigail said with a wink for her husband. "If you think my husband sounds nervous, Your Highness, it is because he and I have placed a wager on today's festivities. And he fears being soundly trounced by me."

Priscilla laughed. If Ophelia was competitive, she had come by it naturally. Her brother was also of the same character and had married a woman with just as much spark. Their wagers were legendary in their circle of friends, but it was always good-natured. And now as the duke and duchess smiled at each other, Priscilla realized there was also an undercurrent to their playfulness: desire.

She blushed and cast her gaze to her feet. Funny how as this feeling was awakened in her, she could see it more clearly in others. What an innocent little fool she'd been not to notice it all before.

"Oh, it looks like they're starting," Ophelia said. "I must go make sure I'm positioned well on the field. Excuse me, Your Highness."

She darted off with the rest laughing at her enthusiasm. The duke turned to the duchess. "What say we get a good place along the side to watch, wife?"

Abigail blushed, as if what he said pleased her, and nodded. They said their goodbyes, as well, and Priscilla found herself alone with Remi again.

She looked up at him with a nervous smile. "Are you participating?"

He shook his head. "My mother feels it wouldn't be fair for the family to play. Just in case people feel they'd have to let us win. Are you?"

"No." She cleared her throat. "I-I gave a headache as my excuse for why I left the ball early last night and didn't come to breakfast this morning. So, I couldn't exactly jump up and raise my hand for such strenuous activity today."

He arched a brow. "And *are* you up for...strenuous activity, in truth?"

Heat filled her cheeks and she had to fight not to look away from him. "I...you're asking about our conversation last night. About your offer to—to help me."

He nodded wordlessly.

She shifted. "I have thought of nothing else."

"Nor have I," he admitted. "Though I do admit I thought I might have cocked things up when you didn't appear from breakfast. If I made you uncomfortable, I do apologize."

She held his stare a moment. "You—you do make me uncomfortable," she said at last. "But it's because you make me feel...things. Notice things. Want things."

His gaze grew sharper. "Do I?"

"You know you do, don't play coy," she said with a nervous laugh.

"Well, if that is true," he said slowly, "then you will have the added bonus that if you agree to what we talked about last night, you will get to explore those feelings you claim I create. If you'd like."

She worried her lip gently. "Yes. I've taken that into account in my decision, I admit. But I would have to ask a few more questions before I could say yes or no."

There was a cheer from the crowd as the game began, with Ophelia immediately rushing forward to whack the shuttlecock with her racket and sending the rest of the participants racing to do the same and keep the birdie in the air.

Remi caught Priscilla's elbow and drew her slightly away from the crowd and its noise. That light touch made her shiver, and she was afraid he could feel it. Afraid she was so obvious in what she wanted while he was experienced enough to be more guarded in his desires.

"What are your questions?" he asked when they were slightly away from the din.

"You—you wouldn't tell anyone, would you?" she asked.

He drew back in what seemed to be genuine surprise. "I would never make what was between us public. I would never tell another soul. Here on Athawick, desire is not punished. Love affairs are commonplace, pleasure is lauded as a positive. But I recognize that isn't true in your country. That whatever we do could have long-lasting consequences if you return home when this celebration is done."

The passion of his declaration sent relief through her. His use of the word *if* when it came to her potential return home, though, created more questions. Ones she wasn't brave enough to ask, so she simply said, "Good."

"What else?" he pressed.

"If I…if I didn't want to do something, would you make me?" she asked.

"Never," he assured her, and briefly brushed her fingers with his own. "You are in charge of what happens to you. I would never proceed in any activity without your express and, I hope, enthusiastic consent. I'm a cad, not a monster. And any man who isn't of the same mind is one you should very much avoid."

She swallowed. His answers were so easy, and there seemed to be no deception in his demeanor. She had one more question. One that burned in her. "You said last night that you…you wanted me. Why?"

He stared at her a long moment. "I just do. Sometimes these things are like a lightning bolt, something we couldn't control even if we tried. I want you because you intrigue me. Because I feel compelled to look for you in a crowd. Because of the way you worry your lower lip, just like you are right now, and it makes me want to do the same. Animal desire is often not to be explained, it is either to be denied or accepted. So the question is…do you accept it?"

She realized she wasn't breathing and forced herself to do so. "Yes. I…I would like to try."

He cleared his throat. "Good. Very good. But I, too, have some rules to this endeavor. Or one rule, at any rate."

She nodded slowly. "What is it? I also would like you to be comfortable and I shall try to make you so."

His brow wrinkled, as if no one had ever suggested such a thing to him before. "Th-thank you," he said. "If I am to do this, if *we* are to do this, I want to make it clear that your hopes for any future dalliance or connection to my brother must be ended."

"Of course!" she burst out immediately. "Oh, I would never think of participating in any kind of intimacy with you and then secretly planning to continue a pursuit of your brother. Even if I thought there was a chance there, it would be wrong of me to do so."

He seemed relieved at her quick acquiescence on that topic, as his features relaxed and his smile became softer. "Good. Then I think we may be agreed."

Her heart began to throb. She had just agreed to engage in… what else could one call it but sexual training? To participate in that sort of behavior with Remi. She nearly fainted at the realization.

"You don't know how much I want to kiss you right now to seal this bargain," he said with a chuckle. "But I think that would be too risky, even if the group seems to be distracted by Lady Ophelia's *very* aggressive play."

Priscilla had all but forgotten the game going on just behind them. She looked past Remi and found that Ophelia had eliminated a great number of her competitors. Her expression was highly focused as she walloped the shuttlecock with her racket once more and sent her opponents scattering to keep the birdie in play.

"Well, we shall know we are agreed without the kiss," Priscilla said, though she was disappointed they could not lock in their bargain in such a way. She did like kissing Remi. So, so much. "But what shall we do now? How do we proceed?"

He smiled. "In privacy is best. Which we will not have a chance for until after the day's events are complete. Will you meet me tonight? Perhaps in your chamber?"

She caught her breath. "I share a room with Ophelia."

"Oh, no then," he said, pulling a face that was a mix of horror and amusement that made her laugh. "What about the library? It will be quiet by the time the ceremony to title Jonah is finished. Will you meet me there at midnight?"

She nodded, though she went a little lightheaded at the thought. This was going to be real. Whatever this was. "Yes," she said.

He had been smiling, but now his face went more serious. A darkness entered his stare, something that pulled her in and made her stomach flutter. "Excellent. I very much look forward to it, Miss Linfield."

"As do I, Your Highness," she said. She glanced back over her shoulder. "Oh dear, it looks as though Ophelia has come through the first round of play and is crowing about it."

"And everyone but my brother is being good natured about it." He gave a smug grin. "Perfect."

She wrinkled her brow, uncertain why King Grantham's annoyed expression as he watched Ophelia twirl on the field of play could ever be considered a good thing. "Since her brother and his wife seem to be a little distracted by each other at present, I suppose I should go encourage her to practice some decorum."

Remi snorted out a laugh as she curtseyed and began to walk away. "Perish the thought, Miss Linfield."

She smiled to herself as she crossed the field to take Ophelia's side and congratulate her. She could feel Remi watching her as she did so. Never before had she been so aware of a man's regard, certainly no man like him.

And tonight she could get to finally understand what regard like that meant. What the flutters in her body meant. What a moment of stolen recklessness could mean. And she couldn't wait.

CHAPTER 9

Remi had never had a problem with putting on all the finery his position required and going out to exhibit. Grantham might grunt and complain about it, but Remi liked it when people looked at him. When he could make them laugh or watch. Many elements of the crown on his head felt heavy, but never that one.

And yet tonight, everything felt a little…tight. He was finding it hard to attend as Grantham bestowed the title of count onto Jonah while their sister beamed on. The title was reward for Jonah's defense of Ilaria's life back in London, of course. But it was also a way to elevate him, as he was a man with no title. A bastard, in fact, exactly the sort of person the courtiers loved to insist would only dilute the power of the crown and a bunch of other rot.

Even now Grantham's head courtier, Stephen Blairford, watched on from the side, his expression dark and judgmental. Grantham had inherited him when their father died, and it was clear the two men often didn't see eye to eye.

But Grantham had won whatever fight had been had. Because of course he had. He was king, after all. And now his brother stood in his full ceremonial garb, the intricately carved burnished silver crown set on his brow, a sword in his hand that he pressed down on one of Jonah's shoulders, then the other.

"For acts of extreme bravery, for saving the life of Princess Ilaria, I dub thee Count Crawford of the Southern Realm. You are accepted as one of our own, as adored as one blood-born of Athawick, and welcomed as future husband of a most beloved sister."

Grantham glanced toward Ilaria, and Remi did the same. He was surprised to find that his normally controlled sister's eyes were filled with happy tears. Relieved tears. Without a word, Remi reached out and touched her hand. She smiled over at him.

He had known she loved this man. She said it often enough. But this was the first time Remi had truly seen how deep that went. And as Jonah rose to the applause of those in the large throne room, his gaze moved to Ilaria. Those feelings were returned, just as deep, just as powerful. Their connection was almost too bright to look at in that moment and so Remi turned his attention away from it and into the crowd.

They all seemed duly impressed by the pomp and circumstance of the grant of title. All of them were watching the scene with breathless rapture. Save one.

He realized that Priscilla was not observing the ceremony. She was looking at him. Oh, of course she ducked her head when he met her stare, but he had seen it. He had felt her regard in that big room full of people. And while he might tell himself, over and over, that he only felt the surge of desire at that fact, there was some small part of him that knew it was a lie. He liked that she sought him in the crowd. That she was focused on him.

He pushed that feeling away and followed the family from the throne room. They would go into a small reception now, so that the invitees and dignitaries could also congratulate the new count.

As they entered the antechamber, Remi slapped Jonah's shoulder. "Congratulations, my lord."

Jonah pulled a face. "Oh, that is going to take some getting used to."

"I'm sure you'll rally admirably," Ilaria laughed before she leaned up to buss his cheek. "I am happy for you, my love."

Jonah shrugged. "I recognize the honor of this, of course." He glanced toward Grantham and Queen Giabella. "I hope you know that. But I am more excited about the wedding in a few days than this. This is just...stage dressing to make our future more palatable for the masses."

The queen stepped forward and grasped both of Jonah's hands. She smiled up at him, her expression that of a loving mother and not the queen of a nation. "And that is why we are so thrilled to accept you into our family, Jonah. Your love for my daughter gives me great happiness. As does Thomas's love for Sasha. I could only hope my two sons would be as lucky in their choice of brides down the road."

Remi glanced at Grantham, and for the first time in a very long time, he saw his brother there and not just his king. They exchanged a look of horror and his brother even almost smiled.

"Mama, I think our sisters were very deserving of love," Remi said with a grin toward Grantham. "Your sons...perhaps not quite so much."

"That is poppycock," Sasha said, squeezing Thomas's arm. "No two gentlemen are more deserving of it than you two. Nor in more need for a partner who will love you unconditionally. Remi so he does not ruin himself, and Grantham so he doesn't forget himself."

Again, Remi exchanged a look with his brother. He could see Grantham was as uncomfortable with this subject as he was. Strange that on this they were in accord when often it felt like little else. Those days of connection had been gone so long that he felt too drawn to this one, sad and small as it was.

"Our guests are waiting for us," Grantham said, offering an arm to his mother. "Let us not keep them any longer."

He guided her forward and into the reception room where the others were now gathered. Remi went next, alone, of course. Behind him the couples followed. He felt that aloneness more keenly as he entered the reception hall and stepped aside so that the crowd could applaud the princess and her newly minted count.

He backed away, watching it all from afar and feeling…raw somehow. His entire family was moving forward now. Marriages and coronations and futures that had nothing to do with him. And where was he? Still in the same place he'd been for years now. Was it satisfying? Was *anything* satisfying anymore?

He asked himself the question just as Priscilla stepped into his field of view, approaching Sasha and Bramwell for a conversation. She glanced at him from time to time, even as she smiled and talked to his sister and her husband.

She was satisfying. The idea of being with her was very satisfying. So he would simply forget everything else and do that.

To distraction.

Priscilla's hands shook and it took her three tries to properly close her jewelry box and latch it. She was still dressed, even as Ophelia sat in her nightgown, having her hair brushed out by her maid.

She arched a brow at Priscilla. "You aren't going to ring for Beth?"

Trying to ignore the rising anxiety in her chest, Priscilla shook her head. "You know, I think I just rested so long last night and this morning that now I'm not tired. I believe I'll go down to the library and see if I can find something boring to read to put me to sleep."

"Oh." Ophelia tilted her head. "Would you like me to go with you?"

"No!" Priscilla burst out, and watched as her best friend's eyes went wide with surprise. "No, I'll be just fine. And don't wait up for me. I'll just slip in and go right to sleep."

Ophelia wrinkled her brow. "Very well. And why don't we get up early tomorrow, take a long walk through the grounds? I feel like we've been on opposite paths since we arrived and I'd love to just spend some time together."

Priscilla tried not to allow her face to show the reaction in her heart. Tomorrow she would very likely not be a virgin and she would want to talk to Ophelia about it. Would she? Would she keep lying? What in the world was she going to do?

"Pris?" Ophelia asked.

"I would love that," Priscilla said.

Ophelia didn't look certain, but stepped up to buss her cheek and then flitted back to the bedchamber. Priscilla took a long breath and then stepped out into the hallway. The journey to the library wasn't long, of course, even with as big as the palace was, but it still felt like it took an eternity. Every time she passed a servant finishing up for the night, she felt certain they could read her thoughts, her wicked plans.

By the time she reached the library, she felt breathless, and for a moment she considered just forgetting the whole thing. She could turn on her heel and march back to her chamber. Remi might be angry, but he would get over it. This didn't mean anything much to him anyway. She was another conquest in a string of conquests. He might genuinely want her, a fact that still felt so odd to her, but it didn't follow that she meant something. When she went home, he would forget her and she...

Well...she would be lost, wouldn't she? Trapped in a dozen worst-case scenarios that kept playing through her head in a never-ending loop.

It was that reminder that made her push her shoulders back and open the door. Remi was there already, standing by the fire. He didn't seem to notice her as she entered the room, so she took a brief moment to just drink him in.

He was still wearing his full formal attire from the presentation earlier in the night, but he hardly looked stuffy or staid. His hair was wild, as if he had spent some time running his fingers through it, and his blue gaze was piercing and focused as he turned toward her and caught his breath.

"I was placing wagers with myself about whether or not you would come at all," he breathed.

She licked her lips, which suddenly felt very dry. "Would you prefer I go so you will not owe yourself?"

He laughed and stepped toward her. "I am very happy to lose." He cleared his throat and his gaze flitted over her from head to toe. "Now, will you close the door, Priscilla? I think it's high time we were alone together."

Priscilla's hands were shaking as she reached back and slowly closed the door behind her. She glanced at him over her shoulder before she turned the key, locking them in together. To Remi's great surprise, his nerves rose up, as if he hadn't had dozens of lovers before, as if he weren't the far more experienced of the two of them.

He moved toward her a step, and she caught her breath and began to pace the room, looking at all the books. "It's—it's a lovely library," she stammered.

He let her walk around for a moment, giving her the space she clearly needed to catch her breath. "Yes," he said at last. "Lovely. Have you visited it often since your arrival?"

She nodded. "I do love a library. Lucky for us, too, because when I told Ophelia that I was coming down to find a book because I couldn't sleep, she accepted that easily." She worried her hands before her. "She won't come looking for me. She was going to sleep. After her performance at the games earlier, she must be tired and—"

He crossed to her in one long step and caught both her hands. She fell silent and stared up at him, her gaze soft and lips trembling.

"You don't have to do this," he said softly. "Do you understand?

You came here, the door is locked, but you don't have to do this if you've changed your mind."

She drew back a little. "I-I haven't. I want to be here. I'm just… I'm just very nervous." She shifted slightly and she stopped holding his stare. "Did—did *you* change your mind?"

She looked so fragile as she asked that question, and for a moment he saw all the hurt on her face, all the rejection she'd felt since coming out, all the fear and regret, all the self-doubt. He saw it all and what he wanted to do more than anything in this world was to erase it. Ease it.

He'd never felt such a strange desire before, except for his family. But never with a woman who was hardly more than a fascinating stranger.

He cupped her cheeks, threading his fingers into her hair. Gently, he tilted her face toward his and then lowered his lips. He took his time, reveling in the hitch of her breath, the ache in his chest, the way she curled her hands around his forearms and gripped him tightly.

His lips brushed hers after what felt like a wonderfully torturous eternity. She gasped against his mouth and he took advantage of the parting of her lips. She opened to him with a whimper and he drowned in the sweetness of her flavor. She was guileless in the way her arms moved up to wind around his neck, the way she lifted into him to get closer, the way she darted her own tongue against his with uncertainty. And yes, he'd kissed those with more talent in the art.

But he'd never felt such a burning desire as a result of just a kiss. It was like when she traced his tongue with her own that she found some secret way to light him on fire. He wanted to claim her, to mark her, to brand himself with her so that he would never forget how desperate she made him with just a simple kiss.

The room was spinning out of control and he fought to regain purchase. He pulled back without releasing her from his embrace and then kissed her once more, this time with a closed mouth. "I haven't changed my mind," he whispered.

She smiled up at him, relief and anticipation mixed, and he nearly came undone right then and there. How could she be so lovely and tempting? Even to a jaded bastard like himself?

"Then how do we begin?" she asked.

He laughed and dropped his head to her shoulder. "Well, I feel a poor teacher. I thought that kiss *was* beginning."

She shifted a little, and when he looked at her, her cheeks were bright red. "Oh, I...I didn't..."

"It's all right, Priscilla," he said gently. "Do you like kissing?"

"I do," she said, and then worried her lip a little. "When it's with you."

"You didn't like it with others?" he pressed, still holding her. He liked holding her, truth be told. Her full curves molded against him in such a lovely way.

She sighed and slipped from his arms at last. She moved to the settee and sat, her expression anxious. "It isn't as if there were many," she said. "Just one man...a boy, really, and I was little more than a girl. His family was visiting mine and we were in the stable and he kissed me. It was a bit...slobbery."

He pulled a face as he sat beside her. "Then not very nice."

"Not at all."

"Did he pursue you after that?"

She tilted her head. "Of course not," she said. "I wasn't of interest to him, not really."

"You're so certain," he said.

She shrugged. "Well, I am an old maid, aren't I? I suppose if he had been interested, if *anyone* had been interested, that wouldn't be true."

"Come, you are too clever not to know the ways of the world better than that. There are dozens of reasons a man might not be free to pursue a future with a woman he truly desired. Money, position, interfering relations."

"Are those the reasons you haven't pursued a future with a woman *you* truly desire?" she asked softly.

He stared at her a moment. She was asking a pointed question, one he'd never answered. He had no intentions of answering it today. But oh, how he wanted to in this strange, visceral way that felt more dangerous than kissing her in a library and offering to teach her pleasure.

"So one man, one kiss," he said, changing the subject. She didn't pursue the matter further. "And nothing else?"

She shook her head. "No."

"Well, then we should really start there, shouldn't we?" He pressed a hand deep into the settee cushion next to her. He leaned across and brushed his nose along the length of her own. Once again, her breath hitched in that responsive way that set him on fire. "There are so many different kisses, Priscilla."

"Are there?" she asked.

"Yes. There is something chaste...or almost so." To punctuate that, he pressed his mouth to hers, closed and gentle. She moved for more, but he withdrew and almost laughed when she frowned. "I shouldn't be kissing you, it's not entirely proper...but I do it anyway because I'm...me. And by doing it, I make a promise of more, don't I?"

She nodded, unsteady and slightly unfocused again. He responded by leaning in again and pressing another of those almost-chaste kisses to her lips. This time she didn't demand, but she did lift a hand to cup his cheek. The feel of her soft fingers running the length of his jawline made his entire body ache deliciously.

He drew back. "And then we escalate," he said. "I open my mouth, I ask you to let me in. It's a dance, a deeper promise of what is to come. I want you to feel it. You don't have to match me or meet me. Just *feel* me."

Her pupils dilated to almost impossible blackness. When he leaned in, she shut her eyes on a shuddering sigh. He drew his hand into her hair again, tilting her for the best angle, enjoying how she relaxed against him, utterly trusting that he would take care of her.

Which he very much intended to do.

He took her mouth again, at first gently, and then the tension began to build. He traced her lips and she parted them, her fingers tightly gripping his jacket again. He probed with his tongue, slow and easy, then harder, more insistent. A dance to show her what would come later. With his mouth, with his fingers, eventually with his cock.

Her breath grew shorter and shorter and she began to whimper, a low, needy sound that sent electric pleasure straight to his rapidly hardening cock. He wanted to hear her make that sound as she pulsed over him, her head thrown back in pure ecstasy. He wanted to press his fingers into her flesh, grind her down over him as she sucked his tongue and took every part that he poured into her.

He was losing control. He realized it as he blinked and pulled back. He *never* lost control. Ever.

Her eyes came open and she stared at him with bleary pleasure. "What other kinds of kisses are there?" she asked.

He shook his head with a pained laugh. "So many, Priscilla. We haven't even gotten to the ones that aren't on the mouth."

Her eyes went wide. "Oh…oh."

"But that is further down a lovely road." He pulled away a fraction, mostly to regain some purchase over himself. He cleared his throat as he looked at her. "I wasn't quite aware of how innocent you are."

She blushed. "I am. I can't deny it. But everyone starts out as innocent, don't they? Everyone must learn and experience."

He nodded slowly. She wasn't wrong. But this…was? He knew it, even as he danced around it. Surely if he…the English would call it *ruin her*. If he ruined her, it would destroy her chances at a future she might still secretly wish to have.

"I shouldn't do this," he mused out loud.

Her eyes went wide, all remnants of pleasure leaving them. "Oh no, please! How many times have you said that to yourself, Remi, and then done whatever you knew you shouldn't anyway?"

He wrinkled his brow. "Well…a great many."

"Then make this one of those times. You aren't doing anything I'm not asking you to do. That I don't want you to do, even more than I did when you first offered me the option. Please."

It was the *please* that tore him to pieces, that stripped away any decency that continued to try to convince him not to do this. God, that word sounded sweet from her lips. Undeniable.

He cleared his throat. "Then tell me, Priscilla, how you like to be touched."

CHAPTER 10

*T*ell *me how you like to be touched.*

The words hung in the quiet room between them, punctuated by the intensity of his stare, like she was the only person in the world who mattered to him. She swallowed hard, gasping for breath as she had been since the moment she walked into the room.

"I…I told you I haven't been touched," she said.

He shook his head slowly. "How do you touch yourself?"

Her eyes boggled as she realized what he meant. "Intimately?" she whispered.

"Yes."

"I-I don't," she admitted, and it suddenly felt like a failing. That this man would certainly judge her too foolish for him and reject her.

Instead, his eyes lit up, like she had just offered food and he was a starving man. "Then *that* is the first lesson," he said.

She watched, wide eyed, as he eased a little closer. The heat of him rose up around her, overpowering but welcome just the same. She wanted to be warmed by him, overrun by him.

"May I touch you?" he asked.

She nodded, watching as he dropped a hand to her knee. He

bunched her dress in his fingers and lifted, edging the fabric up past her ankle, her calf. Higher. Eventually he lifted it around her lap and left it there. He smiled at her as he dropped to his knees before her, caught her behind the knees with both hands, his fingers burning into her through her stockings.

He yanked her forward on the settee, so that she was slouched, then pushed her legs wide. She turned her face, staring off toward the bookcases so she wouldn't see him looking at her.

"Priscilla," he said, her name hypnotic coming from his lips.

She shivered as she forced herself to meet his gaze again. He was looking at her face, not where she was exposed. Not where he was exposing her further by lifting her gown to rest on her stomach. She was still wearing drawers, of course, but that felt like a flimsy barrier, indeed.

"When I kiss you, do you feel an ache in your body?" he asked.

She bit her lip. Talking about this felt impossible, how in the world was she to do more? But she had to, she had to be brave, didn't she?

"Here," she whispered, and brushed her hand over her breast, across to her heart. "And…and there. Where you are."

"Here?" He gestured to the space between her legs without touching her.

"Yes." She had to be almost purple, she could feel it from the heat on her cheeks. God, he was torturing her and yet she didn't want to escape.

"Do you ever feel the ache at other times? Like when you looked at that wicked little book you and your friend found, for example?"

Her eyes went wide. "How—how did you know that?"

"Because it's a natural feeling," he said. "Almost everyone gets it. That wild draw to another person, a stranger or a friend. That desire when we see something intimate or wicked. That thing that makes us hot and needy. Desire is not something to be ashamed of, no matter what anyone tells you about it."

She considered that. Desire hadn't been something she'd really discussed with anyone before. A little with Ophelia, perhaps, but never in much detail. Her friend had seemed reluctant and that had ended the conversation. Certainly she couldn't imagine talking to anyone else and not receiving judgment and perhaps even institutionalization.

"Now the trick is," he continued, "what to do about it. You ought not have your pleasure rely solely on a partner. It denies you so much. You can be your own source of it, whenever it is prudent to find it. And by doing so, you begin to know your own body and what it needs and wants."

He caught her hand as he spoke and then settled it between her legs. She flushed and tried to pull it away, but he held her there gently.

"Don't be afraid," he whispered, and in that moment she wasn't. She met his gaze, holding there to find purchase, and then let her hand rest where he had left it. She was warm there through the layer of her undergarments. "Wiggle your fingers, apply just a little pressure."

She did as she'd been told and was surprised that a tiny flash of pleasure jolted through her. Sensation unlike any she'd ever had before. "Oh!"

"Yes." He leaned in and glided his hands beneath the bunching of her skirt. He found the little ribbon that held her drawers in place and untied the bow, continuing to watch her as he tugged on the fabric. She felt mesmerized watching him, unable and unwilling to say no. She lifted her hips instead and let him strip that last barrier of propriety away.

He looked at her then, spread out before him, and let out a long, heavy breath. "God, but I'm going to enjoy this. Far too much," he murmured. "Put your hand back."

Her fingers shook as she did as she'd been told, wedging her hand into the space there. She was warmer still without the drawers, and there was a humid quality to the heat. She flexed her fingers and was surprised to find them coated with something slick.

"You are very wet," he choked. "And that is a good thing, I assure you. Your body gets wet with excitement and anticipation. To ease the way for a lover." He leaned in closer and she felt the brush of his cheek against her knee, he was so close. "I'm going to help you now, Priscilla. But tell me to stop if you don't like something I do. Or ask for more if you need it."

She couldn't respond verbally, only nod and stare as he reached up to cover her fingers with his own. Now they were both coated in the wetness from between her legs. He seemed to revel in it, letting out a low groan as he pressed both their fingers more firmly against her entrance.

The little ripple of sensation she'd felt when she touched herself earlier became sharper with his help. He shifted to his knees and focused intently on her sex. With one hand he kept rolling her fingers against her, with the other he peeled her open, holding her there so that the feeling grew more intense than before. It was an ever-increasing feeling, overtaking her with the continuous waves of his touch. She found herself lifting into his hand, into her own, seeking some relief from this building pressure.

"What do you want, Priscilla?" he asked, his voice rough. He never looked at her face, just continued to focus on what their hands were doing.

She struggled to find breath, to remember words as this sensation continued to lift her higher and higher. What did she want? She had no idea, except that all this seemed to be building to something and she wanted to know what it was.

"I-I don't know," she gasped out.

He glanced up at her, his pupils dilated, his breath as short as hers. "Let me show you."

He increased the pressure of their joined hands, focused it more fully, and the sharpness of the pleasure increased yet again, to what she would have said was an unattainable level. But before she could revel in that too long, the world shifted, changed, and she changed with it.

Her entire body began to quake and she arched against their fingers as wave after wave of incredible pleasure rushed through her. She cried out against it and he leaned in to kiss her, silencing her with his mouth even as he continued to stimulate her rocking, pulsating body through the crisis. She had no idea how long the explosion lasted. It felt like a lifetime, but perhaps it was nothing more than a moment. Slowly the spasms eased, the pleasure faded to a deep, wonderful warmth, and she relaxed back on the settee cushions with a shudder, breaking their kiss at last.

He drew her hand up to his mouth and kissed it, licking the moisture from both their fingers. She shivered at the idea that he would taste her so intimately. Especially when he let out a low groan when he did. Like he was savoring her, like she was a treat to be devoured whole. He looked positively wolfish doing it.

She waited for him to make his next move. He must wish to take her now, she knew that was the ultimate result of all these games. But he made no move to do so. Instead he shifted to sit on the settee next to her and gathered her against his chest.

"*That* is how you like to be touched," he said softly.

"Apparently so," she said with a shake of her head. "I had no idea such a thing was possible. I mean...I have a few married friends, occasionally they whisper about pleasure. And the book, *The Ladies Book of Pleasures*, it posited that a lady should demand nothing less. But I certainly understand it a little better now."

He was quiet for a moment, and the mood in the room shifted. Where everything had been comfortable between them, now a tension entered the space. He straightened up, releasing her and reached for her discarded drawers on the floor nearby. When he handed them over, she wrinkled her brow.

"That...that's all?" she asked. "You aren't going to...to do the rest?"

He shut his eyes briefly and his hands clenched at his sides. "You do not know the temptation, but no."

A sting worked through her. "I did something wrong, didn't I? And now you don't want me."

He shook his head immediately. "No, not at all. I would like nothing more than to repeat what we just did with my mouth and my fingers and most definitely my cock. But this isn't a race. If you are to learn, then you must practice. So that is what I suggest. Practice what you just learned. Find all the ways you like to be touched, all the ways that bring you to orgasm…climax…what just happened. Keep practicing, over and over."

She shifted at the idea that she could do this herself, in the chamber upstairs. She and Ophelia shared that chamber, but not a bed. And Ophelia wasn't always around. There was plenty of privacy when she required it. Of course, she wasn't certain it would be as exciting without Remi's hand between her legs, fingers rippling over her as she jerked against him helplessly.

Oh, the tingle was back, that tugging need. She squeezed her thighs together, hoping it would ease it, but instead it only increased the desire.

He got to his feet and ran a hand through his hair. "Christ, you have no idea what a temptation you are."

He wasn't wrong. She had never felt like much of a temptation, but he did seem truly riled by her. Still, he moved away, not toward. She pursed her lips and slipped into her drawers. She stood to pull them up fully and tied the knot at her waist as best she could under her gown. As she smoothed the skirts back over herself, she found him watching her.

"Aside from practicing…*that*…what would you like me to do now?" she asked.

He cleared his throat. "I think what I'd like to do next will require a bit more privacy than the library. I'll make some arrangements, but I know that there is an empty chamber in the tower. Probably used once upon a time to house a mad prince or king or something, I hardly pay attention to those history lessons. But it's very nice. I used to go there as a boy to…well, it doesn't matter."

She wrinkled her brow because for a moment as he spoke, there was a deep sadness that entered his expression. It was gone almost immediately, but she couldn't ignore that she'd seen it. Seen through him just a fraction.

"I should…meet you there, then?" she asked.

He nodded. "I'll make sure the room is prepared properly by a servant I trust completely. No one will know the purpose, certainly no one will know it is you who I am meeting with. I promise you that. But we could meet there tomorrow night if you'd like."

"I've started this and I want to continue. I want…more…"

He swallowed hard and then moved on her again. He cupped her cheeks, and for a beat he simply stared down at her, like he was memorizing something about her face. Then he kissed her. Gently. Chastely, like he had shown her at the beginning what seemed like a lifetime ago. But he still lit a fire in her, one that she more fully understood now.

When he pulled away, he smiled. "Better go now. At some point Ophelia will come looking for you and I think being caught with me in a locked library will be a problem."

She couldn't argue that point, so she simply slipped from his arms. She unlocked the door and peeked back at him before she left the chamber. He was standing where she'd left him, his gaze fully focused on her.

"Good night," she whispered.

He inclined his head. "Good night, Priscilla."

She slipped away and back up the hallway, her entire body trembling with every step. She had gone into that room as one person, but she was leaving another. She'd expected that, told herself it would happen, but experiencing it was something else entirely.

And she couldn't wait to repeat it. To go further and deeper with this remarkable man who could make her feel so good. Could make her feel so…so cherished.

She came to a halt at the bottom of the stairs with that thought. "No," she whispered to herself.

Cherished wasn't how he felt about her. Good Lord, what was she thinking? Remi might be kind and gentle with this awakening, but she could not for one moment mistake his feelings. That was the way of true ruin and despair. That was the way of heartache.

CHAPTER 11

Remi had never been an early riser. His father had hated that about him, railed about it constantly. If he examined his motives closely enough, he thought he might find that he did it on purpose to upset the king…but he never examined it very closely.

This morning, however, he found he couldn't lie in bed, sleeping contentedly. He was too troubled. Or perhaps *troubled* wasn't the correct word. He'd been tangled up in thoughts of Priscilla since the library last night. Playing over their encounter in his head, stimulating his hard cock until he came with the memory…and yet remaining oddly unsatisfied by it all. He wanted more. And that was…unsettling.

He loved sex. Had since his first encounter as a young man. Pleasure was paramount in his life and his reputation as a giving lover, if not a lover who stayed, was well-earned. But he didn't brood over it. He didn't relive any particular scenario once he had parted from a woman.

And now he couldn't stop. Even as he shocked his valet by calling for him early, even as he dressed for the day, even as he stormed around the garden trying to clear his head.

Even now as he strode up the hallway, steering himself danger-ously close to the very library where he had watched with apt atten-tion as Priscilla came undone under their intertwined fingers. He might have returned to that room...the scene of the crime...and brooded on it further except that he heard a sound from just up the hall. Raised voices.

His brother's raised voice.

"I recognize *exactly* what it is you wish me to do, Blairford," Grantham snapped. "And you would best recall that I am king, not you."

Remi moved toward the ruckus and pushed open his brother's half-closed study door. The king stood at his desk, knuckles pressed into the smooth oak top, leaning across as he shouted at Stephen Blairford, the head courtier who served the household.

Blairford stood impassively, taking what his sovereign dished out. But for the slight twitch around his eye, Remi would have thought it was meaningless to the man. He had never been one to react around his employer...

And yet not one of the royal children liked him. He had served their father for decades, a story told by the deep lines in his stony face. He liked his position and the massive power it gave him. He had fought to keep that position when the previous king had died at last.

"I understand you, Your Majesty," Blairford said as Grantham bent his head, snorting like a bull. "But you must know I am only thinking of your best interest. Of the best interest of the nation. You have not struck back at these...these...*anarchists*. If you do not do so soon, you could find yourself without a kingdom."

"You tell me that these camps are all over the island," Grantham growled. "And that there are *children* in them. And you wish me to front an assault."

"I recognize the difficulty—"

Remi stepped into the room, shaking his head. "The difficulty.

Please tell me I have misunderstood you, Blairford, and you are not encouraging the king to attack his own people, to attack children of Athawick or any nation."

Grantham seemed surprised at his intrusion, but he pushed his shoulders back. "My brother is right. There is no forgiving a leader who takes on the cloak of a despot. I would deserve to be overrun in those circumstances. I want to negotiate with these people and I will not ask to do so again. Find me a leader and let us make overtures."

"Your Majesty—" Blairford began, tone thick with outrage.

"That will be all," Grantham said, and sat back down. He flipped open a leather folder on his desk and began to read the correspondence. Blairford pinched his lips, but executed a quick bow and then made his way out of the room with only a tilt of the head for Remi.

When he was gone, Remi pushed the door shut. "What the hell was that all about? I thought things had gotten better since London and the attacks there." Grantham lifted his gaze, and Remi's heart sank. "Still keeping secrets, brother?"

"They are mine to keep," Grantham said. "What can anyone do about them but me? I am king."

"Let us advise," Remi suggested, coming toward him. "Let us support."

Grantham glanced up at him. For a moment Remi saw his brother, the man he had been before ascension. He saw the weight of king press down on his shoulders and the desperate desire his brother might secretly feel to push it away. To run away. In that moment he felt connected to Grantham. He, too, wished to run from this life sometimes.

But before he could open his mouth to say that, Grantham's expression changed. Dismissal covered desperation. Coldness overtook the warmth of his brother.

"If you wish to support me, then simply try not to make a scene," Grantham said.

Remi flinched at that. He couldn't help it. "Father used to say that," he whispered.

Grantham had been moving to pick up a pen and his hand hovered near it, frozen. "Well…he might have been wrong in a great many ways. But not in that."

Remi stepped back, as if he could avoid this blow his brother threw toward him. He couldn't. It landed square in the chest and took his air away.

"I wonder what other ways *you* are wrong," Remi said.

"Be careful now," Grantham said, lifting his eyes. "You are speaking to your sovereign."

"I'm certainly not speaking to my brother," Remi retorted. "I think my sovereign might have killed him. The right of a king, I suppose. At least do me this favor: if you will not listen to me, then don't listen to *Blairford* of all people. I don't even know why you keep him around."

"He has experience," Grantham said softly. "In places and things that you could not fathom. I do not have to listen to his bad advice, and I would miss his good. Now if that will be all, I'd like to get back to my paperwork. I have a good deal to do before Mama's…before the queen's next wedding celebration event."

His brother didn't look at him again, even as Remi stared down at him. At last he executed a bow and backed to the door. "Of course, Your Majesty. Anything for king and country."

He pivoted and walked away, shutting the study door perhaps a bit too loudly behind him. In the hallway, he stood for a moment, hating that his hands shook with frustration. He stalked down the hall eventually, toward the back of the house where he could exit onto the terrace. He needed air. He needed to be left alone.

And he needed to get control of his emotions.

～

When Ophelia had bounced onto her bed early that morning, laughing and chatting and reminding her about their promised walk, Priscilla had been…less than enthusiastic. After all, she had been up far too late the night before. Even after returning to her chamber, she had stared at the dark ceiling above, reliving every erotic moment with Remi until she had almost no choice but to touch herself again. The orgasm had been wonderful, though not quite as powerful as the first.

She hadn't told Ophelia all that, of course. She'd just gotten up and tried to shake the cobwebs free as she dressed. They had taken a long walk through the palace grounds, and every step had settled Priscilla's mind a little. Being with Ophelia, it was almost impossible to remain sad or troubled. Her friend's light was just so strong.

So they were returning to the palace with Priscilla in far brighter a mood than she had left in. She clung to Ophelia's arm, laughing at something her friend had said.

"God, it is beautiful here," Ophelia said after their laughter had faded. "I can see how one could be content in Athawick forever."

Priscilla pursed her lips because that sentence made her mind go where it ought not. To Remi. If she were to be in Athawick forever, she would see Remi.

"Pris?"

She blinked. "I'm sorry, what did you say?"

"I asked you if you still think you'd want to be queen over this island," Ophelia said, and her brow wrinkled. "I meant it to tease, but you had such a look on your face."

Priscilla jolted. Queen of this place. God, she had almost forgotten her original idea of capturing King Grantham's attention even if that had only been a few days ago. Aside from when she saw the king, she never thought of him. She never really had, except to ponder how he might assist her future.

In retrospect, she could see how foolish that might have been. A man could be attractive and the king was certainly that. But that didn't mean one was attracted to him.

"I…I don't think I shall ever be queen here," she said.

Ophelia's face lit up suddenly, but then she wiped the expression away. "Oh no? But you were so certain you and that pompous Grantham were a good match, at least in theory. What changed?"

Priscilla shifted. "He…he made it clear he had no interest in me."

Ophelia stopped at the edge of the garden and stared at Priscilla. "He did *what?*"

Her friend's defensive anger was plain in every line of her body, and Priscilla held up a hand. "He wasn't rude. He just…he just was very obvious in the fact the he thinks nothing of me. I am invisible to him."

Ophelia grasped her forearm. "Oh, please don't say that. I know the feeling of being invisible is a painful one to you. I hate that a fool like him could bring it back to the surface. Someone ought to call him out."

"Oh no, please don't," Priscilla said. "Honestly, it didn't sting. I think the fact that it didn't proves the point that I wasn't meant to pursue him, doesn't it? So I've let go of the idea and I want you to let go of your righteous anger toward him on my behalf."

Ophelia didn't look certain, but she started up the path again. "Very well. Because you asked me to, I will try to control myself and not give him the set down he so richly deserves. But then what will you do?"

Priscilla swallowed hard. "I think I must continue with the other plan we discussed."

Ophelia sucked in a breath. "To become a man's lover."

Priscilla nodded.

"I may be biased in this matter, considering what I experienced," Ophelia said quietly.

Priscilla took her hand. "I'm sorry. We don't have to talk about it if it upsets you."

"What upsets me is the idea of you giving yourself to some man who doesn't value you or care about your wellbeing or pleasure."

Priscilla closed her eyes and recalled the spasms of pleasure Remi had milked from her not twelve hours before. "I'm not sure that the two options are mutually exclusive," she said carefully. "A lover might essentially buy the company he keeps, but that doesn't follow that he wouldn't be tender or giving or focused on the person in his bed."

Ophelia stared at her as if she didn't understand the concept. "What…is going on?" she asked slowly.

Priscilla caught her breath. She could tell her best friend about what had happened with Remi. Part of her desperately wanted to do just that, in order to get advice but also just be able to say out loud how those things he had done had made her feel.

But Ophelia already looked so concerned for her wellbeing, so uncertain about this entire thing…what if she said what she'd done and Ophelia judged? Or worse, told someone out of some misguided attempt to protect her? Then everything with Remi would come to a screeching halt and she definitely didn't want that.

"Nothing is going on," she said, continuing to walk up the path to the palace and forcing Ophelia to do the same. "I've only been pondering the situation and trying to parse out what I shall do, that's all. I'm trying to see it from its most positive outcome." She smiled at Ophelia nervously. "Isn't that what you normally do? Come now, if I cannot depend upon you to tell me how it will all be fine…"

Ophelia caught her hand and squeezed as they reached the garden at last and weaved their way through the maze of bushes and plantings and sweet smelling flowers.

"Oh, it will be fine," Ophelia said. "I *do* believe that. Things tend to work out as they should…eventually. And I will support any decision you make and try to help you in every way possible. Don't let my worries increase your own."

Priscilla was about to press the issue when they reached the top of the steps that led to the large wraparound terrace that extended around a huge portion of the back of the palace. Her attention toward Ophelia faded as she glanced across the expanse of terrace to find Remi standing at a table, staring off into nothingness.

Her breath caught as the breeze stirred his hair a fraction. He was so outrageously handsome, and as he flexed a hand at his side, she couldn't help but think that those same fingers had done such magical things to her the night before.

And yet, once those lustful feelings eased a fraction, she also noticed something else. He appeared...upset. That was a rare enough thing that she found herself taking a long step toward him.

Ophelia jerked as Priscilla accidentally dragged her forward too.

"Oh goodness, I apologize," Priscilla gasped, releasing Ophelia's hand. "I was distracted."

Ophelia followed her stare and arched a brow as she realized who Priscilla had been staring at. "I see that," she said softly.

Priscilla looked over at her. Once again, she was tempted to tell her friend something, anything to make her understand. But instead she just forced a smile. "Why don't you go in? I would like to speak to the prince about something we...we discussed at the gathering last night."

Ophelia hesitated a moment, her gaze drifting between Priscilla and Remi. Long enough that Priscilla feared she might demand to stay as chaperone. But at last Ophelia shook her head and sighed. "Just...be careful."

Priscilla tensed. After a lifetime of doing just that and still suffering all the consequences, the last thing she was doing now was being careful. And it felt wonderful.

"I will be," she lied as Ophelia walked away to the terrace doors and slipped inside.

Immediately Priscilla turned back to the temptation she could not deny and walked toward Remi. He hadn't seemed to notice her and Ophelia during their brief conversation. They had been halfway across the large terrace, after all, and he was obviously distracted.

But as she made her way across the expanse that separated him, he appeared to sense her attention on him, and he glanced toward her.

When he realized she was moving toward him, she saw his expression relax. Saw a flutter of pleasure move across his unusually tense features. And that called to her as much as anything else. If she could ease whatever troubled him…even a little…

Even if she knew it would only destroy her in the end.

CHAPTER 12

"Your Highness," Priscilla said as she finished the final few steps across the terrace to Remi's side. She executed a small curtsey.

"Miss Linfield," he drawled, and his gaze flitted over her from head to toe. "What a *pleasure* to see you this morning. Where did you come from?"

"Ophelia and I were walking the grounds this morning," she explained. "And they were enchanting."

His jaw tensed. "Indeed, it is an enchanting place. That is strange, for I didn't notice you two even though I was staring out at the garden."

She moved closer. "You were...you seemed distracted, Remi. Is everything well?"

His brow furrowed at the question, as if she had taken him aback with the observation. "I'm fine. I'm always fine."

She shook her head slowly. "I'm certain that is not true. No one is fine at all times."

"I'm expected to be," he said. "To be the court jester. And so I am. This is the way of the world."

His tone was so bitter that she almost flinched. Instead she closed the rest of the distance between them. After a quick glance around to ensure they were alone, she touched his hand gently. "What is it? What has upset you?"

He stared down at her, their gazes holding for what felt like a lifetime. Then he smiled, that false expression he shared with the world when he was playing his games. She could see how it was a mask now, covering a great deal more depth than he would choose to share, perhaps even with her.

"You needn't trouble yourself," he said.

She tightened her fingers against his. "You are helping me. Won't you allow me to offer you the same support?"

"I'm seducing you, Priscilla," he said, sharp and pointed. "Don't make me out to be some hero."

"You're not a hero," she agreed. "You're human."

Those words seemed to surprise him, for he was silent for some time before he cleared his throat and motioned her to sit at the table. Once she had, he took his own place and clenched and unclenched his fingers before him.

"What is…what is your place in this world, Priscilla?"

She drew back at the question. "I…I suppose I'm not sure. I was raised a gentleman's daughter, with the expectations that went along with that. I thought I would become a gentleman's wife, likely matched for monetary and positional gain more than affection. When I failed at that, well, that is how we came to be here. And I will be forced to forge a new path…or follow one that is thrown out before me."

He nodded slowly. "I realize this is a difficult time for you, but in some ways I envy your position."

"Envy me?" she repeated in shock. "A failure at the marriage mart who must now choose between spinsterhood or becoming a courtesan?"

"I envy that you have any choice in the matter at all," he said. "Again, I don't diminish that you are in a difficult position, but the path you walk in the future may end up being one you chose entirely. And it could take you anywhere in the world potentially. I...I have always known my role."

"Prince," she said.

He sighed. "Spare. I was raised to be the backup plan if, God forbid, something happened to my brother. I look at my family...my sisters have both found love, against all odds. They will race off for futures with their husbands. Yes, there will be some expectations when it comes to duties here, but they are free now. Grantham has taken his title, so his path is clear, as well. They all have their places, they are all changing and I...I am ever the same. So I find myself wondering...who the hell am I?"

She watched him for a moment, exploring the tiny twitches of his lips, the sadness around his eyes that he normally covered so expertly. He was no longer the playboy prince in this moment. He was just Remi. And she knew deep in her soul that he would not have let many people see that truth of him.

"Who do you want to be?" she asked.

He blinked. "What do you mean?"

"If your sisters were allowed to choose their place in the world, if the king is taking his...then it seems you are poised to do the same. After all, King Grantham will marry eventually."

"Yes. He will do his duty and produce the line that will carry on the monarchy."

"Then you will no longer be the spare," she said. "So who would you *like* to be?"

He shook his head. "I don't know."

"How exciting," she said as she lifted a finger to trace the line of his jaw. He made a face and she laughed. "It *is* exciting, Remi. You can be whoever you wish to be, however you wish to be it."

He didn't seem certain about that, but the openness in his gaze faded. He was putting a wall back up between them, locking her out of the struggle he was obviously having in his heart. She found herself longing to be let back in. To have a more permanent place in that secret corner that she had just seen.

But that was foolish.

"So…how are you this morning?" he asked. "You had an eventful night."

"I did," she said, heat filling her cheeks. "Thanks to you."

"You are very welcome." He smirked and leaned a little closer. "And did you do as you were told and practice?"

The heat grew higher and she knew she must look like a plum. She was searching for an answer when the terrace door opened and the queen stepped out. Priscilla leaned away from Remi instantly and gave him a meaningful look. He glanced over his shoulder and saw the impending interruption, and nodded slightly.

"Good morning," the queen said.

Priscilla and Remi got to their feet. She curtseyed and he bowed before he leaned forward to buss his mother's cheek. "Mama, don't you look divine this morning."

"Thank you," Queen Giabella said to her son, though her gaze remained on Priscilla, speculative. "Good morning, Miss Linfield."

"Your Majesty," Priscilla said. "I was walking your wonderful estate grounds this morning with Lady Ophelia. It is a magical place."

The queen's gaze lit up. "It is that," she agreed. "Did you find the apple grove?"

"No," Priscilla said.

"It is truly beautiful in the spring when the blooms pop," the queen said. "We are too late for that now, of course, and too early for full fruit. But it's still one of my favorite places."

"I shall have to look for it when next we explore," Priscilla said.

"Or Remi could show you," the queen said with a mild look for her son. "He has always enjoyed the grove."

Remi's gaze narrowed on his mother. "Of course," he said. "It would be my pleasure. Now I'm certain you didn't come out here to talk about apples, Mama. Is my presence required?"

"It is, I'm afraid. I do apologize, Miss Linfield."

Priscilla shook her head. "Not at all. I realize the prince has many duties to attend to, as does the rest of the family. I will see you later, Your Majesty, Your Highness."

Remi took his mother's arm and moved to lead her away, but not before he winked back at Priscilla. "You most definitely will, Miss Linfield."

She worried her lip as he disappeared into the palace with his mother. His playful demeanor warmed her, of course, as did his reminder that they would see a good deal of each other that night. But she was still troubled by the glimpse she had seen of the real man beneath the mask. The one who she very much wanted to help...even though she knew it would only lead to heartache to become too close to him.

Remi felt the tightening of his mother's fingers on his inner elbow as she guided him into a parlor and closed the door. There was a light in her eyes as she released him and paced across the room, pivoting to spear him with a stare.

"I thought I was required for some official reason," he said, trying to keep his tone as mild as possible when she was almost bouncing with excitement. Clearly he had not been careful enough with Priscilla. His mother's intentions were now written all over her face.

"I think that your future is the most official of reasons," the queen said. "And I don't want you to think I have forgotten about it just because we are all aflutter about Ilaria's wedding tomorrow."

Her words reminded him of Priscilla, of her assertion that he was in a position to be whomever he desired. That had never felt true and his mother's bright excitement on this topic didn't change his thoughts on the matter.

"Well, you are not allowed to be *aflutter* about me," he reminded her. "Your focus should be that very wedding. And then we must give equal attention to the coronation of Sasha as an official

Princess of Athawick. You cannot put your attention on me and my future until…oh…at least next autumn."

The queen shot him a look. "Do not be ridiculous, Remi. Everything in our world is…" She hesitated and there was a twitch to her cheek, a rare revelation of emotion that she normally controlled. "…it's changing. You cannot hold yourself aside from that."

"I'm not," he insisted, even though that was exactly what he was doing. She had always been able to see through him too easily.

"Have you put any thought into marriage?"

He tensed. "I suppose I knew this day was coming."

"What do you mean?" she asked, but there was a guilty quality to her stare now.

"Grantham had his plans for Ilaria that fell through thanks to her falling in love with Jonah and Sasha falling in love with Bramwell. A tangled little web of who should have married who for title and position. But of course you two would have to put your energy into the next in line. You are eyeing me for a political union? Why doesn't Grantham do it himself?"

The queen's lips pursed. "I never said a political union. Of course we have hopes to strengthen our position with the English with a marriage to someone linked to a title, but I have learned my lesson after nearly losing both my daughters. At any rate, Sasha did marry Bramwell and she will soon be a princess in title as well as in our hearts, and that does solve the problem somewhat."

"Then why harass me about it?"

She drew back, and he realized how sharp his tone was in that moment. She cleared her throat softly. "Your hearts and your futures are worth more than some short-term gain. I am asking you, Remi, if you have considered a union for your *own* happiness, as much as for some invisible border that only exists on paper."

Remi drew back. His mother had been raised to marry a king— she had never had a choice in the matter. She'd always been taught to be calm and prudent, but at that moment her eyes were bright with emotion.

"I have…not," he said, correcting his tone. "Do not mistake me, Mama, I am incredibly happy for Ilaria and for Sasha. They have found whatever they label as love and it seems to lighten them both. I would wish nothing less for them. But…but not everyone is destined for such a happy ending. Most people are not, especially in circles like our own."

Her expression softened. "Remi," she said gently. "I realize that you did not have an easy time growing up. Your father was…" She stopped herself briefly.

"He was a cold, cruel man who was not fit to shine your shoes," he said, just as quietly. "Who didn't care about his children or anything else but himself. We can speak freely about him now, Mama. He is in the ground for over a year."

She drew in a long, shaky breath. "Yes, he was all of those things. And in some ways, you received the worst of his behavior."

Remi bent his head. His relationship with the last king had been complicated to say the least. "I saw how he treated Grantham, how he treated you. And I felt his utter disgust and disregard for me grow daily from the time I was fifteen until nearly the day he died."

"I know," she said. "And I'm sorry."

"You needn't be," he said, walking away so that this uncomfortable conversation might end. He certainly didn't want to have it or to be reminded of the experiences she was describing. "It's over now, there's no need to discuss it further."

The queen was silent, and eventually he turned to look at her. She was staring at him closely, pain in her eyes. But she inclined her head. "If you don't wish to do so, I wouldn't dream of forcing you." She cleared her throat. "So let's talk about something else."

"Thank you," he said.

"Miss Linfield."

He ran a hand through his hair. Somehow talking about her seemed as fraught as talking about his father. Hardly a change of subject at all. "What about her?"

"You had your heads close together on the terrace a moment

ago," Queen Giabella said. "I have not been able to spend much time with the young lady, but from what I have seen, she seems lovely."

"She is lovely," he conceded. "And that is where your match-making mind must stop. She's…she's not my type."

That was such a lie. Perhaps she hadn't been at one point, but at present she was the only woman who was his type.

His mother arched a brow. "I suppose not. You tend to chase after women who will make your brother rip out his hair. Ones that there is no chance of a future with."

"There's no chance of a future with any of them. At least right now." He moved toward her and caught her hands. "Mama, enough. I know what you want of me, what you and my brother expect. But you will not control me any more than you controlled Ilaria or Sasha. So stop trying."

She huffed out a breath and threw up her hands. "Fine. Then what do you suggest I do?"

"Enjoy the wedding this week and the coronation later this year. Play cribbage with Dash." Her expression tensed at that suggestion. "Worry about the king."

"Why would I worry about Grantham?"

Remi hesitated. He could tell her about their encounter in the study, but it would only make her worry. And piss Grantham off, which was fun but also had consequences. So instead he shrugged. "Why wouldn't you? He is so grouchy, I'm surprised he hasn't scared the entire kingdom away."

He could see she was trying not to laugh at his assessment. "He has a great deal of weight on his shoulders," she scolded without heat.

He nodded. "That he does. And so you should focus all your meddling on him."

She rolled her eyes slightly. "Very well, I hear you. I will not push you. For now. But I am still going to get to know Miss Linfield better."

Remi ought not to want that. After all, there was something

awkward about his mother spending time with the woman he was slowly debauching. And yet…he liked the idea of them getting to know each other. They were both so warm, he had no doubt they would get along.

"Do as you wish," he said, waving a hand as if it meant little to him.

She moved toward him and pressed a kiss to his cheek. She held his gaze for a moment. "You know I only wish for your happiness, Remi."

"As I do for yours. Neither of our futures are cast in stone, are they? Perhaps there is great happiness ahead for us both."

He had meant for the sentiment to give her pleasure, but instead she dropped her gaze away. "Let us hope so. And now I must go. I'm meeting with Dash and Ilaria for a few final arrangements for the wedding."

"Off you go then," he said, waving her away playfully.

She went with just a quick glance back at him. When she was gone, he sagged a fraction, leaning on the back of the closest chair as he dragged in a long breath. He had dodged his mother's interference, at least in part. And yet he felt not a sense of triumph but of… loss. Like he had missed out on something by not offering her more details about his life, his worries, his feelings.

He had to get himself together, that was all. It couldn't be that hard, he just had to remember who he was. And what he wanted… from life, and from Miss Priscilla Linfield.

CHAPTER 13

Priscilla's hands were shaking as she climbed the last few steps up the winding staircase that led to the east tower of the palace. It was quiet in this little-used part of the castle, and that should have been comforting. It also meant she could hear every pounding beat of her own heart and she couldn't blame the racing rhythm only on the exertion of climbing the never-ending stairs.

She paused at the top of the stairs and looked around. The top of the tower was round, of course, and there was a door a few steps in front of her. It was open a crack, probably left that way by Remi to encourage her to enter.

"You can do this," she whispered to herself. "You *must* do this. You cannot go back now."

She drew in a long, deep breath and stepped into the chamber. Immediately she gasped as she looked around her. For whatever reason, she had pictured a bedroom in a tower to be dank or cold or plain. This was most definitely not that. A bright fire burned in a stone fireplace, richly made tapestries covered the windows and curved walls, and in the middle of it all was a huge bed. Obscenely huge, if one was to get to it. There was a table closer to the fireplace, and a tray of wine and cheese was set there.

As she moved farther into the room, Remi stepped from the shadows. "Good evening," he said softly.

"Good evening," she parroted back.

He smiled. "So what do you think of my tower? Fit for a dragon?"

She lifted one hand to her chest and waved the other one around the chamber. "It's wonderful, Remi! But a great many servants must have been part of this. Is there no danger that they'll talk about who you might be bringing to a deserted tower in the middle of the night?"

He moved toward her. "I assure you, only my valet was involved in the creation of this setting, and he was paid very handsomely for his silence and his hard work. He is accustomed to being discreet."

Those words reminded her of his vast experience and she found herself wondering about all those women he had loved and forgotten. Wondered how long until she was one of them.

"I suppose he…would…have to be, if your reputation is to be believed," she said, turning her back on Remi as she roamed around the room. "And this seems to be the perfect place for an assignation."

He was silent for a moment, but then he said, "Yes. In the library you would have to be quiet, but here you can express your pleasure all you'd like. It was built for…" He hesitated. "Well, I shudder to think why this room was placed up here and made so fine. It was done hundreds of years ago, and *that* doesn't bode well."

"But tonight it will be for more pleasurable pursuits," she said.

He nodded. "Very much so. Would you like something to drink or eat before we begin?"

She glanced at the table and its offerings again. "I don't think I could eat a bite and I'm already a bit dizzy. I think drinking wouldn't be the best idea, even just wine."

"Very good. Then why don't we move to the bed?"

He motioned toward the giant bed, and she worried her lip as she crossed to it, sat gingerly on the edge and looked up at him. To her surprise, he didn't step over to join her or make any move to touch her.

"The stairway and area leading to the door echoes," he said instead.

She blinked, not fully understanding. "Is that...is that a euphemism? Or some kind of suggestion that I don't understand in my innocence?"

He tilted his head back and laughed. She was mesmerized by the look of it for a moment. The tendons in his neck flexed, his expression relaxed, his eyes were bright as he grinned at her. He was so unfairly beautiful.

"No," he said when he had stopped laughing. "I only meant that I heard what you said to yourself before you came in to the room. That you couldn't go back. And I want you to know that isn't true. I told you before and I shall repeat it again: you can say no any time you like. There would be no recrimination or punishment from me."

She swallowed. "I realize this is meaningless to you."

"I didn't say that," he said with a shake of his head. "I would be intensely disappointed if I didn't get to do all the lovely things I plan to do here with you. But you get to decide what happens to your body, not me."

She considered that a moment. It was surprising and also comforting to know that this man cared about her wellbeing and her consent. With his power, he could take what he desired and never face a consequence. That he was so careful about exerting it spoke highly of him and the kind of man he was.

She cleared her throat. "When I said that in the hallway, I-I wasn't talking about you," she explained slowly. "I was...reminding myself that I have reached a point of no return. That this is my future and I had best take the opportunity you are presenting to me to make it something more in my own control."

His brow furrowed and at last he did sit next to her. He caught her hands, his warm fingers stroking gently along the top of her knuckles. "If you want a different path, I can help you find it. I could help you find a husband. Here in Athawick. I could do that. I...would."

He meant that to be supportive, kind, but the sting it caused in response ripped through her powerfully. She didn't want Remi to go off and find her some reluctant man to share her life. She didn't want him to have to beg and bargain on her behalf so he could play a white knight rescuing her from a tower like the one they sat in.

"I want this," she said softly. "I want what you promised me already."

He held her gaze intently, reading her. She had no way to keep him out—he was too focused and talented at seeing through people. Seeing through her. So she let him. Let him see it all and felt stripped and vulnerable in spirit the way she hoped to soon be in body for this man.

She expected him to say something, to offer more false comfort or explanation. Instead he cupped her cheeks and then his mouth was on hers.

She tilted her head slightly, angling to be closer and felt him smile against her lips before he parted them and drove his tongue inside. A flutter of desire rippled through her with that claiming, melting her barriers and her questions and leaving nothing behind but him and the way his mouth felt on hers.

She kissed him back, bolder today than she had been before because she understood what he wanted more. She understood her own desires on a deeper level, too. He had taught her that and she would be eternally grateful for that tutelage. But she wanted more. Deep in her heart, she feared she wanted too much.

She pushed those thoughts away and grasped for the lapels of his jacket, lifting against him with a murmur of pleasure. His fingers flexed against her cheeks in response, and when he pulled back he was panting, his pupils dilated.

"I would like to remove your gown. I want to see you for what I have in mind tonight."

She tensed. It wasn't that she hadn't known eventually she would be naked. What they were going to do would require it, according to what she'd read and understood. But she hadn't been naked in front of a man before. She was hardly ever naked in front of anyone, as she tended to put on her underthings before her maid, Beth, came in to dress her.

"You are staring straight ahead, eyes wide as saucers," he said with a chuckle. "Obviously running off into thoughts in your head. Tell me."

She pushed to her feet and paced away from him, as if creating physical space would somehow make things clearer or easier to say. Of course it didn't.

"I just don't know what you'll think of me naked," she admitted as she dared to look at him once more. He had stood by now, as well, but was not following her or demanding her return to him. "And I'm not sure how I'll react."

He shook his head. "First off, my mouth waters when I picture all those lovely, lush curves unwrapped for my pleasure," he said. "I cannot wait. And as for how you'll react, I'm certain you'll be hesitant at first. But hopefully I'll make you comfortable enough that it will pass. That, my dear, is part of my duty as a lover. If you find a man who doesn't take that seriously, cut him off swiftly."

"It is kind of you to think I'll have the option to be so choosy in my bed partners." She sighed.

"You should be," he insisted, and now he did move toward her. Close enough to touch her, though he didn't. Yet. She knew it was *yet*, she could practically see him vibrate in a desire to touch her. "In fact, you must promise me you will be or else I cannot properly train you in anything else."

She thought he was teasing her, but when she met his eyes she saw how earnest he was. This was actually important to him. So she nodded slowly. "Very well. Then what do I look for in a man? A lover."

His mouth tightened briefly, but then he relaxed it. "Any man lucky enough to have you as a lover should tend to your needs first.

He should be thoughtful in and out of the bedroom. And you should never have to chase him for his affection or attention. Any man who is less than that..." He made a slicing motion back and forth in front of him with his forefinger.

What he described sounded...lovely. She had always had to chase for love, from the moment she knew to long for it. In her family, in gentlemen who she had an interest in during the early days of her coming out, when she still had hopes for a future. The only person she didn't have to chase for affection was Ophelia.

And she supposed...Remi. He had always given her his attention easily, eagerly, passionately.

Her hands shook as she turned her back to him and offered him the long line of buttons along the back of her gown. "It seems you fit the bill, Your Highness. So you may pass."

He chuckled as he smoothed his hands down the length of her spine. That sound made her entire body clench, and this time she understood the tingle of pleasure that followed. Multiplied when he unfastened the first pearl button at the base of her neck. His fingers brushed the bare skin beneath, and it took every ounce of control in her body not to just lean back into him, melt into him.

He unfastened the next, the next, and finally he parted the fabric and let his fingers dance beneath the flimsy fabric of the chemise beneath. He dragged his nails lightly against the sensitive skin, leaning in to kiss her there as she shivered and whimpered his name.

"Ready?" he asked, even as he began to push her gown forward.

She fought the urge to lift her hands, to block the removal of the silk and satin fabric that pooled at her feet all too easily the moment he got it free of her arms. Now she was just in her chemise and she stared down at the length of her body without turning. The chemise stopped just at her knees, so her legs were revealed.

"Look at me," he whispered.

There was no denying that utterly hypnotic tone, so she did as he asked, facing him slowly. He had taken a step back as she moved and now he stared at her, eyes wide, almost like he'd never seen anything like her before. A lie, of course, he had been with many women before her. He'd likely be with many after her.

But in that moment she felt singular and special.

Also very exposed. Once again, she had to fight not to lift her arms and cover herself. "Wha-what do you think?" she stammered.

"You are stunning," he said. "And all I want is to sink into all those curves and make you cry out my name like you did in the library last night. I want to feel you wrapped around me, Priscilla. I want to feel your heat, I want to drown in it."

She was shaking. How could she ever resist him when he was so focused on her and his words were so…powerful?

"Yes," she moaned. "Yes, yes, yes."

He said nothing else and instead reached forward and looped a finger around the strap of her chemise. He pulled it down slowly, taking his time with one strap, then the other. The garment fell forward, exposing her fully from the waist up. Now she did lift her hands, covering her heavy breasts as she turned her face away from him.

"Please don't cover yourself," he said softly.

She worried her lip and a rumbling sound of pleasure escaped his chest as he continued to watch her, patiently waiting for her to fulfill his request. She drew a few long breaths. He wasn't wrong that she would have to get over this anxiety. And who better to do it with than a man who was so gentle about it.

She lowered her hands and, as she did so, hooked her fingers into the folded layers of her chemise to push it the rest of the way off. All that was left now were her drawers. He stared at her for a beat, two, and then moved closer.

"You make me dizzy," he said, reaching out to trace the slope of her throat with the back of his hand.

She blinked. "I don't know how. You aren't new to this."

"I'm new to you," he said. "I want to learn every inch."

He held her stare more intently as he lowered his hand, stroking her skin slowly, gently, until he dragged his knuckles over her exposed nipple. Immediately it puckered and she dipped her head back with a gasp.

"More?" he asked, his voice sounding so far away.

"Yes," she ground out. "Please."

He cupped the same breast, filling his hands with her, brushing his palm over her and then squeezing. She gripped for his forearms, clinging for purchase as he teased her. He cupped the other breast and thumbed her nipple over and over, plucking her as she writhed and clenched her thighs together.

He wrapped an arm around her waist and tugged her flush against him. He was still dressed and her nipples scraped across his jacket, sensation pulsing wildly through her as he kissed her once more. She found herself arching against him, mewling against his tongue as he backed her toward the bed they had abandoned. She shivered as her backside hit the edge and she collapsed back into a seated position. He leaned over her, still kissing her without covering her.

Finally he withdrew. "I'm going to take the rest off," he said.

She nodded and watched his hands, mesmerized as he slid them from her face to her shoulders, down over her breasts, her stomach to untie the ribbon at her waist. Once she was free, he tugged. She lifted her backside a little, letting him pull the fabric away down her legs. When he tossed it aside, she shivered.

She was naked. And he was just *looking* at her like she was a goddess. Like she was a treat he wanted to devour. Like she was everything.

Did he look at every woman he bedded this way? Was she so foolish that she couldn't scent a game in the air? Or did he focus so intently and then lose interest?

She pushed at the thoughts, trying to quiet her mind and just enjoy his attention. She couldn't long for more, so there was no point in dragging herself through hell for it.

He shrugged from his jacket and let it fall behind him. Then he loosened his cufflinks and set them on a nearby table, rolling his sleeves as he returned to stand before her. She caught her breath at the sight of him. His bare forearms were so…strong. She wanted to trace them with her fingers, then her tongue.

"Lie back," he grunted. "Head on the pillows."

She blinked as she tried to focus on what he'd said. A similar order he'd given the night before, when he'd slouched her down on the settee and helped her touch herself until she lost all sense and reason.

She wanted more than that tonight, but since she didn't know how to ask for it, she simply followed his instruction. She scooted back onto the bed, resting her head on the pillows like she would go to sleep. But she didn't feel tired, she felt tightly wound and needy, aching for him. Aching for release.

She waited for him to remove the rest of his clothing, to be as naked as she was. Truth be told, she was looking forward to that moment. Her experience of nude male bodies was limited to sculpture gardens and paintings. Not nearly as satisfying as real flesh and muscle and bone. Or at least, she assumed so.

Only he didn't divest himself of anything else. He even left his cravat elegantly tied as he sat down on the edge of the bed next to her and just…looked at her. She groaned her disappointment and he arched a brow with a laugh.

"That seems a bad start. What is upsetting you?"

"You're so…so…put together," she said, fighting the urge to fold her arms like a petulant child. "And I'm stark naked and spread out on this bed like a wanton."

His smile spread across his face, not gentle, not indulgent but very wicked. He leaned over her slowly, caging her in by pressing a fist on either side of her head on the pillow. His weight pushed her deeper into the bed, even though he wasn't lying directly on her.

"That's the fun of it, Priscilla," he murmured, stroking the side of his nose along the edge of hers. "Think of what you're doing. You are laid out like a feast to me. I am in control in this tower. You're...mine."

As he said that last word, he dropped his mouth to her throat and pressed a hard, fast kiss there. "Every inch of you is mine. You are helpless to me. And you can trust me to just...surrender. That I will see to every pleasure you need. Your servant as much as your master."

She was shaking as she watched his dark head move lower. Now his kiss was dragged across her collarbone, and his hands opened and slid around her body as he moved lower.

"But," she gasped, lolling her head to the side as he swept his tongue over the swell of her breast and then traced the hard outline of her nipple. "Oh God, don't stop doing that."

He chuckled against her flesh and sucked her into his mouth. She fought to maintain some level of mental acumen, but it was virtually impossible when his mouth was doing that and his hand had moved up to tease the opposite breast like he had been earlier.

"But what?" he asked against her flesh.

She lifted to him, her hips brushing his chest as he hovered over her, making magic with his tongue. She dug her hands into his hair, the crisp locks tangling around her fingers. He grunted, like that touch pleased him.

"But...but..." What had she been planning to say? It was so hard to remember when her entire body was on fire for him. "But if you're fully..."

He switched his mouth to her other breast, his bright blue eyes lifting to watch her as he stroked his tongue over her nipple. "Fully what?" he asked, voice muffled by what he was doing. "Fully erect? Fully present? Fully..."

"Dressed," she gasped out. "I may not know much, but if you're going to take me, you can't be fully dressed."

He paused in his ministrations and lifted his head. "That sounds like a challenge, but I assure you it isn't a difficult one. Priscilla, if I wanted to fuck you—"

She moaned at that direct, vulgar word. She'd read it before, knew what it meant.

"If that was what I wanted, my being dressed couldn't stop me. I could pull you into one of the alcoves during a ball and have you, and no one would ever be the wiser."

She swallowed hard. "How?"

He arched a brow. "I would press you against the wall," he said, his pupils dilating with every word. "Lift your skirts. If you were wearing drawers, I'd rip them down the seam as you whispered all your protests, but in truth you'd be excited by it."

She *was* excited at that idea. She could picture it. "And then? That deals with my clothing, but not yours."

"I'd just unfasten the placard on my trousers. And if you were pressed against me, burying your head in my shoulder to muffle your very pretty moans, I would be rock hard and very ready for you. All it would take would be to lift you up a little, align us, and then I would be sliding home in you. Grinding into you, feeling you flutter around my cock the way you fluttered against my fingers last night."

His breath grew shorter, harder as he spoke. His gaze wild and as wanton as she, herself, felt. She heard a little broken sigh escape her lips and he smiled down at her.

"So…is that what you plan to do tonight?" she whispered, licking her suddenly dry lips. "To unfasten yourself and just…have me?"

He wrinkled his brow. "A rather ignominious way to be taken for the first time, I think. You certainly deserve better. I might just do what I described at some point. I would love to do what I just described and so much more. But tonight…tonight is not about that."

"Then what is it about?" she asked, shaking beneath him.

He bent his head again, but this time he nuzzled the undercurve of her breast, his lips brushing her ribcage, his fingers pressing gently into the soft flesh of her belly.

"Making you come undone," he murmured.

"You have done that already," she gasped, closing her eyes as he edged lower on her body.

Priscilla hadn't ever thought much about that body he was teasing. Tasting. She hadn't spent a great deal of time exploring it until he commanded her to do so, and she had realized how easily she could give herself a version of the pleasure he created.

She was bigger than some other women. More Rubenesque than the works of modern artists, who loved to paint a more slender frame. Now, as Remi's fingers pressed into her soft flesh of her hips, as he traced the curve of her stomach with his tongue, she reveled in all her curves. He certainly seemed to do the same as he stroked his cheek against her thigh before he pushed them wide.

Just like the previous night, she was exposed to him. It didn't feel as odd this time, to have him look at her so intimately, though he was much closer this time. He rested his head against her thigh before he reached up to trace her with a fingertip. She jolted at the contact, lifting to him with a wordless moan. He watched her, his gaze intense as he pressed a little harder, circling her clitoris with his fingertip but never quite touching it. Drawing her to the edge of madness without ever giving her the sweet relief from it.

"Do you want to come?" he asked, his voice low and rough.

"I think that's obvious," she gasped, and lifted her hips toward him. "Please!"

"Very well. Only this time I'm going to do it with my tongue."

CHAPTER 14

Priscilla could not fathom what Remi's wicked words meant. She might have asked him, only he didn't give her time. Instead, he showed her.

He leaned up closer, pressing his mouth between her legs. His mouth was warm against her flesh and the pressure was exciting. It wasn't quite so intense as when he peeled her open and touched her, but she liked it.

He drew his mouth away and pressed his hands to her, rubbing the outer lips of her sex with both thumbs. She lifted against him, meeting his rhythm as the pleasure began to warm, to spread, to intensify. Yes, this was what she liked, more than the other. This was what she wanted, what made her wet and needy and shaky for him.

He watched her closely, his gaze burning into her as she relaxed. Her breath grew shorter and she ground against him, seeking what he could give.

Only then did he open her, exposing her sex to him. He continued to massage her sensitive outer lips, but now he returned his mouth to her. This time he traced her entrance not with his fingertip, but with his tongue. She jolted, the intensity of the sensation deeper and more powerful. She pushed to her elbows, watching in wonder as he licked her.

The pleasure became even more intense with every swipe of his tongue, and when he focused his attention on her clitoris, sucking instead of licking, she barked out a sound she had never heard herself make due to the sharp sensation. He moaned softly against her, sending vibrations through her sex. She ground up into him, flopping back onto the pillows again.

He was relentless, sucking her, licking her, teasing her. She would begin to edge toward release and it was like he sensed it and would pull her back away, keeping her from orgasm. She was sweating by then, panting. Her legs shook, her toes curled.

He lifted his head, his chin coated with her juices, his hair wild from her fingers and she nearly came just from seeing him like that. He smoothed a finger over her.

"I'm going to put a finger inside of you," he said softly.

She sucked in her breath and sat up again. "Inside?"

He nodded. "It might hurt a little, since you have never been tried. And some would view it as a taking of your virginity. So I must ask...do you want this?"

She pondered the question a moment. Her body screamed yes, but she focused with her mind. If he was saying this would be viewed by some as a point of no return, she had to be mindful of what her answer meant. She would be giving herself to this man. Surrendering to a future as a lover, to a future built around the pleasure Remi was teaching her and perhaps little more.

Right now that didn't sound terrible. And if he was the one giving her the pleasure, it sounded downright heavenly.

"I want this," she affirmed. "I want...I want you and everything you can give and show and introduce. And I trust that you'll be...careful."

His brow wrinkled. "Careful. I've never been accused of that before. But yes. With you, I will be exquisitely careful. I will take care of you like you were fine bone china, as priceless as emeralds.

No one else in the world may be able to say this, but *you* can trust me."

Her lips parted at that promise, earnestly given and clearly meant. It bonded them, she felt it in an instant as the truth of it washed over her.

But before she could treasure that realization or overthink it, he lowered his mouth back to her and sucked her clitoris once again. Her head lolled back, thoughts emptying from her mind as she gave over to him. He lapped gently, with just the right pleasure to build that peak without ever throwing her over the other side of it. And when she was gasping and moaning and begging, he pressed his index finger to her entrance and took her to his first knuckle.

She gasped at the sensation of his body invading hers, even on this small scale. There was a tiny bit of friction to the action, but no pain. She tensed her inner muscles around him, testing what it would feel like.

"Christ," he muttered, dropping his mouth back to her sex. He continued to pleasure her with his tongue even as he stroked that finger, easing in farther, farther, until it was fully seated inside of her. He lifted his eyes. "Grind," he ordered.

She nodded and began to do so, arching against his mouth, his finger, squeezing against him harder and harder. He moaned against her, thrusting his finger gently. And just as she thought she could take no more, he placed a second digit at her entrance and further claimed the channel.

The discomfort burned a little higher now as she stretched to accommodate him. But this time he offered her no respite from his mouth. She was torn between faint pain and outrageous pleasure and the combination was wildly intoxicating. There was no time for nerves or fear. He had teased her for what felt like a lifetime, but as he fully claimed her with both fingers, curling them inside of her, his tongue worked harder. She tugged at his hair as her control wavered. Her heels dug into the mattress as she arched higher.

And the pleasure he had been denying and offering came roaring over her with an intensity that was undeniable. The waves were hard, harsh, powerful. She squirmed beneath his still-seeking tongue, clenching against his thrusting fingers as she shattered into a thousand pieces beneath him.

R emi had given a great many orgasms since his first sexual encounter. The pleasure of his partners was always paramount to him and he took a great deal of pride in the moment where he watched them spasm in bliss.

But he had never experienced anything like what he felt as he watched Priscilla unravel beneath him. She was utterly guileless, completely free as she cried out, twisting and grinding and demanding more from him in a way he doubted she would dare to do in her right mind. She would talk herself out of such demands, tell herself she didn't deserve them.

But in the throes of passion, she was bold. And it was glorious to watch.

At last she collapsed, her body still twitching, her expression relaxed and pleased. Only then did he slowly withdraw his fingers from her sheath. He checked for blood, but found none. Good. He had readied her enough that the invasion of his fingers hadn't damaged her.

She was watching him, her expression becoming a little wary. "*Am* I still a virgin?" she asked.

He shook his head. "Depends on who you ask. I haven't claimed you with my cock. To some that is the ultimate stealer of so-called virtue. But in my mind, you are not. However, the only mind that matters is *yours*."

"What we did does not feel very…innocent," she said slowly, and her gaze dropped to his cock, which was very hard beneath his breeches and clearly outlined there. "But I would still like to experience the rest."

She reached for him, pressing her palm against the length of him. He jolted at the pleasure that touch created. God's teeth, her natural desire, drive, would unman him. And he would revel in it... too much.

Right now he did not feel exactly in control. His heart was racing, his hands were shaking, and there was a sensation in his chest, in his heart, that he had never felt before. Perhaps because she *was* a virgin, and that was territory he had always avoided. Whether or not he valued that status the same way others might didn't matter. It did mean something to be the first man to touch a woman. To introduce her to pleasure.

So perhaps that was what he felt. That responsibility he usually avoided. Either way, he moved away from her seeking hand.

A flicker of hurt crossed her face at that action. "I...is that wrong?"

"No," he assured her, and leaned in to kiss her. He knew she would taste herself on his lips, felt her shiver as she deepened the kiss. Once again, he was on the border of being lost, and he pulled back. "But I'm trying not to go too fast."

She blinked up at him as he pushed from the bed and walked away, attempting to gather himself before he said or did something that could not be played off. Before he laid claim in a way that would bind them more than merely fucking her would do.

"I...I appreciate that," Priscilla said slowly. "But I doubt any other man who takes me as a lover will be so thoughtful. And though I'm very much enjoying these lessons on my pleasure, must I not also learn how to give as much as I receive? Perhaps even *more*."

He shook his head. "No, no. Now you listen here. If you take a lover who is not thoughtful to your pleasure, or one that expects you to give and only give...you should kick him in the shin and exit with your head held high. That is the lesson here."

"But I will have to give him *some* pleasure," she argued. "And I would like to give you some, too."

"You have," he said, and it was true. "Watching you come undone is a pleasure I will relive many times to come." Her lips parted and he realized he had said too much. He cleared his throat. "I am not planning to neglect the parts of your education that you are referring to. For my own good, as well as yours. I just want you aching for me by the time I finally take you."

She pushed from the bed and walked to him, utterly naked. Completely alluring. She wrapped her arms around his neck and he was not strong enough to put her off. He settled his hands against the bare curve of her hips, his fingers just caressing the top of her backside. She lifted onto her tiptoes and kissed him once again. He let the kiss escalate, reveling in the hum of his blood as she writhed against him.

Finally, she pulled away. "I already ache for you."

He couldn't resist her. It was impossible. He just needed a little more time to prepare so he didn't destroy himself in the process.

"Tomorrow," he said gently as he pushed a few tangled locks away from her face. "Come back tomorrow, after the wedding is over and the celebrations have ended. We will do *everything* you desire."

She nodded slowly. He could see the flicker of her disappointment that he wouldn't give in to her demands right now, but it was tempered by her excitement. "Very well," she said softly as she parted from him. "Then will you help me with my dress?"

"Of course."

She took her time dressing. He thought it might be her way to torture him. To remind him that he was turning away from…great God, all that temptation. But once she was fixed and smoothed and buttoned, she gave him one last glance.

"I-I know I'm not the kind of woman you…you desire…" she began.

He clasped her wrist and dragged her against him before she could finish that horrible thought. "Now wait a moment," he insisted. "That is not true. If I have not made it clear, I very much desire you. I dream of you. The moment you leave this room, I'm going to do wicked things to make this absolute throbbing in my cock ease for a little while. And then I'll think of you again and it will start back up, never to be satisfied until I finally sink into you."

Her eyes were wide as he said those things, those truths. Slowly, she swallowed. "Then why don't you do that? Why all the waiting?"

He stared down at her, her face lifted to his, her hands pressed against his chest. She looked almost angelic in the dancing firelight and he felt even more like a devil next to her.

"Because if I lose control," he said softly, "I...I would be overwhelmed. I feel the edge of it every moment I'm with you, including this one. That danger zone where it would become difficult for me to maintain any level of control. And as entertaining as this is, as wonderful as I wish to make it for you, I cannot afford to be overwhelmed."

Her lips parted, but there was no fear in her eyes at that declaration. He regretted his honesty almost immediately. He had opened his chest for her, even if only a tiny bit, and he needed a way to close it back off. To put her at a distance.

So he pivoted her toward the door and lightly slapped her backside. "Now, off you go. I'll see you tomorrow for the wedding and for everything else that will come after."

She moved to the door and hesitated there, watching him for a moment, like she was memorizing him. Then she sighed and whispered, "Goodnight, Remi."

"Goodnight," he returned.

She left, and a wave of regret washed over him. Regret that he had let her too close, regret he couldn't do it more. Regret he hadn't taken her. That one was directed by his still aching cock, and at least it was something he could take care of.

He moved to the settee by the fire and slouched there, unfastening his trouser placard with one hand and letting his hard cock free in the warm air. He stared at himself, at this instrument he had only ever used for his own pleasure, for the pleasure of his partners. Tomorrow he would actually...change someone with it. Selfishly, he feared, no matter how much he told himself, told her, it was for her education.

No, he wanted to take her because everything he'd said to her tonight was true. He ached for her. Her, not some anonymous body to sink himself into. *Her.*

"Fuck," he muttered because even such a benign thought of Priscilla made him even harder, more ready.

At last he gripped himself, smoothing his hand over his shaft slowly, absently swirling the droplet of moisture that leaked from his cock. Little sparks of pleasure followed those touches, little hints of what was to come.

He stroked a little faster, not quite serious yet, just a bit of a tease before he lost himself. He shut his eyes and let himself fantasize. The images that excited him were almost always the same: memories of a sweaty night in his mother's former kingdom of Everlay when he was twenty. How was he to know he was attending an orgy? It would have been rude to leave.

He thought of watching others take their pleasure. He'd always enjoyed that and had indulged himself plenty in the activity in London's infamous Donville Masquerade.

He thought of sinking into some anonymous woman's body from behind. It didn't matter who she was, just that her wet and willing body clutched at his cock as he thrust into her.

Into his hand, at any rate. Only tonight, none of those scenarios fulfilled the aching need. Oh, they excited him, of course. It felt good as he spit on his palm and began to stroke in earnest. But it was also...hollow. Not completely satisfying. He needed more, somehow, but he didn't know how to capture it.

He grunted in frustration, picturing himself taking that anonymous woman even harder and faster. In his fantasy he leaned over her, wrapping her long locks of blonde hair around his fist, arching her back. She looked over her shoulder, and it was Priscilla.

He stroked faster at the realization, at the expression of pure pleasure on her gorgeous face as she ground back over him. Pleasure shot though him, up his shaft, through his balls, in every fucking nerve ending in his body.

But it was only when that pretend image of Priscilla whispered, "I'm yours" that he came in long, jerking strokes. He couldn't breathe as he writhed on the settee, flexing his entire body with a release so intense that the edges of his vision blurred.

He collapsed back when it was over, panting, trying to find purchase. He didn't know how many times he'd come in his life. A great many—too many, some would say, even in more progressive Athawick.

But he'd never felt like that when he touched himself. Never felt like that when he took someone else. Just a pretend image of Priscilla meeting his eyes and he had been lost.

And as he cleaned himself up with a handkerchief and tried to get himself together, he couldn't help but wonder if the real experience of being with her would help him be found...or if it would yank him from his path forever. Into a wood from which he might never return.

He feared he might not want to. And that was the most terrifying part of it.

CHAPTER 15

When Priscilla had been invited to the royal wedding celebration, her father had been as supportive as he was capable of being. He had lamented that she would make a fool of herself or, conversely, would only fade into the background entirely. And all the while Caroline had smirked, the puppet master watching as the strings she pulled were brought to life. It seemed that the window for what would make him happy in her behavior was very narrow, indeed. Oh, it had been all her life, of course—he'd always been disappointed in her. But his anger, his exasperation toward her? Those seemed to have grown since his marriage.

But the one thing he had been convinced of, and she guessed it was thanks to the Duchess of Gilmore, was that Priscilla had to have a beautiful gown for the wedding, itself. He had acquiesced, and now she stood in the dressing room, staring at her reflection in the mirror, wearing that very dress.

It was a finely made of ivory silk and the bottom half of it was covered in pale green floral-patterned lace. The short-sleeved overcoat was a darker green with a perfectly created bow at each shoulder and a stunning peacock feather pattern that trailed along the entire back. Her hair had been lifted and pinned and curled so that it framed her face, and then paste emeralds had been strategically placed within the locks so that they sparkled in the candlelight.

She had never felt prettier, and she loved that this would be the gown she would wear when she at last made love with Remi. She shivered at the thought, just as she had been shivering at memories of his mouth on her since last night. Nothing could relieve the desire those memories created, not even time alone with her shaking hand.

"What is that look?" Ophelia asked as she came to stand beside Priscilla.

If Priscilla felt pretty, Ophelia was stunning. Her gown was a pink silk, crisscrossed with a darker pink lace across the bodice. Every line of the dress accentuated her lovely figure, every curl of her hair pointed an observer's gaze to her exquisite face. There was no way that every man in the room wouldn't be watching her today, even if they were meant to look at the bride.

And Ophelia would care for none of it. She would notice none of it. She would not seek out anyone in the crowd like Priscilla would. She wouldn't daydream of a prince's hands on her. She was just too confident and certain of herself to worry about what a man thought of her.

Priscilla almost envied her, except that she liked having her night with Remi to look forward to.

"Did you hear me?" Ophelia asked, wrapping an arm around her. "You have the strangest expression—are you well?"

"I'm very well," Priscilla said, and the smile that crossed her lips wasn't forced. "Very excited for the day's events. And the night's."

Ophelia's brow wrinkled. "It's only a wedding."

"A *royal* wedding," Priscilla corrected with a laugh. "Even you cannot be so jaded that you aren't a little excited."

"Very well, a little," Ophelia agreed.

She glanced back toward the bedchamber where their maids were tidying up after the preparations. She slipped to the door and shut it, giving her a moment of privacy with Priscilla. Immediately, Priscilla's anxiety rose. Her friend was looking at her so strangely.

"You have been…odd lately," Ophelia said. "Since you told me you were more determined than ever to make a man your lover in order to secure your future. And then there is the way you look at Prince Remington…"

Priscilla straightened. "Look at him? I-I don't know what you mean!"

"He looks at you, too," Ophelia said softly. "From across rooms and dining tables and terraces. Always looking at you with the most interesting expression. Will you tell me what is going on between you?"

Priscilla shifted. Lying had never been her strong suit and certainly never with her friend. That was why she had avoided this subject until this moment. Ophelia would see.

But maybe she *had* to see, after all.

"He's…he's helping me," Priscilla said in such a small voice that she was surprised Ophelia could hear her.

But she did, if the way her eyes went wide was any indication. "*Helping* you? What the devil does that mean?"

Priscilla cleared her throat, trying to find some tactful way to describe what was happening between her and Remi. Some way that would force Ophelia to see her side rather than argue with her. But her hesitation seemed to provide an explanation more than her words could have. Ophelia staggered back.

"Are you two…" She huffed out a breath. "Is he taking you to bed?"

Priscilla waved her hand toward the shut door. "Scream a little louder, Ophelia, perhaps the maids would like to hear every accusation."

Ophelia shook her head, but she did temper her tone. "Answer me."

Priscilla's foot had begun to tap restlessly beneath the hem of her gown and she shook out her arms in time to the action. "Yes. Well, almost," she whispered.

"Almost?" Ophelia repeated. "You are going to have to explain."

"There was a bed," Priscilla said softly. "And a settee. But we haven't fully…consummated our…time together."

"I thought you would talk yourself out of this," Ophelia murmured. "And when I woke up and saw you weren't in your bed a few nights ago, I assumed you were reading in the library or talking a walk to clear your head."

"I *was* in the library," she admitted. "And my head is very clear now."

"How can you joke?" Ophelia asked. "This is serious business, and I should know."

Priscilla stepped forward and caught her friend's hands. "Dearest, I know your experience was not a good one. There was a great deal of bad that came out of it. But it is not that way for me. Remi is…he's always careful with me, he always tends to my needs, and I *like* being with him. I *like* how he makes me feel."

Ophelia blinked. "I can…hardly imagine such a thing."

"But I hope one day you will," Priscilla said, and drew back. "Oh Lord, I sound like the wise, experienced friend now."

"I suppose in this, you are," Ophelia mused. "What do you mean you haven't consummated things between you?"

"He has…taught me a great deal about my own pleasure." Her cheeks felt desperately hot and she covered them with her hands with a shake of her head. "Oh Lord, this is not a conversation I thought I'd have in this moment. But he hasn't yet taken my virginity. Tonight, though. After the wedding."

Ophelia stared, and for a moment Priscilla thought she saw something she never would have guessed she'd see. Ophelia was *jealous*. Jealous of her pleasure, jealous of her fun. But it was gone instantly and her dearest, closest friend gently caught her hands. "I hope it is everything you want it to be."

Priscilla nodded. "It will be. He would allow nothing less. And it will also be very good for me. By the time I'm done, I won't be afraid of what a man will do. I'll look forward to it. So when I return to London, I can find a protector and no longer be afraid of what my family will do. Or not do."

"I still worry about this course of action," Ophelia said with a sigh. "But if you are enjoying yourself, I could never say you should stop. You deserve the pleasure you have described and the happiness I see on your beautiful face."

Priscilla blushed, for she had not realized her excitement was so plain.

Before she could respond, though, Ophelia squeezed her hands tighter. "But I beg of you to be careful. I know better than most that it is easy to confuse a physical connection with something deeper. You cannot involve your heart if there is no future here. And you must not risk your body in ways that cannot be undone."

Priscilla swallowed hard. Ophelia meant a child, and that made her think of a baby in her arms, Remi at her side. For a moment she was…happy at the thought. And that was exactly what Ophelia was warning about. Because there was *no* future with him. Remi had made that clear from the beginning. If he wanted her, that was magical, but it would never be more than that.

She ignored the pain that accompanied the thought and smiled at her friend. "I will be very careful, love. I promise. Now we must go. I'm sure your brother and Abigail will be impatiently waiting for us."

Ophelia nodded, and together they left the chamber, arms linked. But as they joined the party at the bottom of the stairs that would take the short walk to the chapel on the palace grounds, she still found her troubled heart returning her over and over to the future Ophelia had forced into her mind.

Remi reached the chapel only a few minutes later than he was supposed to be there, but he found his family already gathered in the vestibule. As he stepped inside, he caught his breath.

Ilaria stood in the middle of the group in the most beautiful gown he had ever seen her wear. A magical concoction of silk and satin, embroidered with gold. It shone in the candlelight that brightened the entryway.

Ilaria turned toward him as he came to her. Her hair was wound with more gold, including the crown atop her head. Their mother's wedding crown—he recognized it from the case where it normally sat, just in front of the wedding portrait of Queen Giabella with the late King Alistair.

Normally he would say such a thing would bring bad luck, but he could see from his sister's rapt, joyful expression that there would never be luck required for her happiness. It lived because she and Jonah created it every day. By loving each other.

And for the first time in his life, Remi believed that emotion was possible. True. Real.

"You are stunning," he breathed. "My God, Ilaria."

She smiled, her eyes brimming with happy tears as she leaned forward to kiss his cheek. "Thank you, Remi."

"Jonah will fall over when you enter the church," Sasha gushed. "I almost did so myself when I saw you."

Ilaria's cheeks brightened. "I cannot wait to see him, to call him husband."

"You haven't waited," Grantham grumbled beneath his breath, but he was smiling as he said it and Remi elbowed him playfully. For a moment, he wasn't king but simply brother, and it was a welcome return.

"Enough now," the queen said, her eyes brimming with tears. "We should enter the chapel and begin."

Remi kissed Ilaria one final time before he took his mother's arm to escort her into the chapel. Sasha stepped up behind them, and Thomas appeared from the side where he had apparently been standing to allow the family their private moment. The footmen opened the doors, and Remi drew a breath as he guided his mother up the aisle toward their seats.

The church was filled with dignitaries and guests from Athawick, Everlay, England and a great many other countries, all straining to see the royal family in their finery. He helped his mother to her seat, a slightly elevated one to the side of the chapel where the royal family could see everything. Remi stood beside her and found his gaze moving around the large church, seeking Priscilla, of course. He needed to see her.

She was a few rows back from the front of the church, sitting with Ophelia and the Duke and Duchess of Gilmore. The rest were looking toward the front of the chapel, but her gaze was already on him when he found her.

He drew in a breath. She was wearing an ivory gown, heavy with green accents, and though he couldn't see her eyes clearly from the distance across the church, he knew they would pop and sparkle thanks to the way the fabric matched them. She bent her head, a slight smile on her face, and he found himself smiling too.

Until he felt the gentle nudge of Sasha's elbow in his side. "Look at you, all atwitter with love," she whispered.

He wrinkled his brow. "I'm not…I'm not in love."

She leaned back. "I didn't say you were. I just meant you were so happy for Ilaria and now you're just grinning and lit up like a candle. I meant that you seem to believe in it now even if you have declared you didn't before."

He cleared his throat. Good Lord, he was going to make a cake of himself before this was done if he didn't get himself together. He caught her hand and squeezed briefly. "I believe in your love for Thomas and his for you. I believe in Ilaria and Jonah. And if that is all the love that exists in this world, I would be very happy because that means it has been bestowed upon the two most deserving sisters."

Sasha stared up at him, her eyes bright with tears. "Thank you, dearest. And know that I would only wish such a love for you and for Grantham one day. Perhaps even for Mama."

He nodded. "Grantham and I may be lost causes, but I agree that I would be very pleased if Mama could find happiness."

They might have continued the conversation, but before they could, the doors near the altar opened and Jonah stepped out. He was dressed in full military regalia from his days in the Royal Navy, and he smoothed his jacket nervously as he and the priest moved to the front of the church. Once he was settled, the organ above began to play a traditional Athawick wedding song.

The doors to the back of the church opened, and Ilaria entered on Grantham's arm. She was practically floating as they came down the aisle together, her eyes trained entirely on Jonah.

Remi looked back to his future brother-in-law and found that the captain was equally focused on Ilaria. His expression was rapt and intense, and Remi was shocked when Jonah lifted a hand and swiped what appeared to be a tear from his cheek.

Once again, the power of their connection was on display. And it warmed Remi. He glanced at Priscilla. The congregation had stood to welcome the king and princess, and Priscilla's hands were clasped before her, a bright smile on her face as she watched the procession.

His heart stuttered.

He had read about the heart doing such a thing in books before, of course. But never had he experienced it. Even now, he frowned as he felt that great swell of emotion. Honestly, he was becoming maudlin. He was only happy for his sister on this day, and he was conflating that with some kind of feeling for Priscilla that wasn't there. He liked her, he might even call her a friend. He most definitely wanted her. But that was all there was to it.

And as he forced himself to focus back on the ceremony beginning before him, he knew he couldn't forget that, couldn't let himself become convinced there was more to it. To do that was to risk a great deal of pain for her…and for himself.

CHAPTER 16

If the ceremony to marry Captain Jonah Crawford, Count of the Southern Realm of Athawick, to Princess Ilaria was emotional and beautiful, the reception to fete them afterward was joyful and uproarious. Priscilla couldn't help but swing in time to the happy music as she stood off to the side of the dancefloor watching the bride and groom laugh as they indulged in a traditional Athawickian folk dance. Princess Ilaria moved naturally, as she had probably been dancing these moves since she was a little girl. Captain Crawford was a bit less fluid, but he was enthusiastic and he couldn't stop smiling at his bride, which made the entire exercise enchanting.

Priscilla found herself breaking her gaze from the couple and trying to find Remi. She'd been doing that all night. In truth, she had expected him to come to her when the reception began. He'd been watching her so intently during the wedding. Only it had been an hour now and she had scarcely seen him in the crowd, let alone encountered him.

She feared he was avoiding her, but tried to push that silly thought away. Why would he? Of course she had a dozen answers for that, a dozen reasons why a handsome man like him, a sought-after man like him, would decide he was bored with a wallflower like her.

She chose to push them all down and try not to work herself up. It wasn't working, but she tried.

"Miss Linfield!"

Priscilla turned at the enthusiastic greeting and was surprised to find Queen Giabella approaching, a wide smile on her beautiful face. She noted how much Remi looked like her. Aside from his blue eyes, he had inherited his mother's high cheekbones, the quirk of her smile. Priscilla was comforted by those things somehow.

"Your Majesty," she said, curtseying deeply. "What a happy day. My most sincere congratulations."

The queen's face lit up even further. "They are most joyfully received. How could they not be when I look out at my daughter and her new husband and see how deep their love is? It seems things worked out exactly as they should."

Priscilla nodded. After all, it was commonly known that Princess Ilaria had been thought to be matched with the Earl of Bramwell upon the family's arrival in London months ago. There had been a minor scandal when it was announced that not only was Ilaria engaged to another man, but that her adopted sister had eloped with Bramwell, herself. But the romance of the two stories had seemed to exceed the outrage over the switch. Now it was something no one dared speak about.

"How are you enjoying your time in Athawick, my dear?" the queen asked.

Priscilla smiled. "Greatly, Your Majesty. It is such a beautiful place and the people are so kind and welcoming."

"I'm so glad. We've enjoyed having you, though I feel I've been remiss in getting to know you."

Priscilla looked around the room, which was filled with many more important guests than she was. Why the queen would suddenly take an interest in her was confusing to say the least. "Certainly," she said slowly. "What would you like to know?"

"You are related to the Marquess of Sheraton, are you not?"

Priscilla tried to keep her expression neutral. "I am. He is my grandfather. My father is his second son."

"I think I met the marquess in London. Perhaps at a ball."

"I would not doubt it. He is quite at the center of good Society," Priscilla said, again fighting for a neutral tone so this lovely woman would not see that she and her grandfather were at odds at nearly the same level as she was with her father and step-mother. The queen would certainly not be so kind if she realized that.

Queen Giabella nodded. "And you are good friends with Lady Ophelia. You came with the party of her brother and his wife."

"Yes, they were kind enough to invite me." Now Priscilla needed no false reaction. Her smile was entirely genuine. "I have known Ophelia since we were little girls. She is the dearest friend one could ask for."

The queen gazed off into the crowd toward where Ophelia stood by the side of the dancefloor, chatting with the Duchess of Gilmore. She laughed and her beautiful face lit up, drawing the attention of many a man around her.

"She is like a flame, isn't she? People seem drawn to her." The queen smiled slightly. "Even against their will."

Priscilla's eyes widened. "Oh, if you mean like a flame in that she brightens and warms all those around her, of course yes. But if you mean that she might burn—she would never."

Queen Giabella's gaze returned to her. "You are good to defend your friend. It speaks highly of you both. But I promise you, my dear, I only have a positive impression of Lady Ophelia. It would be hard not to be charmed by her."

Priscilla relaxed. "Oh, good. I'm pleased to hear it."

"I hear that Prince Remington gave you a private tour of the island."

Priscilla's ears began to ring. That moment when they had left the main tour at the beginning of her visit to the island had been secret…or so she thought. But the queen was watching her, certain and also clearly curious at what answer she would give.

"I…we…" Priscilla began, trying to find some answer.

"Don't worry, my dear. The island has eyes, is all. And Remi has never been known to be careful." The queen chuckled as if this were a part of Remi that she liked rather than judged. "He is a wonderful guide, isn't he? He pretends that he doesn't love our home, but he has the most interesting view of it and its people of all my children."

"Why do you think that is?" Priscilla asked, partly to take the focus off herself and her relationship to Remi, but also because she was truly interested in the answer.

The queen was thoughtful for a moment. "Perhaps because he has had different expectations than the rest. Grantham was always raised knowing he would be king. Ilaria was a princess and further down the line. Sasha was…she has always been accepted by us, but her position was not as clear until lately. But Remi…Remi could be…free. Or at least he chose to be. He would sneak out of the palace gates and go mingle with our subjects. Possibly a little too freely."

The queen laughed, and Priscilla joined in. "I can see that. He is so very certain of himself and what he wants."

Queen Giabella arched her brow. "Yes. Except when he isn't. Don't let that exterior fool you, Miss Linfield. My son has…cracks. Little fissures he rarely allows others to see. It would take a very special person to help him learn how to fill them. I do hope he finds her someday."

Priscilla stared at her, uncertain as to how to respond to that unexpected statement. Certainly the queen could not mean her. But then why would she say something so…personal? So provocative?

"I see the king glancing this way, looking to be saved from conversation. I suppose I should go my motherly duty." Queen Giabella clasped her hand briefly. "I do hope we will be able to talk again soon. Perhaps we could walk in the garden together one morning."

"I-I would be honored to do so, madam," Priscilla stammered.

"Excellent. I'll have Dash...Mr. Talbot, my secretary, find a morning that fits my schedule. Good evening."

The queen slipped away then, into the crowd, leaving Priscilla staring after her in confusion. She swallowed hard and looked for Ophelia. She wanted to talk to her friend about what had just happened, because she almost felt like she must have dreamed it. But when she found Ophelia again, she was not in the crowd, but she was walking onto the dancefloor...with Remi.

Priscilla blinked as the two began the steps of the waltz. "Oh, God's teeth," she muttered.

It wasn't that she didn't trust Ophelia. Of course she did. But her friend knew the truth about what she'd been doing with Remi. And there was nothing more frightening than an overly protective Ophelia. Priscilla could only hope her friend wouldn't create a problem.

Or let slip something Priscilla wasn't ready to feel, let alone show to Remi.

~

Remi had been standing by the edge of the dancefloor, talking to Ilaria and Jonah when he saw Ophelia come toward him from the other side of the room. Her expression was serious as she marched his way, and he tensed in anticipation of her arrival.

"Your Highnesses," she said with a quick curtsey. "My lord."

Jonah flinched slightly. "I'm still getting used to that, I admit."

Ophelia smiled briefly toward him before her attention returned to Remi. "How are you enjoying your evening, Your Highness?"

Remi stared at her. She was not subtle, this one. No wonder she drove Grantham to distraction. He loved dancing around subjects versus addressing them head on. A woman like this would drive him mad.

Remi loved to see it. To feel it directed at him, on the other hand...

He could see Ilaria watching him closely, her eyes slightly wide. The last thing he needed was for his sister to start digging into his life rather than focusing on her own. So he smiled at Lady Ophelia indulgently. "Would you like to dance, my lady?"

She blinked up at him, then her eyes narrowed slightly. She was trying to read him. In response he put on the bright smile that usually deflected any deeper observation.

"Yes," she said slowly. "I would."

He inclined his head toward his sister and her husband before he extended a hand to Lady Ophelia to guide her to the dancefloor. The music lifted and he suppressed a chuckle. Ah, a waltz. Of course it would be that—there would be no escaping the very focused intentions of his partner, whatever they were.

They stepped out together. Lady Ophelia was a graceful dancer, naturally adjusting to his lead seemingly without effort. He thought of Grantham's expression when he'd looked at the young lady, whenever he spoke of her. Even now as they spun around the room, he saw that his brother was watching them. His expression was almost entirely blank, but there was a slight fire to his eyes.

It was all entirely fascinating.

"Do you understand how careful you must be of Priscilla?" she asked, and now his attention swung directly back to her.

Ah, so that was it. From her expression, it was obvious she knew something of what was going on with her friend in that tower. He wasn't upset at that, nor even surprised. What was happening between them was momentous—of course Priscilla would want to speak to someone about it. He was glad she had someone she trusted so deeply.

"Miss Linfield is not so fragile as all that," he said carefully.

"But you cannot play games with her, Your Highness. She isn't some jaded widow or playful courtesan that you can play with and abandon." Ophelia's lips pursed. "I won't see her hurt. Not after everything she's been through."

His brow wrinkled. "What has she been through?"

Ophelia's nostrils flared and she ducked her gaze from his. "I've said too much."

"You've said nothing at all. And while I'm not about to give you details of…of our arrangement—I'll leave it to Priscilla to share or not share what she'd like with you—I also am not about to ignore information that could keep me from hurting her as you imply."

Ophelia met his gaze again, seeking once more. Searching for some answer as to who he was. He didn't know the answer himself, honestly. Not trustworthy, he didn't think. She wouldn't find that, if that was what she wanted.

That was what Priscilla deserved, of course. She deserved so much more.

"Have you researched her family?" she asked softly. "Have you asked her about them?"

He pursed his lips. Priscilla had mentioned them, of course. It was obvious there was something fraught to the subject. Otherwise why would she consider becoming a courtesan over remaining a spinster taken care of by her family or even accepting an arranged marriage?

But he'd never pushed. Partly because he didn't want to cause pain…partly because he knew if he delved too deep then the tenor of what they shared would change.

And yet he couldn't deny that he wished to understand her beyond just the surface. He wanted to…to take care of her. A terrifying concept.

"Perhaps it isn't my place to pry," he said softly.

Her eyes flashed. "When you are ruining her?"

He flinched. "Ruination implies that I don't care what happens to her, or that she doesn't understand. I assure you neither of those things is true."

"Then what is true? Are you just toying with her? Taking advantage of her difficult circumstances and the fact that she sees a path forward that is…er…unorthodox, to say the least?"

He hesitated. It would be easy for him to say that he was simply enjoying the circumstances that had been laid at his feet. That Priscilla's request for assistance allowed him to enjoy himself with impunity, all while telling himself a story that he was doing her a favor.

That was what he'd told himself at the beginning, wasn't it? Only it wasn't true. Not anymore.

"I—" he stammered as the orchestra played its final note and the dancing stopped around them. She continued to stare up at him, expectant. "It is not my intent to hurt her," he said softly. "I think Priscilla is…beautiful, but it is beyond that. Beyond merely desiring her. She is remarkable. And if I can prevent her from pain or harm…I will."

Ophelia's expression softened. "I believe you, Your Highness." She let out a small sigh. "It is a difficult circumstance. Whatever happens, I hope neither of you is left with regrets. I know from bitter experience just how painful that can be and I would not wish it on you or her."

As Remi wrinkled his brow, Ophelia stepped from his arms and executed a quick curtsey. "Excuse me."

She pivoted into the milling crowd exiting the dancefloor and left him staring after her, his mind spinning on her questions…and what those questions had sparked in him.

His connection with Priscilla had begun as something purely physical, something he could convince himself was not for anything but pleasure and to help her. But it was more now. The connection between them was very real and he had to admit that it was growing every time he touched her, every time he looked at her.

That was something he should run from. He had made her no promises, he wasn't certain he was the kind of man who could. And yet he found himself looking out toward Priscilla in the crowd, finding her watching him, her expression pensive. Their eyes met and he didn't want to run.

He couldn't. She was drawing him like a magnet and he was almost helpless to that power.

He was jostled as Sasha and Thomas entered the dancefloor. She shook her head at Remi with a laugh. "Have you lost your partner, Remi?"

"I...don't know," he breathed, looking back to where Priscilla had been standing. She was gone.

"Well, you'd best find her. They're going to play the Friskar jig," she said, referring to another traditional Athawickian dance. "I want to teach Thomas. Join us!"

Remi blinked. Everything in him told him to push away these strange thoughts about Priscilla, these questions that had hatched in his mind. Everything tried to drag him to be playful and cover up emotion with fun. Only he couldn't.

"I...can't," he muttered, ignoring his sister's concerned expression. "I must go."

He pivoted and left the ballroom floor, rushing blindly through the crowd. He had to escape. He had to clear his mind. He had to stop these feelings that he didn't want. Didn't know what to do with.

He had to do it now.

CHAPTER 17

"What did you do?" Priscilla snapped, grasping Ophelia's arm and dragging her toward one of the private alcoves in the back of the ballroom.

Her friend stared at her as she extracted her arm from Priscilla's grip. "I didn't do anything."

"You were *dancing* with Remi," Priscilla ground out through clenched teeth. "Please don't act as if I'm a fool and don't understand why. What did you say to him? Did you tell him you know we are...we are..."

"That he's bedding you?" Ophelia asked mildly.

Priscilla swiftly darted her gaze around. "Mind your tone! Anyone could hear."

"Back here?" Ophelia asked, waving her hand at the quiet space. "You think there are spies back here just waiting to pounce on any gossip?"

Priscilla blinked and truly took in her surroundings. Then she shivered. Remi had said he wanted to do such things to her in this very space. Now that she was standing in the half-darkness, sheltered away from the ballroom, but also so close, she couldn't help but picture him standing with her...touching her...

making her come undone while the partygoers bobbed by unaware.

"Priscilla?" Ophelia's tone was sharp.

She forced her attention back to this moment rather than some fantasy. "You never know who might be lurking," she managed to choke out. "Now please, tell me what happened between you two."

Ophelia grasped her hands. "Nothing," she insisted. "We talked. I felt him out. I want to protect you. I don't want you to be hurt as I was hurt by some man who can talk smoothly and take advantage."

Priscilla saw the fear in Ophelia's eyes. True fear. True worry that was bound up in her own past. "I can promise you from the bottom of my heart that Remi is not like Erasmus Montgomery. He *isn't* tricking me, he isn't making promises that cannot be kept. He isn't using me. If anything I'm using him."

Ophelia let out a long sigh. "He does seem...*genuine* in his intentions toward you. He does seem to...to care about your wellbeing."

Priscilla blinked. She believed that, of course. But to hear that Ophelia had seen it warmed her far more deeply than she wished to allow. "What did he say about me?" she whispered.

Ophelia smiled slightly. "That you are beautiful."

Priscilla felt heat enter her cheeks. "Oh."

"But that it is more than that which draws him to you," Ophelia continued. "Beyond that...well, I think you should speak to him about it."

Priscilla drew back. "What does that mean?"

"I don't know what is between you," Ophelia said hesitantly. "Not truly. Nor could I hope to read the mind of a man who is so expert at playing games to cover his thoughts. Honestly, the only person more frustrating than the prince is the king, himself. He was staring at us the entire time we were dancing."

Ophelia began to ramble about her frustrations with the stern king, and Priscilla tried to attend, but she kept thinking about what had been said about Remi. The answers Ophelia had given about him felt incomplete, and she needed to find him and speak to him directly before she would feel entirely comfortable about what had transpired.

There were small viewing spaces in the alcove walls so those who were resting there could still see the activities on the dance-floor, and she peered out, searching for Remi in the crowd.

But he was nowhere to be seen. Certainly he wasn't roaming the floor, looking for her. And everything about tonight left her with so many more questions than answers. And so many more fears as to what the future entailed. And if Remi would be part of hers even for a few more hours.

It was long after midnight when Priscilla stepped onto the terrace, shivering at the cool air that drifted up from the sea in the distance. But she didn't go back inside where it was warm—instead she moved toward the cold. She needed it to clear her head.

She hadn't seen Remi since he danced with Ophelia. At first she'd tried to convince herself that he was just lost in the crowd, but the longer his absence had continued, the more clear it became that he was definitely avoiding her. Her heart ached. What if he was finished with her?

She stared up at the stars above and sighed. "I wish..." she murmured.

"What do you wish?"

She tensed, for she knew the voice that had spoken as well as she knew her own. *He* was the very wish she was about to make.

Slowly she turned and watched as Remi stepped out of the shadows close to the palace walls and into the light that came from the ballroom behind them.

She cleared her throat. "What would *you* wish for?"

He held her stare for a moment and then looked up at the sky. "I hardly know anymore."

"It's the same for me," she admitted, and bent her head. "Did I… did I do something wrong?"

He stepped toward her at last, and his fingers slid along her back as he moved to stand beside her. The briefest, lightest touch, but she felt it through every nerve ending in her body and shivered.

He rested his hands beside hers on the terrace wall. "No. Never. Why?"

She tilted her head to look at him. "I'm not a fool, Remi. I know you were avoiding me. And you looked so serious when you danced with Ophelia. She refused to give me much detail about what you talked about. At least the details I wanted to hear."

He met her gaze. "You."

It was one word, but it felt like it pulled her world down to nothing, down to only him as she stared up at him in the half-dark. Her heart was what reacted to him. Oh, her body did too, but her heart was stronger. It raced for him, and the emotions that burned inside of it were so very dangerous.

She ought to run away from them, from him. She knew that. She had known it from the start, if she were honest with herself. But she couldn't. Not then, not now. He was too strong a draw, too powerful a force. She was caught in his wake now—she would have to let this thing between them play out.

"Remi," she began, thinking she would talk to him about Ophelia, would confess what she'd said to her, would ask what exactly they had said about her.

But before she could continue, he edged closer to her, his boot moving between her feet, her skirts tangling around his knees. He was too close for propriety and anyone who stepped out of that ballroom would see it.

It didn't matter. Not to her and clearly not to him. "I *have* avoided you tonight, that is true. But it is because every time I get near you I want to…to…"

He reached up and traced her lower lip with his thumb. At some point during the night he had abandoned his gloves so it was his skin that touched hers. She let out a broken sigh of relief and antic-ipation.

"Will you come to the tower?" he asked, not stepping away but dropping his hand at last.

She swallowed hard. "Yes. I've been waiting all night to do so. Aching for you."

He closed his eyes briefly at her repetition of his words to her the night before. "Well, I can very much offer you relief. I'll go up first and ready the room. Ten minutes?"

She nodded because she couldn't form words anymore, and then watched him pivot on his heel and stride away from her without so much as a backward glance. But once he was gone from her side, she sagged against the terrace wall.

Something had changed between them, that was clear. And more would change soon because she was about to give herself to this man completely...and she could only hope that she could get some of herself back when it was over.

Remi lit the last candle in the tower room and looked around. The chamber was perfect. Romantic and comfortable and...*theirs*. He had begun to think of this room as theirs in the short time they had been coming here together.

The door behind him opened, and he turned to watch her enter. It was as if his world hyper-focused on her. He had never been so drawn to another person in his life. He doubted it would ever happen again. This was only her, only him...only them.

Their gazes met and she reached back to close the door behind herself, locking it carefully. She moved toward him, and he saw how nervous she was in her taut expression and the way her hands shook at her sides.

"I-I need to ask you something before we begin," she said.

He nodded. "Whatever you need."

Her breath hitched at that promise. The one he intended to keep even if he could keep no other. Including the one he had been trying to make to stay away from her. That one was impossible so here they were.

"What *did* Ophelia say to you about me?" she pressed. "I asked her and she was vague at best."

He arched a brow. "She told me to be careful with you."

The color left her face and she bent her head. "Oh, I hoped she wouldn't. It is with the best of intentions, but..." She lifted her hands to her cheeks. "How humiliating."

"Because it means I know she knows about us?" he asked, stepping closer.

She nodded. "Yes, I did tell her. I'm so sorry."

She was so quick to dismiss herself, to apologize for her own needs. Once again he thought of what Ophelia had implied about her family. What in the world had happened to Priscilla that made her such a cauldron of doubt?

"I...never thought you would hide it from her. You told me once that you two were close as sisters. Of course you might wish to share something so...changing."

She sucked in a breath. "Does that mean...*you've* told anyone?"

He hesitated. If he said no, she would take that to mean he didn't find what was between them changing. Of course, it was the opposite. He didn't share this growing bond between them with anyone because it was *too* changing. If he said this out loud to anyone he cared about...they would know. They would see.

He would see. He wasn't ready for that.

"I haven't," he said, and moved toward her. He saw the flicker of both relief and disappointment cross her face. She turned it away from him but didn't step back.

"Will you...will you take me now?" she asked.

He should have just said yes. That was what he was meant to do. That was how to keep this purely physical, to trick himself into believing there was nothing else there beyond desire. But she looked so vulnerable in the firelight, her gaze cast down, her hands shaking. She wanted this, yes, but he also saw her desperation.

And he couldn't ignore that. He wasn't a monster, or at least he didn't want to be one.

"You are so driven," he said as he took her hand and threaded his fingers through hers. "And I know it's about more than just desire."

"Of course it is," she said, darting her gaze up. "We both know what this is, we made it clear from the beginning. I need you to teach me, to help me. And yes, I want you. God knows I can't stop wanting you."

He nodded slowly, and when she tried to look away, this time he tucked a finger beneath her chin and kept her focused on him. The rogue in him told him to just take. To make sex the barrier between them. To be involved in her pleasure and nothing else.

But he couldn't just be that rogue now. Not with her.

He sucked in a shaky breath. "Priscilla, tell me about your family."

She looked confused and then horrified. She jerked away from him, staggered back and folded her arms like she could shield herself both from his question and from her answer. "You lied to me."

He blinked. "What?"

"You told me Ophelia only said to be careful, but she said more. What did you two talk about in regards to my family?"

He shook his head. "She didn't say anything or tell me anything. But she was a reminder that there is more at stake here than merely pleasure. At least for you."

Once again Priscilla flinched, and he hated himself for the barrier those words created.

"And suddenly that makes you care about my past or my circumstances?" she asked.

Now *he* recoiled. "*That* is what you think of me?"

She blinked, her mouth opening and shutting.

"If you believe I only care about fucking you, you ought to walk out of this tower right now and never look back," he said, stepping closer. He heard the catch in her breath. Felt the tremble to her body even without touching her. "Because you deserve a hell of a lot better than that, even if it's just from a lover who means nothing else to you."

Her bottom lip trembled, and he felt her cracking. About to break. He took no pleasure in that. He could tell this was going to hurt. He hoped he could soothe afterward, but the pain that came before…it seemed there was no avoiding it.

She bent her head and then leaned forward to rest her forehead against his chest. Her breath came in shallow bursts and he lifted a hand to stroke the back of her head gently.

"You want to know?" she whispered, her words almost not carrying despite how close they were.

"I do," he said, and meant it. He'd never meant it before.

She looked up at him with a sad smile. "Fine. Then let me tell you the whole sad little tale. And then you can pity me rather than want me."

CHAPTER 18

Priscilla drew a few long breaths, wishing she could make herself calmer, wishing she could make this seem like it meant nothing so that Remi would stop looking at her like she was glass and he was afraid to break her. What would he think when he knew she was already broken?

"They look like a very good family from the outside," she said. "I am the granddaughter of a marquess, the daughter of a second son. They have money and influence and everything that is valued by those in my sphere. And yet..."

"And yet?"

"My grandfather set everything in his world up as a competition," she said softly. "My father had to fight his brothers, both the younger ones and the older, for every scrap he ever got. Including food sometimes, or so I have been told."

Remi flinched, and she thought she saw some flash of understanding cross his face. He hardened the reaction. "That must have been difficult for him."

"I'm sure it was," she agreed. "And I feel for him, of course. But the result was that he has always been competitive. Nothing I ever did was enough for him. And when I came out, it was worse. He demanded I find the highest title, the best match. The ultimate connection so that he could triumph over his brother, who will eventually become marquess."

"I honestly don't understand why you *didn't* match in those early years," Remi said. "You are so lovely and bright."

She blushed and ducked her head. "You seem to be the only man who believes that, as we have discussed. Even if you weren't, my grandfather had not given his spare much, so there was little to present as a dowry for me. As a result, the pickings were slim. Hardly a duke in sight. And my father was as harsh a judge of any man who looked my way as he was of me. It was a doomed prospect from the beginning. The years stretched on but a lady's value on the marriage mart does not increase with her years, does it? At least not on English shores. Alongside all my other problems, there were prettier, younger, richer girls coming out every year I failed and I was…I was lost in the shuffle, relegated to the wall."

Remi sighed. "I will not sport with your intelligence and say I understand."

"How could you? You're a man, for one. You are allowed to be unattached for far longer and not be seen as broken. *And* you are a prince, so you could wait until you were eighty and there would still be beautiful women clamoring to be your bride."

"Because of my title," he said.

"Yes, but…" She smiled despite the difficult subject. "I'm sure you will be very handsome at eighty. A man like you will age like wine."

He smiled slightly but then retook her hand. He lifted it, unfastening the button of her glove and then peeling the silky fabric away. He tossed it aside and began to massage her palm.

She shut her eyes both at the feel of his warm skin against her, but also the rhythmic way that he touched her. God's teeth, that felt good.

"You haven't answered my question," he said softly. "You're dancing around the question about what it is that drives you to what you're doing, why your family isn't a safe place for you."

"No," she began, but he chuckled and held up a hand to stop her.

"My darling, there is no one on this earth who is better at deflection than yours truly. I recognize it when I see it. A father who demands perfection or excellence is one thing...and I don't want to minimize the effects because I know they can be...they can be damaging. But Ophelia's concern went far deeper. So what else is there?"

She hesitated. She could deny him the truth, but with his vast resources, that wouldn't keep him from knowing what had happened for long. Wouldn't she rather control the way he heard the story? "My...my mother died."

"I'm sorry," Remi said and reached for her hand, holding it briefly.

"She and I weren't close," Priscilla admitted. "Governesses raised me, and then she allowed my father to take the lead when I came out into Society. She got very sick, very suddenly, and then she was gone. And my father's main reaction was to be irritated that I would lose a whole Season to the mourning period."

Remi recoiled. "Great God."

She shrugged. "You see what I am dealing with. He 'mourned' his one year and one day for appearance's sake...and on the second day he married again. A woman named Caroline, who is all of two years older than I am."

"I see. And do you get along with her, at least?"

Image after image of Caroline's cruel and manipulative actions raced through her mind. She tamped them down as she whispered, "She took great pleasure in being hurtful during my years as a wall-flower. She hates me still and manipulates my father's negative feelings toward me." She ducked her head. "Since their marriage, his contempt for me has only grown."

"Priscilla," he breathed, and she could see that he would move on her, comfort her...pity her. "And your father married this horrible woman?"

"He doesn't care about how I'm treated. He refuses to believe that Caroline has lied about me to potential suitors. That she has sabotaged me at every turn and continues to do so."

"Why?" Remi breathed. "Why would she do that?"

"From what I can tell, it's for…sport," Priscilla breathed. "Just to see if she can."

"Does he not care about the consequences…even if it is just for himself?"

She pursed her lips. "He talks often about being thrilled that with a young wife, he will be able to sire children again and hopefully they will not be as disappointing as I am. Because of her, I have begun to receive fewer and fewer invitations. And though he has all but given up on me, my father became enraged just before Ophelia invited me to join their party for the royal wedding, and he—"

She cut herself off and turned away. Remi caught her elbow and pivoted her back gently. His face was lined with concern for her. And she feared exactly what she had said would happen. She feared she saw his pity. "What did he do?"

She swallowed. "No one knows. I didn't even tell Ophelia the truth."

His nostrils flared. "Tell *me*," he whispered. "Tell me everything."

"He told me I was worthless. He…he told me I was better off… better off dead. That at least the family would receive attention and sympathy for that. And when I tried to turn away, he…hit…me."

She shut her eyes and tried not to relive that awful afternoon that she had been keeping at bay in her mind for weeks and weeks. The pure hatred in her father's stare, the mounting frustration in her failure and his own. And finally the crack of his fist…not his palm…his fist, across her body that had sent her flying to the floor.

"He stood over me, and I thought…" Her voice broke, and she realized she was crying. Tears she hadn't allowed herself to shed slid down her cheeks. "I thought he might kill me. Caroline stood in the doorway, smirking at me as he walked away. I went to Ophelia's house that night, but I…" She caught her breath as she thought of that night. Of Ophelia's questions. Of course her best friend could tell something was wrong, but Priscilla had hesitated.

"You couldn't tell her the truth," he supplied when she couldn't. His lips thinned and yet again she had the feeling that he understood that on some level.

"No," she whispered. "Not that she didn't pry and cajole and demand." A flutter of a smile crossed his face, but he didn't interrupt her. "I finally admitted things were getting worse, without providing details. And that's when she invited me here. The idea that I would be part of an elite group invited to the island seemed to appease my father slightly."

"Did he ever address what happened?" Remi asked.

She shook her head. "No. My father has not spoken to me since, even when I returned to the house. He let Caroline discuss my plans for Athawick." She shut her eyes. "She lorded it over me so cruelly. She implied that if I could not find success here, I might not like what I found waiting for me in London when I came back. Whether she meant relegation to the country or being cut off entirely or something worse, I could not say."

"And that is why you thought to pursue Grantham," he said.

"Foolish, of course," she said, and shook her head. "Now I see that. The very idea that I could attract him...or be attracted to him seems ridiculous."

"I am relieved about that," Remi admitted softly. "Though I hate the reason. Still, to land a king would have been the largest feather in any cap."

"It would have appeased them," she agreed, but then she bent her head. "Or not. After all, it is entirely possible that nothing I ever do will be good enough."

Remi was quiet a moment, then took her hand again and this time lifted it to his chest. "I am so sorry, Priscilla. The behavior you've described is so cruel...so terrible. You didn't deserve that. You understand that, don't you?"

She met his gaze. "Sometimes I'm not sure what I deserve. At any rate, so few receive what they deserve, it doesn't matter. Terrible people get rewarded, good people are lost. There seems to be no meter for justice on the wheel of fate. Which is why we must control what we must. I cannot go back home and trust that the situation won't be worse. I need to come to an arrangement for myself almost immediately, so that I can leave my father's home and be protected against his whims."

Remi flinched slightly, and he didn't look as if he liked this plan anymore. Or perhaps he wasn't certain she could pull it off.

"You do need to be protected." He drew her closer, folding his arms around her. She relaxed into him. Now the worst of it was out. The truth, the one she had kept inside for weeks, was out. And it did feel a relief, as if she had finally popped a boil. The pain lessened. But the damage was still there.

But in Remi's arms it just felt…smaller somehow. She could believe, foolishly perhaps, that with him anything was possible. That somehow they could soar above all the pain she had just revealed, all the pain she knew he concealed, and be…happy together.

He kissed the crown of her head and then drew back so he could look into her eyes. "I have taken advantage of you," he said softly. "And of a situation I didn't fully understand. We don't have to do anything here tonight, Priscilla."

She sucked in a breath. "Oh no, please don't say that!" she burst out. "Remi, you might not have known all my motivations, but we have always been honest with each other about what this is. Does it matter more now that the reason I wish to become someone's mistress is to escape my family? Does it truly change anything that you have the sordid details?"

He pursed his lips. "Priscilla."

She pulled from his arms and shook her head. "Then forget the future I need to plan. If you don't want a part in that, then have a part in this: all my life I have sought to be more. To be better. To be perfect. And I've failed at every turn. The only place I have ever felt...felt so warm, so welcomed, so taken care of...was in your arms."

She said the words and realized how true they were. This man... this beautiful man who should have been so far above her in social stature had plucked her up and cradled her close and made her... happy. She was happy when she was with him. And lost without him.

"Remi, I want you," she whispered. "Not for some bargain, not to be trained, not for any other reason but that when you touch me I feel alive in a way I've never felt my whole life. Please don't take that away from me."

She moved toward him, pressing her palms against his chest, sliding them up and loving the way his pupils dilated with pleasure. "Please make me yours. Just for a little while. Just as we planned."

He leaned in, pressing their foreheads together, his eyes closed. His breath was short, his grip tight on her hands. "I should be better than this," he began, and she thought for a moment that he would deny her out of some twisted sense of honor. Instead, he opened his eyes and locked his with hers. "But I'm not."

He cupped her cheeks and then his mouth was on hers, hard and demanding, passionate and hot. She lifted against him with a whimper, releasing all the tales of the past, at least for a moment as he swept her away with pleasure.

He wrapped an arm around her waist and dragged her closer, their bodies molding as he deepened the kiss even further. She felt like she was melting in his arms, going boneless and weightless under the steamy pressure of his mouth, the darting certainty of his tongue, the roving swipe of his hands.

She broke the kiss, her hands shaking as she leaned them against his chest to create a sliver of space. "I want to see you," she whispered, shocked by her own boldness.

He arched a brow. "Do you now?"

She nodded. "You've gotten to explore every inch of me and every time you are fully clothed. But I want to see you, Remi. To see your…I don't know what to call it…your…your body. I want to touch you tonight."

He swallowed hard, as if that request…demand…meant more than she knew. He stepped back, removing his warmth from her. For a moment, she thought he might refuse her. He would distract her, of course, she would come, but he would not let her have him the same way she had been had.

Slowly, he shrugged from his jacket and tossed it aside. He lifted his hands and untied his cravat. When the edges of it were dangling at his neck, he crooked his finger. "Unwrap it," he ordered.

Her heart was pounding as she stepped up to him and caught each edge of the cravat. Slowly she unwrapped it from his neck and at last tugged the long swath of fabric free to flutter to the ground. Before he could ask anything else, she unbuttoned the first button of his waistcoat, a finely stitched thing done in the colors of the Athawick flag.

She slid her fingers beneath the vest and hissed at the warmth of him trapped there. She would be burned alive by him before this night was over. She couldn't wait.

She slid her nails along the front of his shirt as she pushed the waistcoat away. His gaze held hers, watching, hooded, his pupils dilated until the blue was almost gone entirely. Her hands shook as she unfastened the first button on his shirt, the second, the third. The linen fabric gaped, and she whimpered at the tiny glimpse of olive skin beneath.

He let out a shaky breath and, in one smooth motion, tugged the shirt from his waistband and over his head. He dropped it to his side and smiled at her while she stared.

And stare she did. This was the first time she'd seen a man thus and it was…worth the wait. He was lean and muscular, built like a Roman god or a Michaelangelo statue. Only he was real. He was a flesh-and-blood man standing in front of her, there to be touched and to touch her in return.

She extended a hand and let it hover over his chest, uncertain what to do or how to do it. He chuckled, a low and feral sound, before he caught her wrist and dragged her hand flat against his pectoral. She hissed at the feel of his skin beneath hers, the way his muscle rippled when she flexed her fingers against it. She dragged her palm lower, down the apex of his body, over the taut ripples of abdominal muscle and to the waistband of his trousers.

"I want the rest," she whispered.

"Good God," he muttered in return, his eyes widening. "I've unleashed a monster."

"Only for you," she said, and knew it was true. She could not imagine any other man sparking such desire in her, such boldness. She'd never felt brave enough with any other person, that was certain. She feared she might not ever again.

That some part of her would always belong to Remi.

She pushed the fear that accompanied that thought away and instead worked at the placard of his trousers. His member was hard beneath—she could feel the harsh line of him when she brushed the heavy fabric in her attempts to unfasten him.

He grunted in a sound that was half-pleasure, half-pain.

"Why don't you allow me this part?" he asked, and backed away. He sat on the settee near the fire, slouching low as he unfastened his boots and pulled off first one, then the other. When he stood, it took him only a brief moment to strip the buttons of his placard open. The flap fell forward as he hooked his thumbs into the waistband and her eyes widened at the final revelation of what was beneath.

"My cock," he said softly as he shoved the trousers down and kicked them out of the way. He was naked. Fully, gloriously naked.

She blinked. "Wh-what?"

He smiled. "It's my cock. You said you didn't know what to call it."

She jerked her gaze to his face. "I did?"

He nodded. "It's a lovely compliment to stun you into this state."

"As if you don't exactly know your power," she murmured, and stepped closer. "Can I touch it? Your cock?"

He made a rough sound in his throat. "Yes, yes, yes…"

He trailed off as she dragged a fingertip over the head of him. The flesh was so soft, almost silky, and she folded her hand around it. Beneath that softness was steel, though. The hard thrust of him that filled her palm. He caught his breath and she stared up at him. "Too much?"

"Not nearly enough," he gasped. "So much more. I want too much more."

"So do I," she whispered.

He nodded slowly, his face twitching as she stroked him from base to head. Then he caught her wrist and removed her hand. "As much as I would love to teach you the ins and outs of manually making a man scream, there's a great deal else to be done."

She pushed her lower lip out in an exaggerated pout. "You never let me have any fun."

He lifted both eyebrows. "You're going to have plenty of fun, I assure you. Now let me unfasten you."

She laughed as he unhooked the buttons on her fancy robe. Unlike his clothing, which he had tossed around like it didn't matter, when he slid the beautifully embroidered piece of her gown away, he took it to drape across the back of a nearby chair. Protecting her as always. When he returned, he faced her away from him, leaning in to kiss the little bit of exposed skin at the base of her neck before he went to work on the line of buttons along the back of her cream gown.

He had done this so many times now. She should have been accustomed to the brush of his skin on hers, the whisper of his breath as he parted the gown and leaned closer.

"You were so beautiful tonight," he whispered as he glided the gown down without turning her to face him. "From the moment I saw you in the church, all I could think about was you."

She squeezed her eyes shut. This man had been a rake for years, playing his games, taking his pleasure. And yet she believed him. He wouldn't lie to her, he never had.

He thought she was beautiful. He wanted her, truly wanted her. And when he was with her, he forever took care of her and her needs, pushing his own aside. She felt protected, sheltered in his arms.

And she loved him because of all that he was and all that he made her feel. She loved him. There was no surprise when that thought passed into her mind. There was only a sense of peaceful rightness to it. She loved this man whose hands drifted down her hips and then balanced her as she stepped out of her dress. She loved him as he guided her back to lean against his bare chest and wrapped his arms around her.

She would always love him, even though she had no expectation that what was between them could mean more than this affair, this set of lessons so that she could give herself to another man, other *men*, who she would never love.

He turned her toward him at last, and his brow wrinkled. "Are you well?"

She bent her head. Trust that he would see her feelings. He seemed to do it so effortlessly. "I'm very well, Remi. I've never felt better."

His lip curled in a possessive smirk. "Tell me that later. After."

She couldn't help but laugh as he captured her mouth once more. She leaned into him, loving how her silky chemise brushed against his bare chest. The undergarment was short and tonight she hadn't worn drawers because of the lay of her dress. That meant her bare thighs touched his, tickled by the coarse hair there.

He let his hands drag down her back and then they curved around her backside. He tugged her closer, letting the hard cock she'd recently had in her hand press into her belly. She lifted against him with a mewl of pleasure and his tongue drove harder in response.

He backed her across the room and stopped at the edge of the mattress. Only then did he stop kissing her. He stared down, as if memorizing this moment, memorizing *her*. Then he slid his hands to her arms and lifted them above her head. In a quick movement, he pulled her chemise off and tossed it away.

She was as naked as he was. She had been this way with him before, of course. He had seen her body twice in this very tower, explored almost every inch of her. Made her quake and cry out and learn more about her own flesh and bone.

But standing here now, flush with him, nothing between them, she felt like it was the first time again. She lifted a hand to cover herself, and he frowned. "Too much?"

She swallowed. "It's just different now. I know what you're going to do and I'm…nervous."

"It's natural to be nervous," he said, stroking the back of his hand across her cheek. "But I promise that everything I'm going to do will feel good. And if it doesn't, we'll stop."

"Until a certain point," she said.

He shook his head. "There is no point of no return, sweet. You say stop, we stop."

She gazed up at him, that love she felt swelling even higher. "I don't think you're as much of a rake as you pretend," she whispered. "I think you are, at your heart, the very best of men."

His mouth fluttered, but then he glared at her playfully. "Spread that slander around and I shall meet you at dawn."

"I hope you will," she said, and reached up to touch his lips with her fingertips. "You would be beautiful in the dawn's light."

He grumbled low in his chest before he dipped his head and his mouth found hers again. This time there was a drive to his touch. There would be no more fits and starts. This was truly happening.

She was about to be his in every way.

CHAPTER 19

Remi lifted Priscilla up on the edge of the high mattress and she gasped as her bare backside hit the cool coverlet. He pressed each hand on the top of her thighs and guided her open, creating a space for him to step inside. She wrapped her legs around his hips, her arms around his shoulders, and just reveled in the feel of him there. There had never been anything so powerful. Perhaps there never would again, so she savored it, savored him.

"You make me forget myself," he groaned against her mouth. "Forget that I have to take my time."

She shook her head. "You don't."

He pulled back and arched a brow. "I will, though." He kissed her again and then motioned back to the pillows.

She pursed her lips. She liked sitting as she had been, wrapped around him as he kissed her with abandon. She felt more an equal in this moment. But he knew best. She scooted back and rested against the pillows, tracking him as he joined her on the bed. He caged her in with a hand on either side of the pillow, positioning himself between her legs again.

She lifted toward him, trembling with anticipation. He nipped her lower lip gently, but didn't kiss her mouth, instead he dropped his lips to her throat. He took a path she knew, one she had dreamed about since the first time he had done this magical thing to her. Sucking and licking and teasing his way to her breasts, lapping at her nipples, sucking and scraping his teeth against one and then the other. She dragged her hands into his hair as he did it, keening his name in the quiet as he woke the first ripples of pleasure to ease their way through her.

She found herself lifting to him, his hard cock nudging her hip each time. She'd seen the illustrations in that book—she knew where it fit. How in the world that would work, she didn't know, but he knew and she trusted him.

He dragged his mouth lower, over her stomach. When his teeth scraped her hip, she lifted with a gasp of sensation that made him chuckle possessively. He seemed in no hurry to do this, to simply take and claim and change her forever.

He settled his mouth against her sex, and she sighed with pleasure. He lifted his gaze to her, eyes bright with desire and purpose. He watched her as he licked, and she found the strength to keep her gaze locked with his as he did the same. She moved against him, lifting to his tongue as he swirled it around and around her clitoris. Grinding against his mouth and chin as the pleasure began to mount. When he pressed his finger inside, she shivered at the fullness, knowing it was just a shadow of what would come soon. He thrust, stretching her gently as he sucked harder and harder against her clitoris.

Sensation increased as she watched him, as she focused on the thrust of him. He was going to take her when this was over. Press himself into her and truly make her his. That thought was what pushed her over the edge. She arched her back, all her air leaving her lungs as she cried out. He pressed a hand to her hip, holding her steady as he continued to lash her sensitive clitoris with his tongue, forcing her pleasure until she felt weak and warm.

Only then did he lift his head, licking his lips clean of the slickness of her. He rose up on his knees, stroking the length of himself once, twice. Then he aligned their bodies. She expected a hard thrust, a quick taking.

Instead, he stroked the head of his cock back and forth against her, stimulating the still ultra-sensitive pearl of her clitoris. He seemed focused on the act, on building her pleasure again. On watching her writhe like that was the ultimate outcome, not anything else.

"Please," she panted, opening herself wider. "Please!"

He nodded slowly before he positioned himself. She felt the thickness of him at her entrance, the impossible bigness of what was to come. He pushed forward, and she gasped as he breached her the tiniest bit.

"Hurts?" he asked as he brushed his mouth to hers. She tasted herself on him.

"A little. It's…it's different from your fingers."

"Just slightly," he said with a soft laugh. "It will feel better as we go. And if you relax, it will help."

"How can I relax when you're…you're inside of me?"

"Barely inside," he corrected. "And you think about how good I'm going to make you feel. Because I'm going to make you feel so good. Once this is done, you won't hurt again. And then the world opens up."

"How?" she gasped as he slid forward a fraction more.

"So many positions, Priscilla," he promised, his tone a feral growl now, something that burned in her blood as she heard it, "that feel even better than this. You straddling me, grinding down against me, forcing your own pleasure while I watch you shatter."

She caught her breath at the idea, and he took another inch.

"From behind," he growled. "Bent over the dining table. You touching yourself like you like, me taking you while you scream into a napkin to keep the entire household from rushing to see what caused you to make such wicked sounds. And then you can sit at that fucking table later, Priscilla, and know that my cock is still wet from you."

He took more of her, but it no longer hurt. She found herself lifting into him, reveling in that stretch and in all the wicked things he was describing.

"More," she gasped. "Give me more."

He fully seated himself with a heady groan that told her she moved him as much as he moved her. "When you're ready, I could take your mouth."

"Like you've done with me?" she whispered.

He nodded. "God, sometimes I look at that mouth and wonder what it would feel like around me. Dream of it. I want to do so much with you, Priscilla. I want to wake you with orgasms, I want to make you come while you listen to people have polite conversations too close for comfort. I want to have you drinking tea while my come drips down your thighs and you have to clench your legs together to keep from making a gorgeous mess on a fine rug."

She realized she was grinding into him as he spoke. He was thrusting gently and the pleasure of his words was a faint reflection of the pleasure of their bodies moving as one. It built, faster now because she'd come so recently and was already sensitive. She clung to him, nails raking his flesh, moaning his name, crying out against his shoulder as pleasure so powerful that it bordered on pain built and built inside of her. He drew it from her, as experienced in this as in any other way, and when the sensation burst, it was with starbursts before her eyes. She lifted out of control, her trembling body milking him, clutching him inside of her and multiplying the wild feeling of her release.

He increased his thrusts, his mouth heavy on hers, his kiss as wild as his movements. She fought to meet him, to keep up as his breath shortened and he began to moan. She made him do this...this man versed in pleasure...he was losing himself in her. Her orgasm startled her, because it seemed to come out of nowhere. She slammed up against him, their cries mingling in the quiet as he gripped her hands, pushed them hard against the pillows.

At last, he threw his head back, the tendons of his neck defined.

He pulled from her body, thick ropes of release spurting from his cock as he milked it with one hand. It hit her skin, hot and sticky, and she cried out from the sensation. From the emotion.

From all the love she felt for him. From all the desire he had just fulfilled and yet not erased. From the future she wished she could ask for but knew was not in her reach. Still, as he flopped down next to her, as he dragged her into his arms, murmuring empty sounds of pleasure, this was enough.

For now, at least. This was enough.

~

Remi had taken a great many women to his bed. Not an uncountable number, but a great many. He'd very much enjoyed himself every time and had always been very satisfied when he left whatever bed or hay pile or countertop he'd enjoyed himself on.

Tonight, as Priscilla lay in his arms, her eyes closed and her breathing deep with sleep…tonight was different.

First off, he had never come so hard that his legs shook. That his entire body felt stripped to the bone. It was…remarkable. Like he'd given everything in his body, in his mind…in his soul.

Secondly, there was the matter of satisfaction. Oh, he was satisfied. Completely and totally and more powerfully than he chose to explore. And he knew Priscilla had also been satisfied. Multiple times, even. And yet he was left with this…hunger. He still wanted her as she snuggled closer, her bare hip pressing against his. And it was more than just the physical that he craved. He wanted to eat with her and laugh with her. He wanted to wipe her tears. To protect her. He wanted to wrap her around himself, to bury himself as deeply as he would go and never, ever escape this tower or her company.

He shook his head and stared up at the canopy of the bed above. This was madness. Absolute madness. Prince Remington of

Athawick did not feel these urges. He did not surrender to them, certainly. He loved and pleasured and left without a second thought. That was the bargain he'd made with every lover...including this one.

Priscilla flexed her hand against his bare chest, each finger the weight of a thousand pounds in that moment, he was so aware of them and her. He ought to roll away, wake her, make some dismissive comment, send her off to her chamber.

Only he couldn't. Instead he held her closer, marking the way her hair felt as it fanned across his arm. She was so warm in his arms, her body so soft against him. She had been wonderful tonight, unlike anyone else he'd ever been with. She was a natural when it came to pleasure. Time would only make her more confident in her skills, in her body, and then...well, then she would be an unstoppable force.

For someone else. Because that was the end goal for her now. To find a lover who would trade these gorgeous moments with her for safety and security.

He pursed his lips at the thought. He wanted her to have what she wanted, of course, but the idea of her rising up above some other man, riding him with abandon...

Well, it stung. More than it should have. Deeper than he'd thought possible.

"Remi?" He wasn't certain if she said it in her sleep or if she was waking up.

"Yes?" he whispered.

She lifted her head and his gaze was pierced by cool green beauty. "I'm sorry."

He wrinkled his brow. "Sorry? Why?"

"I fell asleep."

He chuckled, seeking some way to temper the mood in the room. Make it more fun and distant. "You *do* snore a bit," he lied. "But after that performance, I find it endearing."

She couldn't fight her smile at his quip before she rested her head back on his shoulder. "Do you judge me more harshly because of what you know about my family? Do you think it will make my path forward harder with potential lovers?"

He cupped her chin and tilted her face up so she would look at him again. "There is *nothing* that could ever make me judge you, Priscilla. Nothing in this world or any other."

Her lips parted and he could see the impact of his words on her. Her eyes filled with tears and her fingers clenched tighter against his skin. For a moment they were fully connected, perhaps even more so than they had been when he was inside of her, their bodies so fused that it was impossible to parse one from the other.

Only this connection was far more dangerous.

He cleared his throat. "When do you go back to London?"

She stiffened slightly. "A week," she said.

"Then perhaps we should start looking for potential lovers... here." Why was it so hard to say that? Why did it feel thick on his tongue, or like he was choking on it?

She drew back slightly. "Here in Athawick?"

He nodded. "You staying here would truly end any danger to you."

She drew in a long breath, a shaking one. "I see. And you are saying you would help me with finding someone here?"

He swallowed. Good God, what a thought. To find her some match as a lover? And then probably have to see her constantly on that other man's arm? Perhaps even hear about how happy that other person was with her in his bed and his life? That sounded like pure torture. Letting her go at all seemed like flaying the skin off his own body.

She sat up, disconnecting their bodies at last, and tugged the coverlet up to cover her breasts. "I suppose there is some benefit in such an arrangement," she said softly. "In never going back there, in never having to face their disappointment or their plans again. In never having to seek out a man who didn't want me to wife but might settle for me as a lover."

He pursed his lips at that description. "Then I suppose we are at an accord," he said softly. "I'll start thinking about options soon. Perhaps in a few days we can discuss them further."

She didn't answer, but swung her legs off the bed. The sheets clung to her as she began to move away, but eventually they dropped aside and he was left with the most beautiful sight of her naked body. She didn't face him, but bent to pick up her chemise.

She pulled it on and then looked at him. "Very good. Thank you, Remi. Your Highness. Remington."

He flinched at that attempt of a return to propriety. Something that had to happen in the end, but by God, not today. He got out of the bed and caught her hand, dragging her against him for a kiss that quickly deepened and grew hotter, sweeter.

When he was able to force himself to part from her, he panted, "I want to see you again. Tomorrow. Here. Please say you'll come."

She stared at him a long moment. He saw the fight on her face. The worry as she glanced toward the tower door. But then she nodded. "Yes. I can't deny you, Remi. I'll meet you here tomorrow. After the events of the day."

Relief washed through him. Too quick and hard and powerful to be safe. He ignored it and swept up her gown. "Let me help you dress."

She allowed it, and somehow he managed to get her back to presentable without laying her out on the bed for another round of pleasure. But as she slipped from the room, her gaze moved over his face, and he saw her...her disappointment.

And it mirrored his own. Not for what they'd shared, but for what they'd lost. Or what they could lose before this was all over.

CHAPTER 20

The next few days moved like a dream. Remi watched the clock in every room, counting the hours, the moments, the very seconds, before he could join Priscilla in the tower. When he did?

It was explosive. Their physical connection was unlike anything he'd ever experienced before. She was an enthusiastic lover, learning to embrace her own desire and his with abandon. He had begun to crave the grip of her sex around him as she came. He dreamed of her expression as she cried out his name and her fingers raked his back.

Did they connect emotionally? Not as much. Since her confession about her father and stepmother, since he had declared he would find her a lover here in Athawick, she had not pushed for closeness again. He ought to have been happy, but—

"Bloody fucking hell!"

Remi was yanked from his thoughts by a massive crash. He pushed from the settee where he had been sitting and went into the hallway to see what was amiss. The sound had come from his brother's study and the shouting was in Grantham's voice.

Remi hesitated. Going down there might only make things

worse. But he couldn't leave his brother in the midst of whatever had made him so uncharacteristically enraged.

He moved to the study and stepped inside, shutting the door quietly behind him. His brother stood at the massive window which overlooked the port below and the sea beyond. His shoulders were hunched, his hands clutched at his side.

"Grantham," Remi said softly.

His brother jumped, and when he pivoted back, his expression was dark and stormy. "What do you want?"

Remi pursed his lips. "I heard you having a fit from down the hall. Probably half the household did."

"Bollocks. I know the household is mostly down at the port shopping. With the ship coming in this afternoon from London, most of them are starting to prepare for their departure in a few days."

Remi flinched. He didn't particularly want to think of that outcome. It meant he was running out of time and needed to do as he'd promised to help Priscilla.

"I suppose you will be pleased to be rid of them," Remi said.

For a moment, Grantham's gaze grew faraway, and then he shrugged. "I will certainly be able to focus more fully when sh—they are gone. God knows I need to."

Remi moved forward. He saw the ornately carved blue box on his brother's desk, its lid removed and papers strewn from it. It was the way the kings of their island had received daily reports for generations. One of the papers was badly wrinkled, as if Grantham had smashed it in his upset.

Remi watched his brother carefully as he picked it up. Grantham tensed. "Those aren't yours to read."

"It isn't just your country," Remi said softly. He read over the sheet and frowned. "There is unrest in the southern region?"

Grantham bent his head. "Yes."

Remi read further. "Do they think it is the same group that

planned the attacks on Ilaria and Sasha in London? The one that wishes for your abdication?"

Grantham shifted. "Father's death was a rock thrown into the sea, and now we are experiencing the waves as they crash on our shore." He ran a hand through his hair. "Transitions are always difficult. I knew that would be true, I'm not a fool. But I didn't expect… this. Nor the response I'm being told to activate."

"Which is?"

"The courtiers and the military are pushing for…" Grantham caught his breath, and Remi saw the true struggle on his brother's face. He hid it so well, but now pain was streaked there. "They continue to claim that to meet violence with violence would swiftly end the protests. That I must set a strong example immediately or risk the situation spiraling out of control."

"Attack our own people." Nausea rose in Remi's belly, just as it had the first time he heard this plan.

Grantham nodded. "Yes. As a last resort."

"So there have been others?" Remi asked.

"Of course," Grantham snapped, the vulnerability replaced by irritation again. "I'm not a monster."

Remi set the papers back on the desk and shook his head. "May I ask you something?"

"You will no matter what I say," Grantham grunted. "So why not?"

"Are you happy as king?"

Grantham pulled back. "*Happy?*" he repeated. "What does that have to do with anything?"

"A great deal. Our family has lived for the service of this island for generations. I'm not discounting it. But does it follow that we must continue that path in perpetuity?"

"What the hell are you suggesting?" Grantham asked, his face twisting.

"Could the people be…right? Could they simply be asking for

the next step in their own futures, one that could actually make *yours* a happier one?"

Grantham's lips thinned. "It must be wonderful to live in such an insulated world where you can so easily change your path. Where you can return from London with your head in the clouds as you have."

Remi backed up a step. "What?"

"Please don't deny it. You've been odd since we came home."

Remi wrinkled his brow. "You're so desperate to avoid talking to me about issues regarding *our* home that you want to talk about this?"

"The topics are the same," Grantham said, folding his arms. "You are a representative of the Crown, so your behavior impacts how we are viewed. So tell me, why have you been so odd lately? Does it have anything to do with Miss Linfield?"

Remi narrowed his gaze. "And what do you know about Miss Linfield?"

"That you rushed to her defense when you believed I had wronged her. That you track her across every room she enters. That Mama has her own thoughts on the matter."

"Bloody hell, Grantham, it isn't as if you don't have your own situation. What about Lady Ophelia?"

Grantham threw up his hands. "You have no need to worry about me, I know what my position is. I may be the only one in this family who does. All I'm saying is that I don't want to have to step in to clean up your mess, Remi. I've done that enough already."

Remi recoiled because his brother could not have stung him more by actually striking him. He backed away as Grantham stared, his gaze even. These were not words said in anger, he meant them. He *meant* that he felt he had to chase after Remi, cleaning up after him.

"Don't you?" Remi asked softly. "Isn't that *exactly* what you want, Grantham? To step in and interfere with everyone else because you can't control anything about your own future? You tried with Ilaria, you drove Sasha to run away to marry, and now you're trying to dangle the puppet strings with me. In the past, you've accused me of being like our father …perhaps you should turn that mirror toward yourself and see if you like what's there."

Grantham stared at him, the only sound in the room the tick of the clock for a solid twenty seconds. Then he pointed to the door. "Get out, Remi."

"With pleasure, Your Majesty," he said, executing a deep bow that was meant with the utmost disrespect.

He turned on his heel and left the room. He had hoped to help Grantham by coming to him, or at least clear his own mind a little so he could find the answers regarding Priscilla. But now he felt only frustration, not relief.

And he had to do something about it soon, or else it would overtake him.

Priscilla exited the shop, her package clutched in her hand. She lifted up on her tiptoes to look around for Ophelia in the bustle. Her friend had stepped into the dress shop to look at a pretty fabric and they had agreed to meet to walk back up to the palace with the rest of the group.

She didn't see Ophelia, but she did catch a glimpse of the adopted daughter of the Athawick royal family, Sasha. Lady Bramwell? Soon-to-be princess? It was certainly confusing with all the titles and honorifics. Whatever name she would go by, she turned, and when she saw Priscilla, she waved.

"Greetings, Miss Linfield!" she called out.

Priscilla smiled and moved toward her, joining her to look out toward the sea. "Good afternoon," she said. "Oh, what a beautiful vista."

"Isn't it? I have always loved this view. And I swear I can see the little dot in the distance of the ship coming in from London. The one that will take away friends old and new."

Priscilla flinched. Would she be on that ship? She had no idea. Remi had spoken to her about finding her a lover here in Athawick so she wouldn't have to go home, but they had not discussed it since. They rarely spoke at all when they were together in the tower, unless it was him telling her how to move, unless it was her panting his name in desperate pleasure.

She blinked to clear her mind. It was inappropriate to be having such thoughts in front of the man's sister!

"The time has certainly flown, Lady...Princess..." She hesitated. "I do not know what to call you, to be honest."

Her companion laughed. "Sometimes I don't know what to call myself. But since I like you and I hope we can be friends, perhaps just call me Sasha when we are alone and follow the queen's lead when we are in public. Mama always seems to know what to do to be properly...er...proper."

They laughed together, even though Priscilla was uncertain of the rightness of what Sasha suggested. She had no place in this world, after all. She'd barely had one before, but soon she would be a courtesan...a mistress...and certainly she would not be welcome to call a royal daughter by her first name after that.

Perhaps she should enjoy it now.

"A good plan...Sasha."

"Now what did you buy?" Sasha asked, motioning to the little box in her hand. "You came from Verrick's Gems, did you not?"

"I did," Priscilla gushed as she pulled the little ribbon that held the box closed and opened it to reveal the necklace within.

"Sea glass," Sasha gasped as she let her finger trace the beautiful pale blue stone.

"It isn't as fancy as gems, of course, but I wanted something to remind me of my time here," Priscilla explained. She didn't add that the glass was exactly the same color as Remi's eyes. So she could wear it and have something of him close to her.

"It's stunning," Sasha said. "You know that the Sea Crown—the one Ilaria wore for one of her engagement balls, it's her favorite—has as many pieces of sea glass as it does actual gems. We value them nearly as much here."

"Well, I will cherish it," Priscilla sighed. She wrinkled her brow. "I was waiting for Ophelia, but she doesn't seem to be coming out."

Sasha laughed. "I saw the Duchess of Gilmore go into the shop behind her. They might be caught up in the fabrics. I could have someone let them know that we decided to walk back to the palace together. I'm sure they wouldn't mind."

Priscilla smiled. "That would be lovely, thank you."

Sasha stepped away a moment, talking to one of the servants who was standing at the ready for her. As the young man scurried off to deliver their message, Sasha returned and motioned them toward the palace in the distance.

For a short time, they walked together, talking of the wedding and the upcoming coronation.

"Will you stay in Athawick until then?" Priscilla asked.

A little sadness entered her companion's face. "No, Ilaria, Jonah, Thomas and I will all return to England in a few weeks on the royal ship. Both the men have things to attend to, and Ilaria and I are still settling into our new roles. We won't return for a few months after that. Not until the coronation date is closer."

Priscilla reached for Sasha's hand without thinking of their disparate roles and squeezed gently. "You must be sad to be parted from your family. You seem so close. It's enviable."

"We are close," Sasha said, and linked arms with Priscilla as if they had been friends for years. "And yes, I will miss them desperately, especially the queen and Dash." When Priscilla tilted her head, Sasha smiled. "Dashiell Talbot, the queen's secretary. But he's a father to me. Is a father to all of them, really."

Priscilla wrinkled her brow. She had seen the man in passing, of course. Watched Remi interact with him on one or two occasions. Mr. Talbot was a handsome older gentleman who seemed driven to see to the queen's comfort even before she knew what she needed.

"I see," she said softly.

"Perhaps you do," Sasha said. "Sometimes parental relationships are...difficult. It was different for me because I was an adopted daughter. But the late king..." She trailed off. "I shouldn't say more. I only wish and hope that Grantham and Remi will not be so caught up in expectation that they do not allow themselves happiness."

Priscilla swallowed. She had wanted to ask Remi about his family in the past few days. But there was such a wall between them emotionally. Now her questions returned.

"Of course, I will miss Remi desperately, too," Sasha said.

Priscilla tensed. "You two are...close."

"It seems you two have become close, as well," Sasha said.

Priscilla jerked her gaze to her companion. Sasha was watching her carefully as they continued to walk, though how Priscilla stayed on her feet, she couldn't say. Her knees felt wobbly.

"He is impossible not to like," she said at last, hoping that would be vague enough.

"I think it might be more than that," Sasha said softly. "And I admit it was why I wished to walk with you today, so we could speak in private."

Priscilla slid her arm free of Sasha's and stopped on the path, backing away as she opened and shut her mouth in shock. "I...I don't...I couldn't..."

Sasha shook her head. "Oh, please, Miss Linfield...Priscilla, don't look so frightened. I like you so much, I think we have a great deal in common and could be friends. And I love my brother." She hesitated. "And I have begun to think that you could say the same."

Priscilla felt like she was choking on air and she was desperate to change this subject. She didn't want Sasha to know what she felt, what would be the point? Remi didn't love her, so her heart was the one at risk. Her heart was the one that would surely be broken in a matter of days.

"I-I cannot deny that I like your brother," she stammered at last. "Beyond that, it would be foolish of me to say."

Sasha's expression softened. "It can be a complicated thing, I know. Ilaria and I both faced difficulties on our paths to happiness, but we are here, and I would not worry about speaking for both of us when I say it was more than worth it. Remi is more than worth it...even if he can be..." She laughed. "Difficult. We'll call it difficult."

Priscilla stiffened at the choice of words. Sasha wasn't wrong, but she still felt a flare of protectiveness.

"He is also kind," Sasha continued. "And funny. And worth it."

Priscilla cleared her throat, and together they began walking again. She was still searching for a response to Sasha, one that wouldn't push her over the edge. One that wouldn't reveal all the things she concealed to protect herself.

"The prince is all the things you say and more," she said as they reached the gate leading back into the palace grounds. "And you're right that he is worth whatever battles one will endure to have him. I only hope he one days finds a woman he is willing to fight for just as hard."

Sasha looked at her and slowly nodded. There was a sadness to her tone as she said, "I see."

"Now, if you don't mind, I think I'll take a brief turn about the garden before I return to my chamber to ready for supper later."

"Of course," Sasha said, touching her hand. "I'm so glad I got to know you a little better. I hope we'll continue that before your departure. And after, for my sister and I will be in London often. We'd love to call on you."

"That would be wonderful," Priscilla said, thinking of what her father and stepmother would think of her becoming friends with royalty.

"Good day," Sasha said with a smile.

"Good day," Priscilla echoed, and then let out her breath in a ragged sigh as Sasha left her side.

She walked around the palace perimeter slowly and into the garden. She saw nothing as she roamed through the flowers and the beautifully maintained paths. Her mind raced too quickly, dragging her through every moment of the conversation with Sasha and every moment she'd shared with Remi.

She stopped at a bench near a fountain and sat down, placing her head in her hands momentarily to gather herself. "What are you doing?" she whispered. "What are you thinking?"

She had no answer for herself and lifted her head again. As she did so, she was shocked to see Remi storm past, without even noticing her. Unlike usual, his demeanor was angry and frustrated, there was no jovial mask to make others comfortable.

"Remi?" she called out.

He froze in the path and pivoted back toward her. His face was dark with emotion and his hands were clenched at his sides. "Priscilla," he breathed. "Did you not go to the port with the others?"

"I did," she said, lifting her package. "Sasha…Lady Bramwell and I walked back together before the others." She stood slowly. "What is wrong?"

"Wrong?" he said, his tone suddenly falsely bright. "What could be wrong? It's a beautiful day and there's no reason at all for—"

"Remi," she said, moving toward him. She touched his hand and he shivered.

He cleared his throat. "I had…I had an altercation with my brother."

She drew in a sharp breath, thinking once again of Sasha's implication that all had not been well with the royal family. That their smiles hid deeper issues. "An altercation?"

"Not physical," he said slowly. "Though perhaps one day it will come to that and I'll be living in that tower as a prisoner, not some mad lover."

She wrinkled her brow at that description, but didn't address it. "What did you argue about?"

He shook his head. "Doesn't matter."

"Yes, it does." She slid her fingers through his. "Remi, you have done so much for me. Won't you let me help you? Just hear you, knowing that I am a safe place to put some of these things you hide beneath good humor and frivolity."

His expression changed, the smile fading, his brow lowering as his stare grew ever darker. In that moment, she saw so much more, so much deeper into his soul. She wanted more, God help her, even though she knew it would only strengthen the connection she felt toward him, the love that was bound to destroy her.

As Sasha had said, it was worth it. *He* was worth it.

"Please," she whispered. "Give me some of this to carry, even for a moment."

He pursed his lips. "We're a royal family," he choked out. "We're perfect, Priscilla."

"No, you're not," she pressed. "You are human. You're *human*, Remi, with every right to joy and beauty and pain and anger."

His face fluttered with all of those emotions in one powerful moment. He erased them, of course. He lifted her hand to his lips, kissed it briefly and then let her go, walking toward the fountain. She thought he might brush her off after all, refuse to share more than his body in the end.

Perhaps that would have been a kindness, because it would have severed her quiet little dreams for more of him.

But at last he glanced at her over his shoulder. "Did Sasha speak of the old king? My father? *Alistair?*" The way he said the name was like it was squeezed out of him. Like it burned. "Because in the end, it all comes down to him."

CHAPTER 21

Remi hadn't thought he would do this. He had vowed long ago to forgo these confessions of the soul. Lightness was his armor, the breeze that blew people away when they got too close.

But Priscilla had already come in past his barricades...even before today. Today, though, as she stared up at him, those green eyes so kind, so accepting, so filled with emotions he had vowed he would never seek...

It was impossible to deny her. Especially when he still stung from his encounter with his brother. From the fact that in a few days she would either board a ship to London or begin a very different kind of journey with another man. Either way, she would leave his side. He would let her go like the fucking coward he was.

Her hand fluttered at her side as he asked the question about his father. She wanted to move toward him. She wanted to comfort him, but she held back, respecting his space. He wasn't certain if he was pleased by that fact or broken.

"Sasha mentioned Mr. Talbot when we spoke, and how he was a father to her...perhaps a bit to all of you."

Remi jolted. Yes, that was accurate. When he was able, Dash had always offered the solace his blood father never extended.

"Otherwise, she danced around the topic," Priscilla said.

"Ah, if only that were possible, to dance around who he was. What he was." He sighed. "I suppose that was a man of his position, to be fair to him. He was raised to be king, to be distant, to be an institution, not a man. And if he had just been cold, perhaps one could have understood."

"What was he beyond cold?" she whispered after he stopped and didn't continue.

"Cruel when it suited him," he said, and a thousand moments flooded his mind, ripped through his heart. "He was forced to marry my mother for political union. He did so and made his heirs and spares, as was his duty. But he also flagrantly kept his mistresses, one even under our roof for a time. He humiliated the queen because it…*entertained* him, I think."

"You would never know it. She is so confident, so kind," Priscilla breathed.

Remi nodded. "She is everything. And I don't just say that because I am her favorite."

She smiled at his quip. One that was true, of course. Everyone in the family knew it. But if he had hoped to put Priscilla off with meaningless trivia about his family, it was not to be. She leaned closer. "What was he to the rest of you?"

Remi cleared his throat, thinking of how big his father could be when he was small. How terrifying. "He railed at the rest of us about duty. Grantham had it worst. He was at turns ice cold and red hot. You never knew what you would find when he opened a door."

"That must have been terrifying," she whispered.

He nodded, thinking of the way he used to scoot as low as he could in his chair at the supper table when his father was in a mood. Like if he just shrank…if he was just insignificant enough…it would stop.

"When we were young, oh yes, it was. As each of us aged, I suppose we all handled it differently. Ilaria became more outspoken, challenging him. Sasha put herself on the outside, accepting the role of servant that he dumped onto her back so cruelly. Grantham became more and more dutiful, less and less free in order to please him."

"And what did *you* do?" she asked gently.

He thought of that shrinking boy and how at some point, he'd realized his best defense was something different than disappearing.

"I got louder," he said, and shook his head. "And bolder. And wilder. If I was enough trouble, he would dismiss me. So I created the largest amount of it as I could, as often as I could. And he hated me for it."

"Hated you?" she said.

"Oh yes. He hated me for shirking my duty. At least on the surface. And yet he also hated me for being freer than he was. He had to hide how irresponsible he was under layers of propriety and cruelty. *I* could be open. So he *hated* me for being his mirror image…and for being able to break free of his chains."

Now she did cross to him, taking both his hands. Even though she wore gloves, her warmth seeped through him. This gorgeous sunshine that she carried inside of her and that pushed away the shadows no one else in his life had ever been able to see. And yet she looked up into his eyes and she saw it all. She saw everything because he wasn't capable of hiding himself when she got near him.

She stripped him down to his essence, and then she liked him anyway.

"I was with him when he died," he admitted, feeling the cracks in himself more deeply than he had in years.

Her expression softened. "You were?"

He nodded. "We were taking turns sitting with him—the end was obviously near. Grantham had stepped out, my mother and sisters were sleeping. It was just the king and me. I thought he was asleep, his eyes were shut, his breathing labored. And then he opened his eyes and spoke to me. He said that…that he wished he'd been more like me." Remi laughed, though it was humorless. "I thought he meant it as a compliment, as a final connection to a son. But then he met my eyes and said…he said…"

He couldn't say those words. Reliving them in his mind was bad enough. But maybe if he got the courage and said them, she would understand what he was. Why he was. Why the future that sometimes glimmered in the endless green of her stare was not possible.

"He said he should have just done what he wanted and never given a thought to anyone else…like me," he said softly. "And then he died. And I stared at him, waiting for him to breathe in again, knowing he never would. And I knew the truth. He might have counted himself more nobly, but I was *exactly* like him. I am as selfish, I am as indecent. He gifted me with his eyes…he cursed me with the rest."

She cupped his cheeks, mindless of the garden, of the public space. "Look at me," she ordered. He did because how could she be denied? "You are *nothing* like him, Remi. You are good."

"So says the woman I am ruining in a tower."

"What you do to me isn't ruining," she whispered. "It is everything. *You* are everything."

She leaned up and brushed her lips to his. He wanted so desperately to clutch her close, to bruise her with his desire, to mark her permanently with his heat so she would remain as scarred as he would be when she was gone. But he couldn't do that here, not here where anyone could see.

"Come upstairs with me," he whispered. "To the tower. Please come upstairs with me now."

She looked up toward the spire where they had kept their assignations for days. "Yes," she whispered, and followed when he caught her hand and drew her toward the house. Toward the inevitable. Toward the end.

~

Remi was on her before he had even closed the door fully, shoving her back against it as it slammed, his mouth burning against hers. His desperation and his heartbreak were as present as his desire, and she took it all because she loved him and that was what he needed. Truth be told, it was what she wanted, too. She wanted to drown in all the things that no one else saw, the truth of him.

He ground up against her, and she shivered at the insistent hardness that pushed into her belly. Immediately, she went on edge, her body readying for the inevitable pleasure they were about to give each other. She had no idea how many more times they would get to do this, and so she reveled in every touch. In the way he moaned her name as he slid his mouth from her lips and down her throat. He sucked there, finding some amazing spot that drove her wild. She dug her fingers into his hair, lifting to meet him as they ground together against the door.

"I want you," she whispered. "All I could think about today was you."

He pulled away, staring down at her as if she were brand new to him. Then he backed away, shrugging out of his jacket, beginning to tear the knot on his cravat loose. "Undress," he ordered, his voice shaking.

She set down the package she still clutched and he tracked the movement. "What did you buy?"

"A necklace," she admitted.

He stopped fumbling with the cravat and held out a hand. "Let me see."

She pursed her lips. Not only was this interruption keeping her from what she wanted, she also wasn't certain she wanted him to see the necklace she would wear like a widow in mourning when he had long forgotten her and their time in this secret place.

Her hands shook as she removed the item from its box and

handed it over. He examined it closely. "Beautiful," he breathed. "Put it on. And take off the rest."

Her eyes went wide. "You want me to make love to you wearing nothing but the sea glass necklace?"

"Absolutely, I do," he said, and set the necklace back on the table. "Take off the rest and I'll help you put it on."

Her hands trembled as she unbuttoned her dress along the front and shoved it down her arms. He was unlooping his cravat but watching her as she removed piece after piece. Her gown, her chemise, her slippers, her stockings...until she wore nothing else. He stripped off his shirt and moved to the settee. At some point, he had picked up the necklace again and set it on the cushion beside him while he tugged off his boots and then kicked out of his trousers. His cock was hard, as ready for her as her aching, wet body was for him.

He slouched a little lower and crooked his finger. "Come here."

She couldn't deny him. She was drawn to him like a magnet, like a bee to a wildflower. In a few steps she stood before him. He slid his hands up her bare thighs and she ached for him, he cupped her backside and she trembled. And when he tugged her gently, she sank her knees into the cushions on either side of him and straddled his lap.

Slouched on the settee, he was slightly lower than she was, and he stared up at her, his gaze intense. "Why did you pick this necklace? Rather than any other beautiful color of sea glass?" he asked as he unfastened the clasp of the necklace.

She shook her head. "Don't make me say it, Remi."

He leaned up and reached around, hooking the necklace around her neck. The chain was long and the charm now dangled just between her breasts. "Say it," he ordered softly.

"Because it matches your eyes," she admitted, hating how her cheeks filled with heat and color.

He cupped the back of her head and drew her down, kissing her harder than he had at the door. She opened to him, her tongue warring with his, her arms coming around his neck. She wiggled in his lap, grinding against the hard cock that was now trapped between her legs, but not quite inside of her.

He threaded one hand into her hair, pins clattering around them. The other hand roved down her back, cupping her backside to help her grind helplessly against him. His nails lightly raked her outer thigh, tugging her closer on the settee.

"Please," she moaned into his mouth.

He nodded rather than spoke, and his hand moved between their bodies. She expected him to align them and simply take. She was certainly ready, as it seemed she always was for him. Instead, he stroked his fingers against her clitoris, smiling against her mouth when her breath went short with pleasure.

"So wet," he murmured.

She dipped her head back as he flicked her clitoris over and over with his thumb. He pressed his mouth to her breast, sucking hard enough that she cried out in the quiet. He swirled his tongue around and around her nipple, his thumb over her clitoris until she was panting and groaning with need.

It was then and only then that he fisted himself, finding her entrance with the thick head of his cock. She pushed down over him, whimpering as he filled her to the hilt. She ground down, her hips swiveling as she sought more and more pleasure.

"Just like that," he breathed. "Use me."

She nodded, bringing her mouth back to his. He cupped her backside with both hands now, helping her move over him, stroking herself just right against the root of his cock. The pleasure was intense, the heat of them combustible. She dug her fingers against his scalp, tilting his mouth up to claim him more fully and he grunted as she took what she wanted.

The orgasm came hard and fast. She buried her mouth against his neck as she pivoted her hips out of control, pleasure ripping through her in unceasing waves. He wasn't finished, of course. Once was never enough. He liked to watch her come, she had realized that early on. It excited him to please her, to feel her flutter around him as she cried out his name.

He lifted his hips from beneath her, balancing her carefully on his lap as he took her relentlessly from below. She leaned back against his knees, watching their bodies roll together like waves on the ocean that had brought her to him weeks ago.

His face was lined with concentration as he licked his thumb and pressed it to her clitoris. He slowed his thrusts and she rippled against them as he rebuilt the wall of pleasure that had just been shattered. It was a wonder, truly. She had never imagined that she could feel this way, that a man could do these things to her. Now she couldn't imagine living without all this passion, all this pleasure, all this love.

She pushed away the negative side of that thought: the truth of the matter that soon she would be separated from him. Not today, not in this room, not when he was touching her just like she liked to be touched.

"Don't think about that," he murmured, and her eyes widened.

"Think about what?" she gasped when he flicked her clitoris with the edge of his nail and an electric jolt of pleasure shot through her.

"Anything but this." He tugged her forward and their mouths met again. His hand was still wedged between them, and he increased the pressure of his fingers, the lift of his hips.

She shattered around him a second time, her moans lost in their kiss, tangled with his own. He gripped both her hips, his fingers pressing hard against the flesh to increase her pace over him. She rode him harder, faster, watching every tightening of the tendons in his neck, the way his lips parted as his breath grew short, the way his pupils dilated as he stared up at her in wonder and pleasure.

"Fuck," he moaned, and tilted her back, removing his cock to pump between them as he came.

She flexed above him, wrapping her arms around his neck to kiss him. She never wanted to stop kissing him or touching him. He sought her with his mouth as much as she did his while he wrapped his arms tightly around her back and molded her fully to him.

When their lips parted, she pressed her forehead to his and their gazes locked, as intimate as any moment when their bodies were fused. And somewhere in that beautiful face, in those startling eyes, she saw a flicker of emotion. A reflection of what she felt, though he hid it so well.

What if he *did* care for her? What if they could love each other and be like this forever? Wouldn't she hate herself for not trying to tell him what she felt? Wouldn't she hate herself for being a coward if it resulted in their being parted?

"Remi," she whispered, smoothing tangled locks from his forehead.

He caught his breath, his expression changing as if he knew what she would say. "Yes?"

"I—"

She didn't get to say the rest, because before she could the door to the tower opened and the King of Athawick entered, her stepmother and father at his heels.

"I don't know why she would be—" he was saying, and then the group stopped, staring as Priscilla barked out a shocked gasp, and then she and Remi scrambled to cover themselves.

Her father and the king began to shout. Caroline glared at her, fire and hatred in her eyes.

In short…all hell broke loose.

The worst part of the intrusion to the tower wasn't the screaming or the disappointment on his brother's face. No, the worst thing about all this for Remi was the deep humiliation on Priscilla's face as she scrambled for her discarded dress and held it up as a shield.

Remi got up, caring not one iota that he, himself, was naked, and held up a hand. "Oy, you two can yell all you like in a moment. Let us dress first. The lady should not be so exposed."

"The lady was exposed by *you*," Grantham growled, and then turned to the two people with him. "Lord and Lady Linfield, please let us step out in to the hallway."

Remi's eyes widened and he glanced back at Priscilla, whose head was bent, her cheeks bright with color. She refused to look at him.

"I will not leave my daughter alone with—" Lord Linfield began.

Grantham leaned closer and a spark entered his gaze. "It was not a request, my lord. Now."

Whatever Priscilla's father was going to say died on his lips. He pressed them so hard together that they went stark white, then grabbed for his wife's arm. He all but dragged her from the room into the hall and Grantham followed, shutting the door behind him with a glare for Remi. When they were gone, Priscilla put her head in her hands with a sharp moan.

"How are they here?" she whispered.

"That is your father and, I assume, the infamous Caroline?"

She nodded without looking up. "Why and *how* would they come here?"

"The ship that arrived today," Remi breathed. "They must have come on today's ship. Christ. We'd best get dressed, there will be hell to pay."

She didn't move, but continued to sit with her head in her hands. He dropped to his knees and pushed her hands aside so he could see her face. Her eyes were filled with tears—they streaked across her cheeks and it broke him. He'd done this to her, after all. He'd caused this pain in a woman he would never hurt for any price, not on purpose.

Yet here they were because he was selfish and reckless.

"Please," he said, wiping tears from her cheeks gently. "All will be well."

"How?" she sobbed. "Your brother the king, my father and the stepmother who despises me have just caught us naked in each other's arms. How will that *ever* be well?"

"I will make it well," he promised, even though he wasn't certain that was a promise he could actually keep.

"I suppose that aside from the humiliation, nothing will change. I was going to become a mistress anyway, wasn't I? So this is an added shame to what so many will consider my fall, but my future remains the same."

"My brother will say nothing," he assured her.

"And yet nothing will stop Caroline from telling the world. She will make sure it is circulated, if only for her own pleasure." She sighed. "No, Remi, there is no getting around it."

He shook his head in disgust. If that was true, then her whole sodding family deserved every terrible thing that would come to them. He had his own issues with his brother, yes, but Grantham would never abandon him, he knew that like he knew his own face in the mirror.

Priscilla stood and set the dress back down on the settee. He couldn't help but let himself look at her, glorious and naked. He drank it in, because surely this would be the last time. She would be secreted away from him from now on, guarded by her friends or her father.

She twisted her mouth in worry. "I am sorry that your brother is angry, though."

Always thinking of him, of course. It was her nature. So much better than his own.

"Oh, angel," he said, reaching out to take her hand. "He's always angry with me about one thing or another. This…was worth it."

She stared up at him, the tears returning to her eyes but this time not falling. "It was very much worth it," she agreed.

She lifted up on her tiptoes and kissed him, and it was like it was the first time. The last time. And when she broke away and went to look for her chemise, it was as if someone had yanked his heart from his chest and then tossed it aside.

They both dressed as swiftly as they could and she fought to get her hair back in some semblance of a proper style. At last they looked at each other.

"Ready?" he asked.

"No," she said with a hollow laugh. "Could we just stay here?"

He looked around at this oasis they had created with their passion and their desire. "I would love that. But he will knock down the door."

"Then we better go," she said with a sigh, and then led the way to do just that.

CHAPTER 22

In the end, Grantham marched them to his study, the entire party grim and wordless. Remi felt his brother's stare on his back as he and Priscilla walked ahead of the others. Somehow the king had convinced Lord and Lady Linfield to be quiet, to hold their attacks and questions until they were in a more appropriate spot.

The silence gave Remi time to think. Priscilla had moaned out a pained question up in the tower. How and why had her father and stepmother come? More to the point, how had *any* of them known to come to the tower to look for them? Grantham hated the place for some reason, and the Linfields couldn't possibly know anything about the palace.

Which meant someone had betrayed him. There was only one servant who knew the truth about his hideaway in the tower, and that was his valet, a man he had thought he could trust for a great many years.

None of it added up.

Grantham shut the study door and then leaned against it, staring at the group of them quietly. "I have asked that the queen and her secretary join us. They will be here shortly, according to my courtier. We have a great deal to discuss."

Lord Linfield folded his arms. "*That* is a vast understatement, Your Majesty." He pivoted toward Priscilla. She flinched but didn't turn away. Her bright face had gone dull, her eyes cast down, her shoulders rolled forward in utter defeat. "*You* have been a disappointment for years, but I never thought I'd see the day that I would call my daughter a whore."

"Watch yourself," Remi snapped out, stepping toward him.

"Says the man who made her one," Lord Linfield said, arching a brow.

"And a prince of this island, to which you are a visitor, sir," Grantham said in his voice that was quiet and, Remi knew, far more dangerous than when he shouted. "So I would mind your tone."

Lord Linfield darted his gaze between the two men, clearly sizing up his ability to bully them and seeing none. So he shifted his attention back to Priscilla. "I demand to speak to my daughter alone."

Remi thought of what Priscilla had said about the physical violence her father had acted upon her in London and stepped between them. "No." He met his brother's eyes and held there. "No."

Grantham's expression was confused, but he took Remi's side regardless. "At this moment, emotions are high. Let us instead get you and your wife settled in a room here in the palace." He looked at Priscilla. She didn't return his stare, but Remi saw the kindness in his brother's eyes. "And *I* will speak to the prince."

"And if I wish to demand satisfaction for this wrong to my family?" Linfield said, folding his arms.

"Yes," his wife piped up for the first time. "We deserve it!"

Grantham took a long step toward Linfield. "Prince Remington is a very good shot, my lord. Are you certain you wish to press that course of action against my family?"

"I-I meant financial compensation," Linfield stuttered.

Grantham twisted his face in disgust. "All will be resolved, I assure you." He moved to the door and rang a bell.

Within a moment, his head courtier, Blairford, had appeared. He looked past the king into the room and then the two spoke softly together. "Lord and Lady Linfield, will you come with me? We have accommodations ready. And Miss Linfield—"

"Will remain," Remi said.

Grantham didn't argue, so the Linfields were removed. Priscilla remained, staring at her feet, unspeaking as the voices of her father and stepmother disappeared down the hallway.

"Obviously there is a good deal to discuss, Miss Linfield. But will you step out a moment? You can rejoin us shortly, but I would like to speak to my brother alone."

Priscilla glanced toward Remi, a question in her eyes. He nodded. "It will be fine. Give us a moment."

She ducked from the room, shutting the door behind herself.

"Do you want to explain to me what the fuck you've done?" Grantham asked as soon as she was gone.

Remi glared at him. "You already know, why demand that I explain it?"

"Because I want to hear it from your lips," he said.

Before Remi could do that, the door to the study opened and Queen Giabella entered, followed by Dashiell Talbot. Remi wasn't certain if he was pleased to see them so that he would have a barrier between himself and the brother who looked ready to fight, or sorry that he would have to reveal his bad behavior to his mother and let her disappointment join Grantham's.

The queen looked from one of them to the other. "What has happened?"

"What makes you think something happened?" Remi asked.

She tilted her head. "Because I know you both. And Grantham's message was quite pointed that there was trouble. Now one of you speak."

Grantham motioned to Remi, a silent order for him to confess like a chagrined schoolboy who had been caught at cheating. Though perhaps that was for the best.

Remi faced his mother. "I will be direct about this because it will speed this along. I have been…I've been taking Priscilla Linfield to my bed," he admitted.

The queen's eyes went wide. "Remington! I saw an attraction there, of course, but I had no idea it had gone so far. What were you thinking?"

"Tell her the rest," Grantham ordered softly.

Remi glared at his brother. "This afternoon we were caught by Grantham, along with Priscilla's father and stepmother."

The queen lifted a hand to her mouth and shot Dash a look. The secretary's expression was taut and frustrated. Seemed Remi had disappointed the whole lot of them. Wonderful.

"Her *father*?" The queen looked at Grantham. "Wait, they were not our guests—how in the world did they come into the mix?"

Grantham threw up his hands in frustration. "They arrived on the ship that came in this afternoon and came into the castle demanding to see their daughter, screeching about the tower. Since I could not locate Blairford, I agreed to escort them there, never believing we would find what they expected. But apparently Remi was careless enough with this fact that they had heard wind of it."

"How they hell would they hear of such a thing?" Remi asked, and then he stared at his brother as a terrible guess entered his mind. "Wait…you wanted to link one of us to an important family in England…Priscilla's grandfather is a marquess. And you brought the Linfields to the tower where Priscilla and I were…were together."

"Are you accusing *me* of arranging this?" Grantham asked, his hands fisting at his sides. "Have you lost your senses?"

"Why not? Your spies could have found out the truth, either from my valet or just by following one us. If you could not force Ilaria into a marriage to further your desires, why not trap me into one?"

He caught his breath as the idea of marrying Priscilla sank in. He'd not thought of the concept much before. He knew what the expectations were for a person of his position and had known he would be forced to wed at some point.

But the idea of taking that plunge with Priscilla was…less horrible than it should have been. She would be his. No towers required to be with her. No barriers or fears to separate them.

"How dare you?" Grantham barked, and yanked him from that quick fantasy. "How fucking dare you?"

"Careful," Dash said softly, and the queen glanced back at him.

"I have heard the word before, Dashiell, though I appreciate your interference." She returned her attention to her sons. "Let us not be hasty. Remi, you must know your brother would not be so cruel."

"Must I?" Remi asked, and hated how his brother flinched as if he'd struck him.

"Think what you will of me," Grantham said. "It doesn't really matter, does it? You are acting a fine role of a protector for a woman *you* put in this position. Not me. Not whoever informed her family. Not her parents. *You.* So don't play high and mighty now, Remington, when you are the one who took advantage."

Remi came forward before he could plan what he would do. It was like something else controlled him as he coiled back and then punched his brother in the face. Grantham rocked back and then lunged at him. Remi was almost glad for it. The tension between them had increased for years, perhaps a good fight was what they needed.

At least it would let Remi bleed out some of these horrible emotions that burned inside of him.

But it was not to be. Dash flung himself between them, shoving them apart. "Enough!" he barked out.

"You need to fix this," Grantham growled at Remi as he backed away from Dash. "It's your mess—clean it up!"

"How?" Remi asked.

Grantham shook his head. "You bloody well know how. For God's sake, Remi, you told me you're not our father. Prove it."

Remi flinched at that accusation, and the desire to fight again filled him. He pressed against Dash's hand in an attempt to continue the brawl.

"Please stop!"

The voice came from the doorway and the entire group of them turned to see Priscilla there. She moved forward and wedged herself between Dash's hand and Remi's chest. His focus shifted to her as she pressed her palms there and backed him up. It was as if her touch bled the fight out of him.

"Stop," she repeated, softer now. "And look at your mother."

Remi did and saw that the queen's cheeks were pale as paper, her hands clasped to her lips. "I am sorry, Mama," he said softly. "I'm sorry, Priscilla."

Grantham cleared his throat and stepped up to wrap an arm around his mother's waist. "I am sorry, Mama."

Priscilla faced the two of them. "*I* am to blame for what is happening. Not Remi. Me. It's my fault."

Remi shook his head. "It certainly is not your fault."

"But I had my part," she said. "You were trying to help me, not hurt me. And no one should say otherwise." She shifted her gaze toward Grantham and the queen. "I cannot imagine what you must think of me, Your Majesties."

Grantham wrinkled his brow. "Although I am not pleased by these circumstances, I assure you that we do not view these sorts of things with as judgmental an eye on Athawick, Miss Linfield. My judgement of you remains as it ever was: positive."

His mother nodded. "And I feel the same."

Priscilla lifted her eyes and stared, disbelief plain on her face. "Then at least let me apologize in advance for whatever trouble you will have with my father and his wife."

"You needn't apologize for anyone else's actions," Grantham said.

"We have handled worse, I assure you." The queen smiled at her, and it was warm and genuine. At least they could offer Priscilla that.

Giabella drew a long breath and then stepped forward. "This is obviously a complicated situation," she said gently. "And I think it might be best if we all take a break and a breath. Dash...Dashiell, will you arrange for a private supper in my personal dining room tonight? For Miss Linfield, her parents, her chaperones, the king, Remi and me?"

Dash nodded. "Of course."

"We will break bread together and figure this out," the queen said. "*Calmly.*" She glanced between her two sons, and Remi bent his head in shame.

Grantham looked equally chagrined. "I think that is a good idea, Mama. Miss Linfield, might I suggest that you retire to your chamber? Perhaps discuss these events with the Duke and Duchess of Gilmore so they will not be surprised by the subject of tonight's gathering."

Her bottom lip trembled. "Yes, I shall do so right away." She turned toward Remi. "I—"

"I won't let your parents near you without someone nearby," he promised softly. "I said I would take care of you and I will."

She nodded slowly. "Thank you," she whispered. "And if you will excuse me, Your Majesties."

Grantham inclined his head to excuse her and she left the room, shutting the door behind her. Remi stared at his family standing together, Grantham and Dash flanking the queen. Their disappointment was so evident. As was their curiosity.

"I apologize for striking you," Remi said. "It was out of line."

Grantham stretched his jaw. "As king, I suppose I should be offended. As your brother, I am impressed by your right cross. And I'm sorry I said something so cruel about our father."

"You might not have been wrong," Remi whispered.

"How long has this been going on?" the queen asked.

"A week of...of what Grantham walked in on. And some time before that, other things." Remi pursed his lips.

Grantham shook his head. "I am surprised, Remi. You have a reputation, of course, but you've always chosen more carefully when it came to your games."

"She was different," Remi said softly, and felt the truth of it deep in his chest. "She is…she's different."

"I see," Grantham said, his brow wrinkling.

"You said something to Miss Linfield before she left," the queen said. "About not letting them near her."

"Yes, and you were adamant that she not be left alone with her parents before I sent them away to their chamber," Grantham said.

Remi shifted. They had to know the truth, of course. There was no avoiding that now. But the idea that he would betray Priscilla's confidence put a pit in his stomach.

"The reason is not one that Priscilla would want shared. It was told to me in secret. May I trust that you three will keep this to yourselves?" Remi asked.

They all exchanged a glance and each nodded.

"Her father…attacked her," Remi said. Grantham drew back, his face twisting in horror. "And that woman, her stepmother, is likely the one to encourage such an escalation. Priscilla feared for her life. It was part of why she came with Lady Ophelia and the Duke and Duchess of Gilmore here to Athawick, though I don't think any of them know the worst details."

"That poor girl," the queen breathed. "What a terrible thing."

"Yes." Grantham's nostrils flared and he stepped toward Remi, their gazes locked. "I will be certain that the Linfields are kept far away from her. That she is *never* alone with them."

"Thank you," Remi said. "I do appreciate that."

"Go upstairs and clean yourself up," Grantham said. "Mama and Dash and I will arrange the supper details. We will figure this out, Remi. Somehow."

Remi nodded and left the room, but in the hallway he drew a long, heavy breath. He appreciated the support from his family, even if it came after a fight. But he wasn't certain the situation could *be* worked out. Not after he'd made such a muck of it.

Priscilla trudged into her chamber. What had begun as a wonderful day of exploration at the port, then the time in Remi's arms, was now...destroyed. She kept going back over and over to the door being flung open and her father, Caroline and the king stumbling into the room. Their expressions...

Worse, Remi's expression. Like he'd been caught in a trap. Oh, it had only flickered across his face for a fraction of a moment, but even that was too long.

"Priscilla, is that you?" Ophelia called out from the bedroom.

She caught her breath and entered the room. Ophelia was standing in the middle of the room with her sister-in-law, the Duchess of Gilmore. They were staring at a selection of Ophelia's gowns.

"Good afternoon," Priscilla choked out as she joined them.

"What do you think for tonight?" Ophelia asked. "The pink, the green or..." She turned and her expression fell. "Good God, what is wrong?"

Priscilla glanced at Abigail, then back to Ophelia, and the emotions roared up in her. She fell into Ophelia's arms and allowed the two women to guide her to the settee. After she let herself sob out all the pain, she finally gathered herself. There was no avoiding what she had to do.

"I…I did something," she murmured. "Ophelia, you know a little, but now it's so huge that I cannot hide it." She ignored Ophelia's horrified expression and quickly told them both about what had happened earlier in the day. She watched the duchess rather than Ophelia, ready to have Abigail look at her with disdain or disgust.

Instead, when the tale was over, Abigail merely reached across and patted her hand. "I'm so sorry that this happened, dearest. Not the first part, it sounds like that was…er…lovely. And I certainly cannot judge on that topic."

Priscilla's mouth dropped open. She hadn't expected that answer. "Oh."

"Yes, oh. But it does sound like you will need champions on your side tonight at this supper, for I know your father and that *wretched* Caroline will be terrible." She pushed to her feet. "I will tell Gilmore, you don't have to worry about that. And I promise you that he will judge you as little as I do. In the meantime, try to rest your mind. We will resolve this…together."

Abigail smiled at the pair and then left the room. As soon as she was gone, Ophelia tugged Priscilla back into a hug. "Oh, Pris! Your father coming all the way to Athawick! How in the world did they find out what was happening?"

"I don't know, but they must have been told by someone about what I was doing." She shook her head. "God, it was humiliating. I was *naked*, Ophelia. In front of the King of Athawick and my horrible parents."

Ophelia pulled a face. "To be fair, I'm not sure that the unfeeling King of Athawick has ever seen anyone naked. Even himself."

Priscilla stared at her a moment and then stifled a giggle. "You are terrible."

"But I made you laugh, so I am also the best of friends." Ophelia sighed. "What do…what do you think your father will do?"

"I don't know. I overheard the king telling Remi that he knew what he had to do. Implying, of course, that he would be forced to marry me in order to quell the scandal and appease my father...and I suppose my grandfather. And they would certainly be appeased, wouldn't they? My father has grasped for more all his life and the marquess only cares about rank. A prince would be his dream come true for a bad bet such as me. What more could they have asked for?"

"But what would *you* think of marrying him?" Ophelia asked.

"I would..." Priscilla bent her head. "I would be truly happy as his wife. I love him, Ophelia. You already knew it, of course, you guessed it, I know. But I will say it to you full-throatedly and unabashedly: I love him. I don't want to leave him and I certainly don't want to become the mistress of some other man, as was our original plan."

"Then this might be the perfect ending, as desperate as it was getting here," Ophelia said, grasping her hand.

"Except *he* doesn't want that. He and his brother physically fought about the subject." Priscilla sighed. "He does care for me, I know that's true. He wants me. But if he married me, there would always be a part of me that knew it was by force. It would be horrible to love him completely and know he saw me as a burden that was foisted upon him by our imprudence."

Ophelia twisted her hands before her. "I can see how that would be true. Oh, Pris, I'm the worst person to talk about this with. I've made terrible choices in my life. I cannot be trusted with my own heart, let alone yours."

Priscilla shook her head. "Don't discount yourself, Ophelia. I understand so much more now how love...or belief in love...could have influenced you. And I'm so sorry that the man in question was not worthy of your heart or your body."

"But the prince is," Ophelia said.

Priscilla nodded. She opened her mouth to say more, but the door to the chamber opened. They both turned, Priscilla expecting to see Abigail returned or perhaps a maid to help her with a tub.

Instead, it was her red-faced father who entered the chamber, with a smirking Caroline right at his heels.

She jumped to her feet, Ophelia quick behind her. "What are you doing here?" she asked. "The king and the prince asked you two to leave me be."

"Are they *both* your lovers?" Caroline snorted.

"Don't you *dare* speak to her that way," Ophelia snapped.

Her father ignored Ophelia and glared at Priscilla. "I would not put what my wife suggested past you now that you have shown your true colors."

Ophelia's expression grew even more outraged at Lord Linfield's words. She glanced at Priscilla, who shook her head in the slightest way, hoping it would send a message for her friend to stop trying to take her side. But of course Ophelia would not stand idly by. It wasn't her nature. "Get out of our chamber."

She moved in front of Priscilla as a shield. Lord Linfield's expression grew even stormier at that, his anger clearly bubbling on just beneath the surface. Priscilla pushed Ophelia aside at the sight of it. Ophelia had no idea how dangerous her father could be. Would he attack her friend? Possibly not. But she couldn't be absolutely certain and she would not, could not, take that risk.

"Please, just go," Priscilla said, waving him toward the door. "You will have plenty of time later to humiliate me, and in front of an audience. The king and queen intend to have a private supper to discuss all of this."

He arched a brow. "All the more reason then for us to decide what kind of front we will put on together."

Caroline stepped up beside him and smirked. "Yes, Priscilla. You mustn't be selfish now. I could not have ever guessed it, but your pathetic desperation could actually benefit our family, it seems. Don't make the fact that you opened your legs for this man be for nothing."

Priscilla turned her attention on her stepmother. "You are not part of this, Caroline. Why don't you go bathe in the blood of virgins or bite the heads off a few puppies or whatever your favorite pastime is at present?"

Caroline's eyes widened. She clearly hadn't been expecting Priscilla to go on the offensive. After all, Priscilla had spent years standing along the wall, taking whatever had been dished out to her, her confidence too low to do anything else. But she had changed. Being with Remi had changed her.

She moved her attention to her father. In the past, she might have simply gone along with whatever horrific plan was being hatched in his mind, if only to appease him. She might have bowed her head and let herself be harmed just to avoid worse. Or to earn love she realized now he would never give her.

But right now he wasn't just talking about harming her, he was talking about harming Remi and his family. "I-I will not stand with you," she said softly.

His eyes went wide. "What did you say to me?"

She swallowed hard. "I will not stand with you, Father. Whatever my future will be, it is mine to decide. I offer you no part in it. Go home."

Caroline snorted. "Are you going to let her talk to you like that, Linfield?"

He glanced back at Caroline and then returned his gaze to Priscilla. "Come here."

"No." Priscilla shook her head and Ophelia stepped up next to her, linking their arms.

"Come here," he repeated, this time louder as he lunged for her.

He caught her arm and yanked her toward him. She stumbled as she tried to push back. Ophelia tugged at her other arm. "Stop it! Let her go this instant!"

"Get out," Lord Linfield snarled at Ophelia. "This is a family matter, get out!"

Priscilla looked toward Ophelia. Her friend appeared terrified, as she should. And as much as she adored Ophelia for taking her side, for always taking her side, she would not endanger her friend any longer.

She pulled her arm away from Ophelia. "Please, just go," Priscilla whispered. "I'll be fine."

"I can't leave you with him," Ophelia said, refusing to relinquish Priscilla's arm entirely.

"Please!" Priscilla repeated, and snared her friend with what she knew was a wild gaze.

Tears filled Ophelia's eyes, but she released her nonetheless and backed away, then ran from the chamber. Leaving Priscilla alone with her father.

"You see, you can be good," he said as he shoved her back into the settee. He took the chair across from her and sat on its edge, elbows draped over his knees as he glared at her. "Now you and I are going to talk about what will happen in a short while."

"I won't demand Remi marry me," she said softly.

Caroline snorted as she came to stand behind Lord Linfield. "As if we believe that is any possibility. Great God, Priscilla, he's a prince and you...you're hardly more than nothing at all."

Priscilla glared at her stepmother. Once again, she couldn't help but be struck by how little those words meant to her now when they would have been daggers not so very long ago. And if that was all she got from this horrific situation, that and the memories of Remi? It would be more than enough.

"So if it is not marriage you two are angling for, then what?" she asked.

Her father smiled. "We'll make a fuss about the marriage, of course. And it will provide us with a fine bargaining chip for a financial settlement."

"No more living on the largess of the marquess," Caroline all but squealed as she squeezed Lord Linfield's shoulder. "Can you imagine, Linfield?"

"If we play our cards right, it could be an upfront settlement and then an annuity on top!"

Caroline glanced at her. "Oh, there is the matter of you. Obviously we couldn't have you running about in Society anymore, not with as damaged as you will be socially. Once it is all settled, you will have to cut her off, Linfield."

Her father's eyes met hers. She saw the slightest hesitation there, but then it was gone. "You are likely right."

Priscilla shook her head. "Are you two mad? Why would you think I would ever in my life stand with you if you propose this outcome? To blackmail the family of a man I..." No, she would not admit that she loved Remi to these two monsters. "To blackmail the royal family and a man I care for and then be thrown into a gutter like trash by you anyway? I said it before, and I say it again: I will *not* stand with you."

"Then perhaps we should do something else with you," her father said. "Ask for a marriage with someone here in Athawick."

"A merchant," Caroline cackled. "Force them to offer a marriage to a merchant. She can gut fish the rest of her life while her prince lives up in the tower."

Priscilla stared at her. Good God, this woman was entirely damaged. "You have been rotted all the way down to your core. I pity you."

Her father leapt up and now he towered over her, rage back on his every feature. "Shut your mouth. Either way, this is not a negotiation, daughter. And you'll see that punishment will still be meted out, no matter whose roof you are living under at present."

Fear overtook whatever bravery she had found inside of herself. She scooted into the corner of the settee, as if the increased distance would make a difference. She stared up into her father's eyes. Eyes of a man who was supposed to love and take care of her, but had only ever hated and used her, discarded her when she did not provide what he expected.

She had no idea what would happen now. The only thing she knew for certain was that she was going to protect Remi and his family...even if it destroyed her in the end.

~

Remi was coming up the hall toward the family wing of the palace for a hot bath and a very large drink when he heard footsteps racing toward him. He turned to face the source and was shocked to see Ophelia staggering up the hallway. Her cheeks were pale and streaked with tears, and she shook as she all but careened into him.

He caught her elbows, steadying her. She stared up at him. "I-I was coming to find the king. Priscilla...her father..."

He nodded. Of course Priscilla had gone straight to Ophelia with the news of the day. He was glad she had a confidante. Though why Ophelia would have such a strong reaction to the news and then search out his brother was beyond him.

"Yes, they arrived today and at a most inopportune moment. I hope that—"

"Her father and that wretched wife of his burst into our chamber," Ophelia interrupted. "He was so angry. He is alone with her now."

Remi released her and started down the hall. "Go to Grantham's study and fetch my brother," he ordered. "Tell him exactly what you told me. Hurry!"

She let out a sob and raced down the stairs. Remi began to run, the pit in his stomach sick and cold at the thought of Priscilla alone with that monster she called father. How had he known which chamber was hers?

And then it clicked. Blairford. He had escorted the Linfields to their chamber. And he had so many spies around the palace...he could have also called them here to Athawick in the first place. For what reason, Remi couldn't say.

Right now it didn't matter. He burst into the chamber Ophelia and Priscilla shared and heard the hard, harsh voice of her father coming from the bedroom.

"If you refuse this order, refuse me after all I've done for you, the result will be worse than a few bruises."

Remi bounded into the room to find Lord Linfield standing over Priscilla, who was hunched into the corner of the settee, holding up her hands as if to ward him off. Caroline Linfield stood by, arms folded, smiling like this was all some wonderful entertainment.

Remi caught Linfield by the arm and yanked him back, sending him flying across the room. He hit the dressing table, shattering the mirror and sending perfumes and brushes and combs scattering across the floor.

Priscilla jumped to her feet, and Remi tugged her against his side as he pivoted to face her father. Lord Linfield was slowly getting back up, his expression almost comically confused by what had just happened. "I have never been struck in my life," he said, dusting himself off.

"I was moving you," Remi said. "If I strike you, you will know it. Just as your daughter knew it, you feckless coward."

Lord Linfield leaned away and at least looked slightly chagrined. Lady Linfield, on the other hand, snorted and asked, "Was that how you got him to bed you? By telling him pathetic tales?"

"If either of you ever speak to my fiancée like that again, I will do more than hit him," Remi barked. He heard his own words, echoing in the room, in his own mind.

Fiancée. It was the solution his family had danced around earlier. And it was the best one. The only one. The right one.

As he spoke that truth, Grantham rushed into the room. He came to a stop and stared at Remi.

Remi stared back, and then Grantham nodded. Approval was clear on his brother's face, but more than that was support. For whatever he did, whatever future he took. Grantham would be there.

"You were given an order, Lord Linfield," Grantham said, catching Priscilla's father by the collar and yanking him toward the door. "So allow me to give you and your wife a royal escort back to your chamber, where you will also be given a guard, since you two cannot control yourselves."

"Priscilla!" Lord Linfield shouted, and Remi turned her away from him. When they were gone, he settled her back on the settee and then walked to the chamber door to shut it. This time he turned the key to give them the privacy he should have remembered in the tower.

She was staring up at him, the pain was clear in her eyes. All her heartbreak and disappointment in her father, in her own life, in the path to this place. And all he wanted to do was erase it. He wanted to bring her joy. Peace. Happiness. Pleasure. He wanted to give her freedom to be herself.

He wanted to give her everything.

"Did he hurt you?" he asked, kneeling before her and smoothing his hands over hers.

She blinked as if his question had brought her back to reality. "No," she whispered. "But he wanted to. He would have."

He shut his eyes. "By God, Priscilla, I could have torn him limb from limb. I ought to at that."

She shook her head. "It would only cause more problems for you than I already have. I cannot go back to London with them, that is perfectly clear. But you needn't be talked into making me what you called me earlier. I will accept the future we already determined. And I will find a lover and—"

He flinched. "I called you fiancée because that is what I wish for you to be."

She hesitated at his interruption. "You feel an obligation to say that. And I appreciate your desire to protect me more than I could ever say but I can't make you do this."

He smiled slightly. "No one can *make* me do anything, I assure you. Just ask Grantham. Or my mother. Or Dash."

She didn't smile in return. "Remi..."

"Please...marry me," he said. And meant it. And held his breath as he waited for her to answer.

Priscilla's ears were ringing, and she stared at Remi, blinking like she could wake from this dream. It had to be a dream. He was asking for her hand.

And yet she knew why. It wasn't from some great love for her, but obligation. Because he wished to save her. But she wanted more than saving.

"No," she said, and it tore her heart out.

His smile fell. "Did you say no?" he asked.

She nodded. "As difficult as it is."

He got up off his knees and sat beside her, taking her hand gently. "If it is difficult, then why refuse?"

She drew in a long breath. "Because I love you."

A flutter of emotion crossed his face. "Well, now I'm even more baffled. You love me, so why would you not wish to marry me?"

"Remi, we began this…this affair because you wanted to help me."

"We began this affair because I couldn't deny myself the pleasure of touching you," he corrected gently. "Helping you was a byproduct. But please, continue."

"Whatever began it, then, we both knew it was never meant to be more. I knew your thoughts on love, I knew that you were not ready to marry and would certainly not choose the daughter of a second son, especially *that* particular son."

"We do not choose our family," he interrupted softly.

She ignored him. "I fell in love with you even before we made love the first time in the tower. I knew I was risking myself, and it didn't matter. But I never intended to use this bond between us to make you take a path you didn't want."

"But I'm asking you to walk that path with me."

"Why?" she pressed. "Because we were caught? Because you fear my safety with my father? Because your brother or your mother demand it?"

"Because…" He swallowed hard. "Because I'm in love with you, too, Priscilla."

She drew back in utter shock and released his hand. "Please don't say that."

"Why? Because you don't believe me or because you're afraid of what that means if it's true?"

She couldn't form words as she stared at him, searching his blue eyes to see if the truth was there. And it was. As bright and beautiful as it felt when she allowed herself her own reflection of it. He… loved her. Somehow.

"How can you love me?" she murmured.

He smiled. "How could I not? You are everything, Priscilla. I love your kindness and your wit, I love your sweetness and your laugh. I love that when you touch me I'm more than my birth, my name, my title. I'm yours. Being yours is and will always be the greatest pleasure of my life. But only if you rescind your prior answer and agree to marry me."

She caught her breath, but he cupped her cheeks gently before she could speak. "Please."

She squeezed her eyes shut and leaned forward, resting her forehead against his shoulder. He smoothed her hair, silent as he waited for her answer. The one that bubbled up inside of her, joyful and filled with promise, even as her disbelief faded.

"Priscilla?" he whispered. "Marry me."

She lifted her head and couldn't help the smile that broke over her face, her joy perfect despite the terrible earlier part of the day. "Yes," she said.

His face lit up, happiness with no hesitation. "Yes?"

He dragged his mouth to hers for a kiss. She lifted into him, welcoming him and feeling the newness of this touch even though they had kissed so many times she had lost track. He jumped to his feet, bringing her with him, and spun her around the room as she laughed.

"You will have to shout that from the rooftops! Declare it to the stars!" he burst out. "Tell my family, tell Ophelia and the Gilmores. Tell the world!"

She pressed a hand to his cheek as he set her down. "I will, I shall, I do," she promised. "Forever."

He nodded and leaned in to kiss her again, this time with wicked promise. "Forever."

CHAPTER 24

There *was* a private supper that night, but Lord and Lady Linfield were not invited. Their exile to the guarded chamber would be permanent until their departure back to London in a few days. Only the family gathered, along with Lady Ophelia and the Gilmores, to celebrate the happiest of news.

Certainly, Remi couldn't stop smiling. He hadn't realized one could be so joyful and yet here he was, watching his soon-to-be bride standing at the fire with Lady Ophelia, her face lit with so much happiness that it made his chest ache with pleasure. She was his. His *forever*. And it was a wonderful thing.

There was only one thing he had to resolve, and so he touched his brother's arm and drew him away from where he had been talking to their mother and the Duchess of Gilmore.

Grantham followed him a few steps away and said, "You seem a bit serious for a man who was all but bounding around my study not half an hour ago, declaring he would wed. Tell me you have not already changed your mind."

"Never," Remi declared with a certainty that seemed to surprise Grantham. "But there is one situation we must discuss: how Lord and Lady Linfield were informed about what was happening here, and how they discovered where Priscilla's chamber was so they could confront her."

Grantham let his breath out slowly. "Blairford?" he said.

"You guessed the same?" Remi asked in surprise.

Grantham shook his head. "He admitted it. At least the revelation of the room."

Remi's nostrils flared. "He could have gotten her killed. What did he have to say for himself?"

"He apologized," Grantham said softly. "And he seemed sincere. He claims he didn't understand that Miss Linfield's location was to be protected. They are her parents, after all. When they asked where she was staying, he told them, unaware of the dangers."

"And how did he explain away the letter that brought them here?"

"He denies that," Grantham said. "And we cannot prove that he did it, after all. A guest could have seen something, another servant. It is hard to say."

Remi stepped closer to his brother. "So you will continue to keep this man in your employ? In such a powerful position?"

Grantham sighed. "Until things become a bit more…peaceful, it would be hard to change. But I want you to know that I am watching the man all the more carefully. I take this seriously, Remi."

"You take everything seriously."

A shadow of a smile crossed Grantham's face. "Come, this is too happy a night to dwell on such things. Let's sit and eat and celebrate your very happy announcement."

Remi nodded. His brother was right that he would not allow his misgivings to keep him from his joy. He would simply keep a more careful eye on Blairford going forward. For his brother's sake as much as anyone else's.

He moved to take Priscilla's hand and lifted it to his lips before he guided her to her place beside him at the table.

"You looked very dire talking to the king," she said softly. "He does not disapprove the match?"

Remi shook his head. "No. Never. And I would do it even if he did."

She smiled slightly at that declaration and asked nothing more as they all settled into their seats. But almost immediately, Remi rose and faced his king. "I believe, Your Majesty, that there is a precedence to these sorts of things."

Grantham rolled his eyes. "One you are about to break at least eleven ways. In addition to the five ways you've broken it already. But do continue."

"I would like the Crown's permission to wed Miss Priscilla Linfield," he said, and watched as the ripple of pleasure moved through every face at the table. "As quickly as possible. Tomorrow. Tonight?"

At his side, Priscilla swatted at his hand. "Stop," she whispered, but she was laughing. God, how he loved that sound.

Grantham looked at her and his mouth twitched, but he quelled even the smallest hint at humor and lowered his brow toward Remi. "So this is not a request."

"No," he admitted. "Unless you lock us back in that tower, I do intend to find a way to wed her, permission or not."

"Then how could I refuse you?" Grantham said gently. "Of course you may wed."

Remi looked down the table at all the smiling faces but ended up staring into Priscilla's eyes. "I do not jest when I say I wish to do it swiftly. Ilaria's royal wedding took far too long to plan, and I have never been good at waiting."

"Apparently," Ilaria muttered, and Jonah laughed at her side. Of course the truth about what had happened between Priscilla and him had spread throughout the family.

"Do you agree with this rush?" Queen Giabella asked Priscilla from the other end of the table.

"I do," Priscilla said, and smiled up at him. "And considering the situation with my stepmother and father, it might be best for more than just our happiness."

It was the Duke of Gilmore who responded. "The king and I have discussed the particulars. Abigail and I will…*escort* your family back to London with us when we leave on the ship in a few days. And it has already been made abundantly clear, and will continue to be, that if they create any rumor regarding you or Prince Remington, there will be hell to pay. I'll see to it personally, as I have a friendship of sorts with your grandfather."

"Thank you," Remi said with a warm smile toward the duke. He then gave the same to his brother. Grantham had not taken credit, but Remi knew he had also paid a visit to the Linfields in their pretty prison and made clear his own intentions if they made trouble.

"A small family wedding would be fine," Queen Giabella said. "If it is what the couple wishes. We can announce it later, but you two will be able to be together now. I certainly do not think you could be kept apart."

"Tomorrow," Remi said again, and elicited a laugh from the group, though he was being completely serious.

"Next week," his mother negotiated. "Please let the household have some respite."

"Next week is fine, Your Majesty," Priscilla laughed, and tugged at his arm. He met her gaze and let out a sigh.

"Yes, it is fine." Remi bowed to the king and then the queen, then retook his seat.

As the family began their supper amidst happy and excited chatter, Priscilla leaned her head on his arm and looked up at him. "Your ardor is far too clear, Remi."

"Not clear enough," he corrected. "And it isn't merely ardor that drives me to haste. It is that I cannot imagine one more day where you are not mine."

"I will tell you a secret," she said, and leaned a little closer. She whispered, "I *am* yours. And I always shall be."

He didn't care that the room was watching or that it was shocking. He cupped her cheek and kissed her, his joy unmitigated, his future clear and his heart sealed to the only woman who ever could have tamed him.

She sighed and turned to move away from the crowd. Only to find herself nearly careening into the broad chest of King Grantham. She hadn't even heard him approach and she staggered back with a gasp.

"You-Your Majesty," she said when she could find her breath. She offered a quick curtsey. "Good evening."

"Lady Ophelia," he said, drawing out her name ever so slightly.

He then said nothing else, but simply stepped up beside her and together they watched the dancing crowd a moment. She shifted under the weight of the silence. The man was an expert at it, that was certain. Also at staring.

She cleared her throat when she could take it no longer. "I-I wished to say thank you for your kindness."

He glanced at her. "My kindness?"

"In allowing me to stay for Prince Remington and Priscilla's wedding."

He grunted rather than answered and returned his attention to the ball. She waited a moment and then added, "You must wish to have your palace back from interlopers."

He grunted again rather than answering, though that particular sound felt more in the affirmative.

She pursed her lips. Great God, but the man was frustrating. Why had he approached her, why was he standing next to her if he was only going to be so taciturn and uncommunicative? Was he just playing a game with her?

She blinked and looked at him from the corner of her eye. Perhaps she was right. Perhaps this man just liked to watch her squirm. The more she mulled over that in her mind, the more sense it made. From the very first time she met him he had been…odd in her presence. Watching her even as he avoided her.

Was it all a game to him?

Well, if that were true, she could certainly play it. Match his energy with her own opposite one. If he wanted to be gruff and untalkative, she could be fluffy and light and playful and chatty, couldn't she? Take the upper hand by batting her eyelashes at him and driving him mad?

It might actually make the next few weeks bearable. She smothered a laugh and turned to face him directly. His expression fluttered when she did, as if she had surprised him. Good.

"Your Majesty, I just must compliment you on your gardens. Every morning I take a long walk and they are truly stunning. It's clear the generations of work that has gone into the blooms. I, myself, have a rather black thumb, I fear. I cannot even manage to keep a bouquet alive for more than twenty-four hours. Perhaps that's a curse." She paused only for a quick breath and continued, loving how his eyes were progressively growing wider as she chattered on. "Not that I believe in such a thing as a curse. I'm far more reasonable a person than that. It's all science, isn't it? Water a plant well and it will grow. Give it food and sunlight and I suppose I'm simply not focused enough to recall to do it. Not that I'm flighty. Heavens no."

His mouth was dropped just slightly open and his gaze was entirely focused on her now. No, wait, not on her. On her mouth. As if he was trying to figure out how it was pushing so many words out at once. Excellent.

"I noted that Princess Ilaria's bouquet was from the garden. What a wonderful wedding that was. They seem truly in love, as do Princess Sasha and the Earl of Bramwell. And of course our dear Priscilla and Remi. Marriages of love seem to be as in fashion in Athawick as they are presently in London. What do you think of that, Your Majesty?"

He opened and shut his mouth several times and then cleared his throat. "I think that I wish to see my family happy," he said slowly. "And they are. So that is good enough for me."

She was actually taken aback by that response. She had never been able to read the king's response to the flurry of romances and marriages amongst his siblings in the past few months. But what he said seemed...genuine.

"My lady, would you like to dance?" he asked.

She caught her breath. They had known each other for months, been present at dozens of these events both at home and here in Athawick and yet he had never requested a dance with her. He'd danced with Priscilla, with Abigail...but never her.

"I..." she murmured and then shook her head. This was surely still part of his game...or if he wasn't playing one, she needed to incorporate it into her own. "Yes," she said. "That would be an honor, Your Majesty."

"Excellent," he said, motioning her toward the floor where the previous country jig had ended and couples were filtering on and off. She thought she heard him mutter something else as he followed her. Something about the only way to make her stop talking.

She smothered a smile. Excellent. If they were to be adversaries, she intended to win the day. And flummoxing him was fun. Certainly more entertaining than the time she'd spent avoiding him and wondering why he wouldn't stop looking at her.

ALSO BY JESS MICHAELS

Regency Royals

To Protect a Princess

Earl's Choice

Princes are Wild

To Kiss a King (Coming Soon)

The Queen's Man (Coming Soon)

The Three Mrs

The Unexpected Wife

The Defiant Wife

The Duke's Wife

The Duke's By-Blows

The Love of a Libertine

The Heart of a Hellion

The Matter of a Marquess

The Redemption of a Rogue

The 1797 Club

The Daring Duke

Her Favorite Duke

The Broken Duke

The Silent Duke

The Duke of Nothing

The Undercover Duke

The Duke of Hearts

The Duke Who Lied

The Duke of Desire

The Last Duke

The Scandal Sheet

The Return of Lady Jane

Stealing the Duke

Lady No Says Yes

My Fair Viscount

Guarding the Countess

The House of Pleasure

Seasons

An Affair in Winter

A Spring Deception

One Summer of Surrender

Adored in Autumn

The Wicked Woodleys

Forbidden

Deceived

Tempted

Ruined

Seduced

Fascinated

To see a complete listing of Jess Michaels' titles, please visit:

http://www.authorjessmichaels.com/books

ABOUT THE AUTHOR

USA Today Bestselling author Jess Michaels likes geeky stuff, Vanilla Coke Zero, anything coconut, cheese and her dog, Elton. She is lucky enough to be married to her favorite person in the world and lives in the heart of Dallas, TX where she's trying to eat all the amazing food in the city.

When she's not obsessively checking her steps on Fitbit or trying out new flavors of Greek yogurt, she writes historical romances with smoking hot characters and emotional stories. She has written for numerous publishers and is now fully indie and loving every moment of it (well, almost every moment).

Jess loves to hear from fans! So please feel free to contact her at Jess@AuthorJessMichaels.com.

Jess Michaels offers a free book to members of her newsletter, so sign up on her website:
http://www.AuthorJessMichaels.com/

facebook.com/JessMichaelsBks
twitter.com/JessMichaelsBks
instagram.com/JessMichaelsBks
bookbub.com/authors/jess-michaels

www.ingramcontent.com/pod-product-compliance
Lightning Source LLC
Chambersburg PA
CBHW050845190726
48286CB00007B/2240